FALLING FOR A STRANGER

The Callaways

————⇒⫸⫷⇐————

BARBARA FREETHY

HYDE
STREET
—PRESS—

HYDE STREET PRESS
Published by Hyde Street Press
1819 Polk Street, Suite 113, San Francisco, California 94109

Printed in the United States of America

Cover design by Damonza.com
Interior book design by KLF Publishing

ISBN 978-0-9906951-2-7

PRAISE FOR THE NOVELS OF
#1 NEW YORK TIMES BESTSELLING AUTHOR
BARBARA FREETHY

"I love *The Callaways*! Heartwarming romance, intriguing suspense and sexy alpha heroes. What more could you want?"
-- *NYT Bestselling Author* **Bella Andre**

"I adore *The Callaways*, a family we'd all love to have. Each new book is a deft combination of emotion, suspense and family dynamics. A remarkable, compelling series!"
-- *USA Today Bestselling Author* **Barbara O'Neal**

"Once I start reading a Callaway novel, I can't put it down. Fast-paced action, a poignant love story and a tantalizing mystery in every book!"
-- *USA Today Bestselling Author* **Christie Ridgway**

"I love the Callaways and *FALLING FOR A STRANGER* just makes me love their family even more."
--*All Night Books*

"One of the greatest parts of *FALLING FOR A STRANGER* is making you believe in love at first sight. If you're looking for a great feel good read with a bit of action and mystery, this book is for you!"
--*The Book Momster*

"In the tradition of LaVyrle Spencer, gifted author Barbara Freethy creates an irresistible tale of family secrets, riveting adventure and heart-touching romance."
-- *NYT Bestselling Author* **Susan Wiggs**
on Summer Secrets

"This book has it all: heart, community, and characters who will remain with you long after the book has ended. A wonderful story."
-- *NYT Bestselling Author* **Debbie Macomber**
on Suddenly One Summer

"Freethy has a gift for creating complex characters."
-- **Library Journal**

"Barbara Freethy is a master storyteller with a gift for spinning tales about ordinary people in extraordinary situations and drawing readers into their lives."
-- **Romance Reviews Today**

"Freethy's skillful plotting and gift for creating sympathetic characters will ensure that few dry eyes will be left at the end of the story."
-- **Publishers Weekly** *on The Way Back Home*

"Freethy skillfully keeps the reader on the hook, and her tantalizing and believable tale has it all– romance, adventure, and mystery."
-- **Booklist** *on Summer Secrets*

"Freethy's story-telling ability is top-notch."
-- **Romantic Times** *on Don't Say A Word*

"Powerful and absorbing…sheer hold-your-breath suspense."
-- *NYT Bestselling Author* **Karen Robards**
on Don't Say A Word

"A page-turner that engages your mind while it tugs at your heartstrings…Don't Say A Word has made me a Barbara Freethy fan for life!"
-- *NYT Bestselling Author* **Diane Chamberlain**
on Don't Say A Word

Also By Barbara Freethy

To my wonderful husband Terry, my partner in this amazing adventure!

One

⟿⟫⟪⟨⟵

Ria Hastings was in the mood for trouble. It was a warm tropical night on Isla de los Sueños, a small island off the coast of Costa Rica, known for its white sandy beaches, water sports, deep sea fishing, and rum drinks. On one side of the island, several large estates sat on the rugged hillsides with spectacular views of the ocean. The rest of the town lived near the beach, where three hotels and a dozen restaurants competed for tourist dollars.

Ria wiped a strand of blonde hair off her sweaty forehead. The temperature hovered around eighty degrees at just after midnight, and the beachside bar was packed with tourists. Ria had been tending the bar since seven, and she was ready to call it a night. She'd been hit on four times already, and while she was used to handling men who were a little too drunk or too interested in her, she was tired of wearing a polite smile, but she would do exactly that for another hour. She couldn't risk getting fired, nor could she afford to draw any attention to herself. She'd been blending into the local scene for months. Now was not the night to stand out.

As she wiped down the counter, her gaze caught on a man sitting at the far end of the bar. He'd arrived two hours earlier with a friend—a loud, charming, and now hammered, sunburned blond by the name of Tim. Tim had been doing tequila shots since ten and was now hosting a trio of beautiful girls at a nearby table. The man at the bar seemed to have no interest in joining his friend's party and had been nursing a vodka tonic for the better part of an hour. He also hadn't responded to any of the women who'd slid into the seat next to him, although his gaze had swung in her direction on more than one occasion.

He was an attractive man, athletically built, dressed in khaki shorts and a navy blue knit shirt. His dark brown hair was on the short side, and he had an air of discipline about him. Military, she thought. Just out or on leave, but close enough to his service that his body was still toned and on full alert.

She hadn't missed the fact that his gaze darted to the door almost as often as hers did, as if he were waiting for someone or didn't want to be taken by surprise. Maybe he was military intelligence.

That idea made her frown. The last thing she needed was military intelligence to show up on the island.

She told herself not to let her imagination run wild. A lot of ex-military guys came to the island to decompress and let off steam. Since the location had become a popular destination for bachelor and bachelorette parties, there was usually a good deal of action available for anyone who wanted to find it.

But this man didn't seem interested in escaping reality with alcohol or with women, so what was his story?

Glancing down at her watch, she told herself she had better things to worry about than a random stranger, no matter how sexy he was.

In a few hours, the plan she'd put into motion six months earlier would finally be launched. She'd gone over the details a thousand times in her head, and while she wanted nothing more than to go off by herself somewhere and review everything again, it was more important for her to maintain her usual routine.

The man at the end of the bar caught her eye again. There was something in his dark gaze that beckoned to her, a pull of attraction, desire, feelings that she hadn't allowed herself to feel in a very long time. She couldn't afford to answer his call. She was too close to the end to get sidetracked by a man, especially a man who set her nerves tingling with just one look.

On the other hand…

As two men approached the bar, she moved down the counter toward her fellow bartender, Martin, a twenty-two-year-old ex-Harvard dropout, who had come to the island to find himself. So far, the only thing he'd found was a love for tequila and bikini-clad girls.

"Switch with me," she said.

Martin's gaze moved past her to the men sliding into stools at the other end of the long bar. "Trouble?"

"I'd just prefer not to wait on them."

"Got it," he said.

She walked toward the handsome stranger. At this moment, he seemed the less dangerous choice, or at least, the less *obvious* dangerous choice. It had been a long time since she'd allowed herself to trust anyone.

"Can I get you another drink?" she asked.

His eyes were a deep, dark brown, and there were shadows in his gaze, things he'd seen, things he didn't want to see again, she suspected. But there was also courage and strength in his eyes, a resilient defiance. He might have been knocked down, but she doubted that he'd stayed down.

"Sure, why not?" he replied, with a lightness that was in contrast to his tense posture.

"I can't think of a reason. Same? Or do you want to change it up a bit? We have an island special you might like."

"What's that?"

"Beso de la sirena, otherwise known as mermaid's kiss."

"Do you see mermaids after you drink it?" he asked, a lighter gleam entering his eyes.

"Some men do."

"It sounds dangerous."

"You look like a man who could handle a little danger."

"And you sound like a woman who knows how to sell a high-priced drink to a tourist." A hint of a smile played around his lips.

So he was smart as well as attractive. "Guilty. So what will it be? Beso de la sirena or another vodka tonic?"

"Vodka, hold the tonic." He pushed his empty glass across the bar.

She made him another drink, then tipped her head towards his friend, who was making out with a busty blonde. "Your friend seems to be ignoring you."

He shrugged. "I can't blame him. They're all very pretty."

"Yet, here you sit by yourself. No one here has caught your interest?" She wiped down the bar with a damp towel. As she spoke, she cast a sideways glance at the two men at the other end of the bar.

They worked as bodyguards for Enrique Valdez, one of the very wealthy men who made his home in the island hills. As much as she didn't want them at her bar, it was good that they'd come in; they would see her doing what she always did. She wouldn't raise any suspicion.

"I didn't say that," the man in front of her said.

"What?"

"You said there was no one here I was interested in, but that's not true."

Her heart skipped a beat at his direct gaze, and her pulse started beating way too fast. She'd made a point of not getting involved with tourists, or anyone for that matter, but this man was more than a little tempting. She'd been lonely on the island, living a life of pretense. But that pretense was crucial to staying alive. She couldn't let desire get in the way.

"Nice line," she said casually. "I've heard it before—about three dozen times."

He smiled. "I'll bet you have. But I'm the only one who meant it."

"Sure you are."

"What's your name?"

Her body tensed. "You first."

"Drew Callaway."

"Do you want to add a title before your name? Maybe Lieutenant or Captain," she suggested. He had the air of leadership about him.

He tipped his head, a gleam in his eyes. "Lieutenant."

"With the…"

"I'm in between services at the moment. Former Navy pilot, soon to be flying helicopters for the Coast Guard."

Navy pilot certainly explained why he exuded both discipline and recklessness at the same time. It also probably explained where the shadows in his eyes came from.

"What tipped you off?" he asked curiously.

She shrugged. "I'm good at reading people. It comes with the job. Why did you leave the Navy?"

He didn't answer right away, a contemplative expression in his eyes, then said, "My time was up. I needed a change of pace."

"Where were you deployed?"

"All over."

"So you saw action?"

"Too much."

She gave him a thoughtful look. "It doesn't sound like you're making a huge change, moving from one kind of service to another."

"I still get to fly, which is all I ever wanted to do, but hopefully not with as many people shooting at me."

"I can't imagine that."

"No, you can't." He sipped his drink, then set the glass down. "Your turn."

She cleared her throat. She'd been living on the island for six months, and in that time no one had balked at the name that was on her fake passport, a version of her real name. "Ria," she said.

"Pretty. Last name?"

"Not important."

"A woman of mystery."

"A woman who likes her privacy."

"How long have you lived here on the island, Ria?"

"Long enough to know better than to get involved with tourists," she said with a brief smile.

"No exceptions?"

"Not so far. People come, they go. I'm still here." She paused. "What brought you to the island of dreams?"

A smile curved his lips, giving him an entirely different look, one that was even more attractive. She felt a knot grow in her throat.

"I dreamt about a beautiful blonde with big brown eyes," he said. "A full mouth, with soft kissable lips and a killer body." His gaze drifted down to her breasts. "I think I found her."

Her nerves tingled under his scrutiny and she had to fight the urge to cover her breasts, not that much was showing in her bar uniform, a coral-colored red tank top over white shorts. Most of the women in the bar were showing more skin than she was.

"You're quite the flirt," she said lightly.

"Actually, I'm a little out of practice."

"Just getting out of a relationship?" she queried, unable

to believe this man would have any trouble getting a date.

"I've been focused on other things. Staying alive, for one."

"I can see how that might be a priority."

"What about you?" he asked. "Are you involved with anyone?"

"No."

"Good."

"Why is that good?" she challenged.

He smiled. "Because I like you, Ria. What time do you get off?"

Her heart jumped at the hungry look in his eyes. "You're very direct."

"I'm leaving tomorrow. I don't have a lot of time."

"Where are you going?"

"San Francisco."

A wistful yearning filled her body. San Francisco was one of her favorite cities. And she'd been away for too long.

"I love San Francisco," she said. "I lived there when I was a child. My grandfather was a fisherman. He'd take me out on the bay every chance he got." She drew in a quick breath, realizing she was talking way too much. "What part of the city do you live in?"

"I grew up in St. Francis Wood, but I'll be living south of Market starting next week. It's the hot area to live in now, right near the new ballpark." He paused. "You didn't answer my question, Ria. What time do you get off?"

She gave him a long look, feeling incredibly tempted. His eyes were so dark and intriguing, his features pure masculine gorgeousness. He had a mouth that looked really kissable, too, and a purposeful attitude that made her think he probably knew what to do with a woman. It had been a long time since she'd lost herself in a man's arms for a few hours. And despite the fact that he was a stranger, she had the strangest feeling that she could trust him not to hurt her. That was a dangerous thought, because she couldn't afford to be wrong.

"Ria?" he pressed.

"Do you think I'm that easy?" she countered.

"Not easy, but I think maybe you're important."

The serious note in his voice shot a shiver down her spine. She told herself not to get carried away. He was just trying to get her into bed. He'd say anything. She couldn't believe a word.

"Why on earth would you say that?"

"I don't know. Ever since I saw you I've wanted to talk to you."

"You didn't ask me what time I got off so you could talk to me."

"Well, that was one of the reasons," he said. "I'm not trying to insult you. If I had more time, I'd ask you out on a date. I'd bring you flowers and take you to an expensive restaurant and buy you a really expensive cut of steak."

"Is that your usual style?"

He gave her a smile. "I don't have a style. And while I would never profess to understand or know what a woman wants, I do have sisters, and they talk and complain a lot, especially when it comes to men and dating."

"How many sisters?"

"Three sisters and four brothers."

"Big family. Where are you in the lineup?"

"Fourth from the top."

"Otherwise known as the middle."

He tipped his head. "Yes. What about you? Big family?"

"No. I'm an only child." It was part of the backstory she'd made up before coming to the island; it was also partly true. "I used to wish I had a big family."

"It's not all it's cracked up to be," he said dryly. "A lot of noise and chaos."

"And love," she suggested, feeling an ache that went deep into her soul.

Her family had always been complicated. Love, betrayal, divorce, death … She supposed that's what made up a life, but it seemed like she'd seen too much of the dark side of love.

"Plenty of love," Drew said. "Sometimes too much. Everyone likes to be in my business."

Despite his complaint, she could see the pride in his eyes when he spoke of his family.

"So, one o'clock, two?" he pressed, raising an eyebrow. "What time are you done here?"

"Two. But I'm not meeting you."

"Why not?"

"I'm not in the mood for a hookup."

"Aren't you? I've been watching you all night, and I'm good at reading people, too, Ria. You're a bundle of nerves. Every time someone walks through the door, you tense. Why is that? Are you in some kind of trouble?"

His words bothered her on two levels, one that he'd read her so well, and, two, that she'd given so much away.

"And I suppose you think I should release some of my tension with you?" she asked, ignoring his other questions.

"I think…" He paused, lowering his voice. "That you are a beautiful woman who knows what she wants and how to get it."

"Who said I wanted you?" she challenged.

"Your beautiful eyes say it."

"You're seeing what you want to see."

"Am I?" He cocked his head to the right as he regarded her thoughtfully. "What's holding you back, Ria?"

"I don't do random hookups. And I have to get up early in the morning. In the daytime I sail boats for Sea Charters."

"So bartender, sailor—what other talents do you have?"

"Wouldn't you like to know?"

"I would like to know," he said with a grin. "Why don't you tell me? Or better yet, show me?"

She shook her head at his charming smile. When she'd first seen him, his expression had been tense, but since they'd started talking, he'd loosened up considerably.

"You're breaking my heart," he said, putting a hand to his chest.

"I doubt that. And there are plenty of women in this bar if you want company."

"I'm only interested in *your* company. You intrigue me."

"I can't imagine why."

"What brought you to this small island in the middle of the sea?"

She thought for a moment, then said the only word that came to mind. "Freedom."

He met her gaze. "Have you found it?"

"I'm close," she said. "When I'm in the middle of the ocean, no land in sight, nothing but blue water and the occasional seagull, I almost feel like I've escaped."

"Escaped what?"

"Nothing I care to share." She drew in a deep breath, trying to calm the tension running through her body, that now had as much to do with her attraction to Drew as with her worries about the next day.

"I understand the desire to escape," he said.

"You do?"

"Yes. I first felt the walls closing in on me when I was a teenager. There were eight kids sharing four bedrooms and two bathrooms. It was always too crowded in my house, kids fighting, crying, yelling, so I'd leave whenever I could. And one day I ended up at the airport. I took a flying lesson, and I was hooked. There is nothing like the land falling away and nothing but blue sky in front of you to make you feel like the world just got bigger." He paused. "We're quite a pair. I need the big blue sky and you need the big blue sea."

She smiled. "Apparently, neither one of us is that good on land."

"Maybe we could be good together," he suggested.

She laughed. "You don't miss an opportunity, do you?"

He finished his drink then got to his feet. "I'm staying in the cottages. Number nine. The door will be open, Ria."

"I'm not coming." She wished her words were a little stronger, a little more forceful.

"Then I'll be disappointed. I turned down the mermaid's kiss, because I want yours."

"Another good line. You're full of them."

"I'm not a player."

"You've given me absolutely no reason to believe that."

"I know," he admitted. "You probably won't believe me, but I haven't done this in a while."

"So, why me?"

"You have a smart mouth, and you're sexy as hell. I'd love to see you with your hair down. I'd love to show you how good we could be together."

His husky tone sent another shiver down her spine. "How do you know we'd be good? You don't know me at all," she said, trying to maintain a strong defense against his charm. "We're strangers."

"For now. But what better way to learn about each other?"

"I'm not looking for trouble."

"There's a light in your eyes that says that's exactly what you're looking for."

She caught her breath, thinking he might actually be right about that.

Drew tipped his head and walked away.

She watched him all the way to the exit. When the door

closed behind him, she let out a breath, wondering how she could possibly already miss him.

He was just another guy—only he wasn't, and she couldn't put her finger on why.

Maybe it was the seriousness that lurked just behind his smile. He wasn't like most of the guys who hit on her. Those she could handle. She knew they'd move on to the next woman before she could finish saying *no*. But Drew had left. He'd thrown down his invitation and walked out the door.

He was going to wait for her. He was pretty confident she'd show up, but he was going to be waiting a long time.

She turned her focus back on work. For the next hour, she served drinks, picked up empty glasses, and watched the minutes tick off the clock. Shortly before closing Drew's friend left with two women flanking him on either side. Apparently, he wasn't going to be alone tonight.

At two a.m., she wiped down the bar and closed out the register. She said goodnight to Martin and walked outside, the scent of flowers and sea all around her. She paused for a moment and drew in a deep breath of sweet and salty air. The heat of the night echoed the passionate need burning through her body, a need that had been lit by the sexy smile of a stranger.

She lived in a furnished rental three blocks away from the resort. The cottage where Drew was staying was only a hundred yards away.

Indecision made her hesitate for a long minute. She hadn't been lying when she told Drew she wasn't into hookups, but tonight she was feeling restless and reckless. She wasn't going to sleep anyway. She was too worried about the morning, and the reality of what she was about to do.

In six hours she could be dead.

She wasn't being a pessimist, just a realist.

Maybe she should spend those hours doing something

that would make her happy, something that she never ever did. It had been a very long time since she'd thought of anything but the plan, the goal. Nothing else mattered but fulfilling the promise she'd made to her sister. But tonight, Drew had reminded her that she was a woman, and she was lonely and scared, defiant and determined—all at the same time.

It was the worst possible time to get involved with anyone.

On the other hand...

She pulled the band out of her hair and let the long waves flow loosely around her shoulders. Then she walked down the path to the cottages, her nerves tingling and tightening with each step.

She knocked on his door, turned the knob and stepped inside. The cottage was one big room, a small sitting area and a king-sized bed.

Drew sat on the couch. He was reading a book when she walked in. It looked like some sort of mystery novel. It was silly, but the sight of that book pushed her over the edge. She'd always found intelligence to be a turn-on, and this man was smart, maybe too smart. He'd read her pretty accurately so far.

But in a lot of ways, she liked his honesty. He hadn't set the scene with candles. There was no wine or champagne chilling. He wasn't trying to seduce her. He was just waiting...

After a moment he set the book down and stood up, his gaze meeting hers. Then slowly he walked over to her. He made no move to touch her or kiss her. He simply looked at her with his shadowy dark eyes, and she felt an incredible pull. All her nerve endings tingled. There was electricity between them—a dark, dangerous attraction.

"I'm glad you came, Ria. Why did you?"

Such a simple question—such a complicated answer. She settled for the basic truth. "I want you."

The fire in his eyes flared. He put his hands on her waist. "I know the feeling."

"For tonight," she added. "That's all I can give you. I need you to know exactly where I stand."

"All I care about is that you're standing here in front of me. You're beautiful, Ria. And I want you, too."

Her stomach clenched at the desire in his gaze. And then he was done looking. He pulled her in for a kiss.

He tasted as intoxicating as the vodka she'd served him, and he kissed like a man who hadn't had a woman in a long time. She met his demanding mouth with the same sense of urgency and need.

A part of her called for caution, but she couldn't listen to that voice anymore. For a few hours she was going to just be a woman, the woman she used to be, the woman she hoped to be again some day.

They knew nothing about each other, and yet there was a connection between them that went far deeper than the touch of their mouths. Something inside of her recognized something inside of him. What that was, she had no idea.

But she didn't want to analyze or worry. That's all she'd been doing for months. She just wanted to lose herself in Drew, to be a woman with no past, to reach that elusive moment of complete and utter freedom. Because there was a good chance in a few hours, her future would be over, too.

―➤➤◄◄―

Drew woke up just before dawn to the feel of a warm breeze coming through the open window and the sound of the birds singing in the trees outside. For the first time in a long time he'd slept a dreamless sleep. The nightmares from the past eight years had receded in his mind. There were no explosions, bloody scenes, screams of pain and anguish—no more horror or grief.

Instead, he felt a hazy, happy feeling, as if everything was suddenly right with the world. He was completely relaxed with an ease that came after great sex and a hard, deep sleep. He almost didn't want to wake up, to face the day, to have to think about the decisions he'd made regarding his past and his future. He just wanted to stay in this warm, wonderful place, the place Ria had created.

God! What a woman. So beautiful with her shoulder length silky blonde hair, brown eyes, sunburned nose, and a mouth just made for kissing. She'd brought a light into his life, a beauty that he hadn't seen in a while. She'd been passionate, generous and fun. They hadn't just made love; they'd laughed, and they'd talked, and the sound of her voice had warmed him.

He'd come to the island to relax, to recharge, to find his smile again, and he'd found it in her arms. She'd smelled like orange blossoms, like the flowers surrounding his beachside cottage, and he'd felt like he could breathe in her scent forever, and forever wouldn't be long enough.

That thought jolted him awake. He didn't think of women in terms of forever. Having just himself to worry about was a lot easier than having to worry about anyone else. But that didn't mean he couldn't enjoy the time they had together.

He rolled over on to his side, reaching for the soft curves he'd explored for the better part of the night.

Ria wasn't there.

He sat up abruptly, realizing how quiet the cottage was. The bathroom was empty, and while his clothes were still tossed on the floor, Ria's were gone. There was no sign of her white shorts or pink tank top. No sign of the lacy pink bra and matching thong he'd peeled off her body just a few hours earlier.

He felt a wave of disappointment. He was leaving this afternoon, but he'd thought they'd have a few more hours together. He wanted to know more about her. He wanted to talk to her, at least to say goodbye. What a strange feeling that was. He was used to leaving first, to avoiding morning-after conversations, but this time Ria had beat him to the door, and he didn't like it.

He flopped back against the pillows and stared up at the ceiling. Memories of the night before flashed through his mind. The heat between them had burned all night long. It had been a long time since he'd felt—swept away. He'd always been one to over-think, over-analyze, but last night his body had completely taken over. He hadn't given one thought to what would happen next, until now.

Now, it was obvious nothing would happen. Ria was gone. He should be happy about that. No goodbyes, no messy emotional scenes, no promises to call or keep in touch. It was in actuality the perfect morning after a one-night stand. The only problem was that he didn't want it to be over yet.

He told himself it was better this way. He was starting his new job on Tuesday, a job thousands of miles away from this island. The next phase of his life was about to begin, and he needed to be looking forward instead of backward.

Getting up, he headed to the bathroom and took a long shower, trying to drive Ria out of his head. But as he soaped up, all he could think about was the way she'd touched him, kissed him, smiled at him, and cried out his name as they'd climaxed together.

Damn! He turned the water temperature to cold and stayed under the spray until he was freezing. Then he stepped out of the shower, dried off and got dressed. He threw the rest of his clothes into the duffel bag and glanced around the cottage to make sure he wasn't leaving anything behind.

He couldn't shake the feeling that what he was leaving behind was the one and only woman who'd touched his soul, and he didn't even know her last name.

Was he just going to walk away?

The question ran around and around in his head.

He finally came up with an answer—*no*.

He had a few hours before his plane left. He would find her, talk to her, maybe get her phone number. Walking outside, he paused, realizing he didn't know where she lived, and the bar/restaurant where she worked didn't open until lunchtime.

Then he remembered that she'd told him she was taking out a boat charter in the morning. He felt marginally better realizing that she'd left early to go to work. Someone at the marina would be able to help him find her, or at least tell him when she'd be back.

The dock was only a short walk away. Colorful sailboats and well-worn fishing boats filled the slips. In the distance was an enormous luxury yacht. He wondered who that belonged to—someone with a lot of money. Probably one of the people who lived in the mountaintop mansions that he'd noticed while bodysurfing the previous day. It would be nice to have enough money to have a home on an island. He didn't see that in his future.

Near the entrance to the pier was a small building with a sign that read Sea Charters.

He entered the building and stepped up to the counter. A young Hispanic man with a nametag that read Juan greeted him with a friendly smile.

"Hola, Señor. How can I help you?" Juan asked.

"I'm looking for a woman. Her name is Ria. Do you know her?"

"Si," Juan said with a nod. "Ria is a beautiful girl, very popular with the customers."

"Do you know when she'll be back?"

Juan glanced down at the large calendar on the counter. "A few hours. I have other guides available if you want to go out."

"No," he said, tapping his fingers restlessly on the counter.

So that was that. Ria was out on the ocean and probably wouldn't be back before he had to catch his plane.

"Do you want me to give her a message for you?" Juan asked, a curious gleam in his eyes.

Drew thought about that for a moment, then shook his head. What the hell was he doing? It was a hookup. That's all. He needed to let it be.

"No, thanks."

As he walked out of the office, a thunderous boom lit up the air, rocking the ground under his feet. He heard a gasp from a group of tourists on the pier. Then the door opened behind him, and Juan rushed out. Together, they looked toward the sea. Over the curve of the nearby hill, they could see smoke racing toward the sky.

"What was that?" Drew asked.

"I don't know," Juan said. He ran down the pier toward the Harbormaster's office, and Drew decided to follow.

A crowd of people gathered outside the office. Rumors were flying, all centering around a boat explosion.

Drew's stomach turned. It was crazy to think the explosion had anything to do with Ria, but he had a really bad feeling in his gut.

"Juan, I've changed my mind," he said. "I need to rent a boat."

The other man looked reluctant. "Better to wait. We should stay out of the way."

"I do search and rescue for the U.S. Coast Guard." He pulled out his wallet and all the cash he had. "I need a boat."

Juan's greed won out. "I'll take you."

It took several minutes for them to launch a boat and maneuver their way through the harbor, as more than a few people had had the same idea and desire to help. It seemed to take forever to get past the breakwater, the reef and then around the island hills.

A good thirty minutes had passed by the time they reached the burning vessel, or what was left of it. It had been completely blown apart, with nothing but fiery debris floating in the water while divers began to search the ocean for survivors.

Drew's chest was so tight he could barely get the words out. "It's not the boat Ria was on, is it?"

Juan's somber gaze said it all. Drew stripped off his shirt.

"What are you doing?" Juan asked.

"I'm going to find her."

"There's nothing left of the boat."

"She could have jumped off before the explosion. How many other people were on the boat?"

Juan shook his head. "I don't know. She made the reservation—probably one or two. I didn't see them board. They left before I got to work."

Drew looked at the debris field and couldn't imagine how anyone could have survived, but he wasn't going to give up without a fight. This is what he did—he saved people. And he was going to save Ria.

He kicked off his shoes and dove into the water. It was a strange feeling to be the one in the water when he was usually the one flying the helicopter that launched rescue swimmers into the sea. For the first time in a long time, he wasn't hovering above the scene, he was right in the thick of it.

For almost two hours, he searched for Ria, but he couldn't find her. He couldn't find anyone.

When a shiny piece of gold floated by him, Drew could

no longer deny reality. It was Ria's necklace, the one he'd tugged at with his teeth as it lay in the valley of her breasts. He grabbed it and swam back to the boat. He felt completely exhausted and overwhelmed by unexpected emotion and a terrible certainty.

He stared at the gold heart with the emerald stone and knew that Ria was gone. Beautiful, sexy Ria was dead. He was never going to see her again. One night was all they would ever have.

Two

Fifteen months later

The distress call came in just before seven o'clock in the morning, a few minutes before his shift was supposed to end. A fire in a fishing boat threatened the lives of two people just off the coast of San Francisco. Drew Callaway and a Coast Guard crew that included fellow pilot Tim Roberts, flight mechanic Connor Holmes and rescue swimmer, Michael Packer, took off five minutes later, with Drew at the controls of the MH65C Dolphin Helicopter.

As they lifted off, the usual burst of adrenaline ran through his veins. Today's mission would be challenging. The wind was gusting at twenty knots with a steady stream of rain. Even worse there was a layer of low fog blanketing the Pacific Ocean, which would make visibility more difficult. But there were two people aboard the stranded fishing boat, who were counting on Drew and his crew to come through, and he was going to make damn sure that happened.

His crew was a well-oiled machine, each person at the top of their game, and Drew was honored to be working alongside each of the men. His friend, Tim, could party as hard as he worked, but on the job, Tim was an excellent pilot, and they both trusted each other with their lives.

Only one time had Tim led him astray and that was their

trip to the island, not that Tim had anticipated Drew would fall for a woman who would end up dead the next day. But if they'd never made that trip, then Drew wouldn't be haunted each and every night by the vision of a beautiful blonde with sweet lips and reckless eyes.

His focus faltered as he thought about Ria. She'd come into his life like a burst of sunlight and had made him feel like he was looking at a future that was much brighter and warmer than his past. But that warmth and light had only lasted a night. In the morning reality had returned, and even now he could feel the thunderous boom that had taken her from his life.

As the months went by, he'd started to get over her, and then five months ago he'd seen a woman on Fisherman's Wharf, and something about her had caught his attention. Her hair had been brown, not blonde, and longer than he remembered, but her body, her walk had reminded him of Ria. She'd seemed so real and alive he'd actually jumped out of his chair at the outdoor café where he was having lunch with friends and bolted down the street after her.

Unfortunately, he'd lost that woman in the crowd, and he'd been shaken by the glimpse of her ever since. But Ria was dead—wasn't she?

Drew's gut tightened as he looked down at the ocean below him. They were thousands of miles away from the spot where Ria had lost her life. But the waves still reminded him of the hours he'd spent searching for her in the water.

The memory also reminded him that in minutes he'd be sending a rescue swimmer down into a turbulent sea to do exactly what he had tried to do—save a life. Hopefully, this mission would be successful.

No *hopefully* about it, he told himself firmly. Failure was not an option.

Within minutes they reached the distressed vessel. It was

taking on water fast, and two people were clinging to the side, as the boat was tossed up and down on the stormy waves. Flames lit up the interior cabin and thick smoke mixed with the rain.

Drew sucked in a deep breath. Was this the same scene Ria had faced in her final minutes? It was more likely she hadn't realized she was in trouble until it was too late. There had been no radio call for help, just one powerful explosion that had blown her boat to pieces.

Drew hovered over the scene as the flight mechanic opened the door and launched the rescue swimmer. For the next few intense minutes, Drew had to battle to keep the helicopter stable as the winds gusted. Flying helicopters was both thrilling and terrifying at times. When he'd first decided to switch from planes to helos, his instructor had looked him dead in the eye and said, "One thing you have to know. Planes want to fly. Helicopters want to crash."

He'd taken the old adage as motivation to conquer the wily bird. He liked being able to fly in and out of tight spots. In the Navy, he'd had to deal with extreme heat and dangerous mountain ranges. He'd flown soldiers into enemy strongholds in the dead of night and rescued the injured. With the Coast Guard, he was able to pluck people out of the sea just before they took their last breath.

If only he'd been able to save Ria.

"Visibility is decreasing. Wind gusting to 25 knots," his copilot, Tim, said.

He nodded. "Five minutes."

"Three," Tim said.

He gave Tim a quick look. "Whatever it takes."

Tim frowned but didn't contradict him.

"Victim one is on board," the flight mechanic said. "Cage is going back down."

Despite his boastful claim of five minutes, Drew knew

they had less time than that. The weather conditions were worsening by the second and saving the other man could cost everyone on the helicopter their lives.

"Damn," Tim swore. "Victim two is in the water."

"Swimmer is going after him," the flight mechanic said.

The helicopter bounced and rolled. Drew battled with the controls.

"We've got to go," Tim said tersely.

"We'll make it," Drew said confidently, refusing to believe in any other scenario.

The helo bucked again.

"No time left," Tim said. "Call him in."

"I'm not leaving her," he said tersely as he fought to bring the helicopter back under control.

"Swimmer has the victim. We're bringing them up," the flight mechanic said.

It was a long minute before the second victim and the swimmer were on board, and then Drew headed for home.

When they landed, an ambulance was waiting, and the survivors were taken to the hospital to get checked out. It didn't appear that anyone had life-threatening injuries.

Drew finished his post-flight responsibilities and then exited the helo. The rain had stopped and the winds had decreased. It looked like the storm was on its way east.

As he stepped onto the tarmac and took off his headset, Tim gave him an irritated look. "What the hell was that, Callaway?"

"What's your problem?"

"My problem is you." Tim glanced over his shoulder to make sure they were alone. "You like to push the envelope; so do I. But what you did risked the life of everyone on board."

"We made it back safely."

"This time."

"*This* time is all I care about," Drew said sharply. He started to walk away, but Tim was right on his heels.

"And what I care about is this reckless streak you're on," Tim said, grabbing him by the arm.

He shrugged Tim away. "I was doing my job. If you don't have the guts for what we do, maybe you're the one with the problem."

"You said 'I'm not leaving her'. There wasn't a woman in sight."

"So I misspoke."

"Did you?" Tim gave Drew a pointed look. "You were talking about the woman on the island, weren't you?"

"No."

"Bullshit! She's been on your mind for over a year. You can't get over how she died so suddenly."

"What do you want me to say?"

"I want you to tell me that you're not going to keep trying to rescue a woman who is already dead. You have to let her go. You have to stop seeing her on every damn boat in trouble. You're not making smart decisions, and you know it. This isn't the first time that you've taken too many risks."

Tim's gaze bored into his, and Drew couldn't deny the truth. For a few minutes back there, he had been thinking about Ria and not the fishermen they'd been sent to rescue.

"I've never seen any woman get to you the way she did," Tim added, shaking his head in bewilderment. "And so fast, too."

Ria had gotten under his skin in a way no other woman had. Part of him wanted to chalk it up to the island, the warm tropical breezes, the heady rum drinks, but he hadn't been drunk that night, and neither had Ria.

"I thought you were getting your head together," Tim continued. "But you're back to where you were right after you left the island."

"I was moving on. But then..." He hesitated, knowing he was about to sound like a lunatic.

"Then what?" Tim prodded, curiosity in his gaze.

"I thought I saw her at Fisherman's Wharf," he confessed.

Tim's eyes widened in surprise. "She's dead, Drew."

"Well, she appeared very much alive to me. Her hair was brown, not blonde, but her face was exactly the same, and when she looked at me, she stiffened. I couldn't see her eyes, she was too far away, but I could feel her recognition."

"You could feel it?"

"I know it sounds—"

"Crazy?" Tim asked, cutting him off. "So what happened next? Did you talk to this woman?"

"I lost her in the crowd."

"If she recognized you, why didn't she stop to talk to you?"

He couldn't answer that question. "I don't know."

"You do know. It wasn't her. Whatever you thought you saw was just your imagination. Just like today, when you believed a balding forty-year-old fisherman was your hot blonde bartender."

"It wasn't like today." His jaw tightened. "I didn't see her on that boat, but I did see her on the wharf."

"You saw what you wanted to see. You're obsessed with her. I'm sorry now I ever took you to the island. I wanted you to relax and have some fun with no strings attached. That's what most people do when they go down there."

"That was my plan, too," he said. "And if she hadn't died so suddenly, maybe I wouldn't still be thinking about her. But ever since I saw her a few months ago, I've been wondering if she somehow escaped the fire."

"Seriously?"

He ran a hand through his hair. "Yes. I called her former employers at the bar and the charter boat service."

"And?"

"They confirmed that she was dead, no miraculous rescue."

"How much more evidence do you need?"

"None," he said shortly. "Look, you don't need to worry about it."

"I'm worried about you."

"I will be fine."

"Maybe I should talk to my friends down there, see if I can get any information on her."

"Like what?"

"I don't know," Tim said. "Maybe she has a twin sister living in San Francisco. What was her name?"

"Ria Hastings."

"Do you know anything else about her?"

"We didn't do a lot of talking that night."

Tim gave him a knowing smile. "She was one beautiful woman. She didn't give me the time of day."

"Why would she? You were wasted and surrounded by women."

Tim laughed. "True. I had a great time down there, as I always do. I love that island. Every visit is better than the last. The women are beautiful and free-spirited, and the rum flows like water."

"I don't think I'll be making any return trips."

"I'll ask around," Tim said. "It can't hurt."

"Whatever."

"What are you doing the rest of the day?" Tim asked as they started walking toward the building.

"Family birthday party this afternoon. My nephew, Brandon, is turning six."

"Is that the kid with autism?"

"Yeah. The party is really for my sister, Nicole, who tries to make Brandon's life as normal as possible, whether he likes it or not."

"Rough gig."

"I'll say. What about you?"

"I'm going to take a run this afternoon, then hit the clubs in North Beach with Paul tonight. Why don't you come with us?"

"I'll think about it," he said, not particularly excited by the idea. He was over the club scene. Same people, same drunken conversations.

"Another woman might take your mind off Ria," Tim suggested.

"So far that hasn't worked," he muttered.

"You haven't met the right woman."

As Tim walked away, his words ran around in Drew's head.

He had met the right woman. She just wasn't alive anymore.

"Tory? Tory!"

Ria turned abruptly at the sound of sixteen-year-old Megan's impatient voice. "Sorry, what did you say?"

"I said—what do you think of the dress, Aunt—I mean, Tory," she stumbled. "Sorry."

"It's okay," she said quickly, not wanting to dwell on Megan's small slip. It hadn't done any damage. There was no one else outside the dressing room in the small boutique. She focused her attention on the very tight, bright red mini dress that barely covered Megan's ass. She realized she'd been lost in dreamland a little too long. Their shopping expedition to pick out Megan's prom dress had gone way off track. She shook her head. "No, absolutely not."

"I think I look pretty," Megan said defensively.

"You look like a stripper."

Megan made a face at her. "You're starting to sound like my mother." As the words left her mouth, a guilty expression filled Megan's dark eyes, along with angry tears. She turned and ran back to the dressing room.

Ria let out a breath at Megan's abrupt exit. Her niece's meltdown was partly her fault. She'd been distracted all morning. Actually, she'd been distracted for the past five months, ever since she'd seen Drew Callaway at Fisherman's Wharf.

After leaving the island, she'd put the tall, handsome pilot out of her mind. At least, she'd tried to do that, but their night together had been so passionate and amazing. The chemistry between them had shocked her, and in a way it had freed her, too. For a few hours, she'd just been a twenty-seven-year-old woman on a beautiful tropical island in the arms of a gorgeous man.

Then the morning had arrived, and with the sun had come reality. She'd put her plan into action, and as far as anyone knew she was dead.

It had all been working perfectly until she'd seen Drew last October. Despite the fact that she'd dyed her blonde hair brown, he'd recognized her. He'd picked her out of a crowd of tourists, and he'd come after her.

She'd panicked and run. Fortunately, she'd lost him. But ever since that day, she'd worried that she'd run into him again. The fact that she hadn't yet should have made her less tense, but in some ways she felt like she was waiting for the other shoe to drop. Every time she saw a man in aviator glasses with wavy brown hair, she stiffened. Every time she turned a corner, she wondered if she'd run into him.

She needed to get over it—get over him.

Walking to the window, she glanced out at the San Francisco waterfront. The morning rain had disappeared, and the sun was breaking through the last few remaining clouds. Tourists filled the streets, and as usual, there was a festive air in this part of the city. She'd come to San Francisco because it was one of the few places where she'd felt safe in her life. She could also blend into the crowd and do the one thing she was really good at—sail boats.

Unfortunately, San Francisco was also Drew's home. She had considered that fact when she'd brought Megan here, but she'd thought the odds of running into him in such a large city were very long. She'd been wrong.

After she'd lost Drew on the wharf that day, she'd gone home and told Megan that they needed to leave town. She'd had their suitcases packed and ready to go, but for the first time in over a year Megan had balked. She'd argued and cried and begged Ria to let them stay in San Francisco. They'd been on the road a long time. Megan had been in two different schools, and they'd already changed apartments four times.

Megan was insistent that they stay put. She was finally making friends, fitting in, and Ria could see the difference in her niece. When they'd first left the island, Megan had been a terrified girl who shrank from shadows and woke up in the night screaming or in tears. But over the months, she'd lost her haunted, hollowed look. She'd started to feel safe, and she'd blossomed into a beautiful young woman.

Ria had weakened under the onslaught of tears and pleas. How could she take away the life her niece was just starting to enjoy?

Deep inside, she knew it was probably a mistake, but she'd agreed to stay until June. Then they would re-evaluate. Hopefully, she would never see Drew again. The one thing she knew for sure was that she could not have anyone from her past in her present.

Ria turned away from the window as Megan reentered the room wearing a long, silky, soft pink gown that clung to her curves and looked beautiful against her olive skin and dark brown hair. Megan had grown two inches in the last year and her shorter hairstyle gave her a more sophisticated look.

It had been traumatizing for Megan to have seven inches of her hair cut off, especially since her favorite memories of her mother were the times they'd spent together before bedtime, when Megan's mother, Kate, would brush the tangles out of Megan's long, thick hair.

But Ria knew that her sister would have shaved her daughter's head if it meant keeping her safe. So Ria had done what she needed to do.

"Well?" Megan asked, a need for approval in her uncertain gaze.

"You look gorgeous," she said with a reassuring smile. "Really beautiful. You'll take Eric's breath away."

Megan beamed at the compliment. "Do you think so?"

"I do." She suspected that the somewhat shy and awkward Eric would be speechless when he saw the stunning teenager in front of her. "This dress is a winner."

"It's a lot of money," Megan said. "Can we afford it?"

Ria hadn't checked the price tag yet, but she would find a way to make it work. "Absolutely. It's the prom. We'll make it work."

Megan ran over to her and threw her arms around her. "Thank you," she said, squeezing her tight.

"You're welcome."

As Megan stepped back, her gaze clung to Ria's. "I'm not just talking about the dress."

"I know." Moisture gathered in her eyes at the grateful look on her niece's face. "Why don't we celebrate finding the perfect dress with the perfect burger?"

"Sounds good. I'll change," Megan said, then returned to the dressing room.

Ten minutes later, Ria's wallet was a lot lighter, but it

was worth it to see the light of happiness in Megan's face. Ria just wished her sister could have been here to see her daughter so excited about the upcoming dance. Unfortunately, she couldn't turn back time, no matter how much she wanted to.

They walked out of the store and down the street to Capone's Burgers, named after the famous outlaw who had ended up in Alcatraz, the island prison in the middle of the bay. Capone's appealed to both locals and tourists, who came to the restaurant not only for the great burgers but also to catch a glimpse of the prison memorabilia.

Ria and Megan slid into a booth and ordered their usual burger, fries and soda. While they waited for their food, Megan pulled out her phone and began to text.

The sight of Megan on her phone, being a typical teenager, made Ria both happy and afraid. In the first few months after they'd left the island, neither one of them had kept a phone or had a credit card or a bank account. But as time passed, Ria had used the false identification papers she'd purchased almost two years earlier to set up a life for them. They couldn't exist in the world without establishing records. Ria needed to work and pay taxes and have health insurance, and Megan needed to be registered at the school. Every time Ria signed a form, she felt apprehensive, but she simply couldn't avoid some links to technology; she just preferred to keep them as minimal as possible.

Megan looked up and frowned. "What's wrong?"

"Nothing," she said quickly.

"It's the phone, isn't it?"

"How many people have that number?"

"Only a few," Megan mumbled.

Ria was twenty-eight years old, and while she might not have been a teenager in a while, she did remember a time when she'd had dozens of contacts on her cell phone. "Just be careful."

"I'm always careful," Megan said, a hint of anger in her dark eyes. "But what's the point of being free, if I can't do anything?"

"It's not for forever."

"Don't you ever get tired of pretending?"

"I can't afford to get tired. And neither can you."

"It's been a long time. Do you really think anyone is still looking for me?"

"I hope not, but I don't know. So after the prom, you're going to lose that phone and get a new number."

Megan made a face at her. "Great. Eric will think I'm an idiot. Who loses their phone three times in six months?"

Ria gave her niece a sympathetic smile. "I'm sure as long as you give him your new number, he won't care. He's crazy about you."

"I like him, too." Megan cocked her head to the right and gave Ria a thoughtful look. "Have you ever been in love?"

The question took her by surprise. "I—I don't know," she mumbled.

"You don't know?" Megan asked doubtfully. "Wouldn't you know if you had been in love?"

Her mind flashed to Drew. But that was silly. She'd known him for less than twenty-four hours. Love didn't happen that fast. Did it?

"Tory?"

"There was a guy, but I didn't know him long enough to fall for him. We didn't have a chance to see where things would go."

"Do you still think about him?"

"Maybe once in a while," she admitted, knowing that *once in a while* had turned into pretty much every day since she'd seen him at the wharf.

Megan's gaze turned serious. "You've given up a lot for

me."

She had given up a lot: her life, her identity, everything. But so had Megan. "You're worth it, honey. We're family. You're stuck with me forever."

"Forever doesn't seem as long as it used to," Megan said with the wisdom that came from experiencing too much tragedy at too young of an age.

Ria had no answer to that statement. They'd both learned how fragile life could be.

Fortunately, Megan's attention was drawn to her phone, and in typical teenage fashion she was distracted by the latest text from one of her friends.

Ria wished she could find the same kind of escape, but she couldn't let herself forget that they were living in a house built of cards, and one wrong move could bring it all tumbling down.

Three

After getting off work, Drew drove across town to his parents' house. He wasn't big on family events, and with the Callaways, there was always some kind of celebration happening, but this party was for Brandon and Nicole, and the two of them could certainly use as much support as they could get.

Brandon had been diagnosed with autism almost three years ago, and while there had been some minimal improvement in his communication skills, Brandon was still very much locked in his head. It was such a change from when he was a baby. It was like someone had turned off a switch in his brain at the age of three. And no matter how hard Nicole and the doctors worked to turn that switch back on, nothing generated improvement.

He admired his sister's efforts. Nicole was a warrior mom when it came to her son. There was no therapy too complicated to try, no doctor's office too far away to travel to, but her efforts had not paid off. And Nicole's intense devotion to her son's recovery was affecting her marriage. Nicole and her husband, Ryan, had separated a few months earlier. Drew hoped that the break wouldn't turn into a breakup. Nicole and Ryan were good together, and they just needed to find a way back to each other.

Not that he knew anything about marriage or even

serious relationships. He'd always preferred his single life. He couldn't remember the last time he'd dated a woman for more than three months. He'd certainly never met anyone who'd made him think about happily ever after, except maybe Ria, but that was probably because happily-ever-after was an impossibility.

He rolled down his window, letting the cool breeze drift through the window. The weather had certainly changed in a hurry. But that was typical of San Francisco. It could be foggy and cold in one part of the city, warm and sunny in another. He was happy to see the sun. He was off until Monday, and he wanted to enjoy the weekend.

A lot of other people seemed to have the same idea; there was quite a bit of city traffic. But eventually he made it to St. Francis Wood, an upscale neighborhood of large houses with front lawns and backyards, a sight that was rare in a city where many buildings shared common walls.

As he pulled up in front of the two-story house where he'd grown up, he felt his tension immediately ease. This house had always been his safe haven. It was where his father, Jack Callaway, had brought him and his three brothers after his mom died, after Jack found love again with Lynda Kane, a divorcee with two daughters of her own.

Lynda had inherited the house from her grandparents, and she and Jack had decided it was the perfect place to merge their two families. They'd solidified the merge by adding a set of twins to the family. For a while, it was a his, hers and ours kind of situation, but eventually they all became Callaways.

With eight kids, the house had always felt crowded, especially to Drew. He was the third oldest boy, but the fourth oldest in the family, putting him right in the middle of a lineup of siblings with big personalities. His oldest brother, Burke, was the perfect one, the born athlete, scholar and leader. Then came Aiden, the reckless rebel, Nicole, the warrior mom, then himself. Emma was next in line; she was a feisty fire investigator, then Sean, who'd broken the family tradition of serve and protect by following his dream of becoming a singer/songwriter. After Sean were the twins, Shayla, a super smart medical student, and Colton, a rookie firefighter.

He loved his siblings and his parents, but he liked them better in small doses. Unfortunately, today's party would be huge. Not only would the immediate family be present, but also cousins, aunts and uncles, and probably a few neighbors. At least there would be plenty of food, he thought with a smile. He was starving.

As he got out of the car and walked down the driveway, he let the feeling of being home wash over him like a warm breeze. He'd carried the picture of this house in his mind throughout his years in the Navy, and all the time he'd spent on the other side of the world. There was something very comforting about walking through the side door and into the warm and cozy country kitchen. His parents had remodeled about ten years ago, but the big oak table where he'd done his homework was still the centerpiece of the room.

Today there were several kids crowded around that table as two of his sisters, Nicole and Shayla, painted colorful animals on the kids' faces. Two other moms hovered nearby, sipping coffee and chatting about their lives while their kids were being entertained.

Nicole's long, blond hair was pulled back in a ponytail, and there were shadows under her blue eyes that no amount of makeup could hide. She wore jeans and a tank top that accentuated her thin figure. She'd lost weight since Ryan had moved out. Drew frowned at that thought. Maybe he needed to give Nicole a little more support.

Nicole gave him a happy smile when she saw him.

"Drew, I'm so glad you came. I know this isn't your thing, but I'm glad you're here."

"No problem. Hey, Shay." He turned towards his youngest sister. Shayla was one of the twins and had a mix of Callaway and Kane in her features. She had the Callaway blue eyes and the golden blond hair of the Kanes.

"Hi Drew," she said, as she painstakingly outlined a butterfly on the cheek of a little girl.

"How's medical school going?"

She looked up and made a face at him. "Exhausting. I keep telling myself one day it will all be worth it. That day seems a long way off."

"It will get here. You're such a brain. You've already cut out at least a year of school." Shayla had a tremendously high IQ and had graduated from college at sixteen. At twenty-four, she was finishing up her third year of medical school.

"I'm surrounded by smart people now, not like when I was growing up," she added with a mischievous sparkle in her eye.

He grinned. "Very funny."

He glanced around the kitchen as Shayla's attention was drawn back to the little girl in front of her. "Where's the birthday boy?" he asked Nicole.

"He's probably in the attic. He ran up there when the doorbell rang. Emma went to get him, but that was a long time ago."

"I'll see if I can help get him back to the party."

"It's fine. I don't need to force anything. I'm going to celebrate for Brandon," she said with determination in her eyes. "I know some people think I'm crazy for having the party, but I just couldn't let his birthday go by without doing anything. Even if he doesn't know, I know."

"I get it, Nicole. No judgment."

"Thank you."

"Where do the presents go?"

"Dining room. There's tons of food. Hope you're hungry."

"Always."

He walked out of the kitchen and into the dining room. He dropped off his present on a side table and then checked out the buffet, which had everything from cinnamon rolls, to salads and sandwiches. His father's parents, otherwise known as Grandpa Patrick and Grandma Eleanor, were standing by the dining room table. Patrick had the same ruddy Irish complexion and piercing blue eyes as Drew's father Jack, and Eleanor had white hair and pretty blue eyes that had become more confused as her Alzheimer's got worse.

Drew was happy to see his grandmother at the party. His grandfather had been talking about putting Eleanor in an assisted living facility the last few months, but after his father, Jack, had put up a fight, Patrick had agreed to wait a while.

"Hi Grandma," he said, leaning down to kiss her on the cheek.

She jumped back, alarm spreading through her features. "Who are you?"

His gut clenched at the confusion in her eyes. "I'm Drew, your grandson."

"Drew," she echoed. She looked at her husband for reassurance.

Patrick put a hand on her arm. "It's all right, Ellie. You know Drew. He flies helicopters."

"Oh, I always wanted to fly in a helicopter." The tension in her face eased slightly. "We should do that, Patrick."

"We should," Patrick agreed. "But why don't we eat first?"

She glanced down at the salad on her plate. "I don't like tomatoes. Why did you give me tomatoes?"

"You don't have to eat them," Patrick said.

As Drew watched his grandfather deal patiently with his grandmother, he felt both admiration and sadness. Patrick had always been a no-nonsense, rough-edged man who never felt the need to explain or apologize, but with Eleanor he was softer, kinder. She made him more human. Drew didn't know what his grandfather was going to do without her.

As his grandparents made their way into the living room where the rest of the party was gathered, Drew helped himself to a sandwich and devoured it while he spooned some salad onto a plate. He was halfway through the salad when Aiden and Sara arrived. Aiden was dressed in his usual jeans and a t-shirt while Sara wore black cropped pants and floral top.

Sara was an attractive brunette, who had grown up next door to the Callaways. After returning home last year, she and Aiden had reconnected and fallen in love. They'd announced their engagement right before Thanksgiving and now they were in the midst of wedding planning mania along with his sister Emma, and her fiancé, Max, who had also recently gotten engaged.

Sara and Emma had been childhood friends, so they were both thrilled at the idea of a double wedding. Drew thought that sounded like double the trouble. He had no idea how his brother, Aiden, was managing to keep his cool through all the bridal talk.

"Hi Drew," Sara said.

"Sara." He gave her a hug while he juggled his plate in his hand. "You're looking beautiful today."

Her cheeks turned pink, and her brown eyes sparkled at the compliment. Sara had always been on the shy and quieter side, and he'd barely noticed her growing up, but she'd certainly come into her own.

"Thanks. Have you seen Emma?"

"I heard she's in the attic with Brandon."

"I'll go find her, so you two can talk," Sara said, giving Aiden a pointed look. She grabbed two cookies on her way by the table.

Drew turned to Aiden, seeing an excited gleam in his older brother's eyes. "What do we need to talk about?"

"The *Eleanor*," Aiden replied.

"Grandpa's boat?"

"Yes. He's going to sell it, and I think we should buy it."

"Are you serious?" he asked in surprise. "I haven't sailed in years. Have you?"

"No, but I used to love it. Burke and I were in a sailboat racing class in high school. We came in second in one of the regattas."

"Maybe you should ask Burke."

"Ask me what?" Burke inquired, as he came through the kitchen door into the dining room.

Burke was the tallest of the three of them, with brown hair that was almost black and light blue eyes. He wore gray pants and a cream-colored button down shirt under a black jacket.

"Good timing," Aiden said. "I was just telling Drew that we should buy Grandpa's boat. Grandpa hates the idea of selling the *Eleanor*, but he needs the cash. He really wants someone in the family to buy it. And I told him I'd see if I could round up some partners."

"I can't believe he's selling the boat," Burke murmured.

"He said there won't be any more trips on the water with Grandma, and he doesn't want to sail without her. Too many memories."

"That sucks," Drew said, saddened by the whole situation.

"We can make a bad situation better if we buy the boat for the next generation of Callaways," Aiden said. "He'll give us a good deal."

"It's still going to be expensive," Burke said. "Have you considered the monthly expenses, any repairs the boat might need? I don't think they've sailed it the last few years. Where is it anyway?"

"It's in the marina by the Bayview Yacht Club."

"I'm surprised it's in the water. He must pay to rent the slip."

"He said he's been letting friends use it," Aiden explained. "And as for the rest of your questions, we can figure out the answers as we go along."

Drew smiled at Aiden's comment, which perfectly illustrated the differences between his two brothers. Burke liked to plan, to weigh pros and cons, then make a decision. Aiden liked to jump first and think about whether jumping was a good idea later. They'd always been opposites, and Drew had often ended up being their mediator.

"You should have done a little homework before you came to us," Burke told Aiden.

"I just came up with the idea. Give me a break."

"Why doesn't Dad buy the boat?" Drew asked.

Aiden shrugged. "Lynda gets seasick, so it doesn't really work for them, but it could work for us. Burke, don't you remember that summer we raced in high school? It was a blast. There are a bunch of regattas coming up this spring. We could be racing by May. Wouldn't you like to breathe some fresh sea air for a change?"

"How do you have money to buy a boat?" Burke asked. "Isn't every spare dime going to your wedding?"

"Sara's dad is taking care of the wedding expenses. He's compensating for being a lousy father for most of her life," Aiden replied. "And I have enough cash saved to invest in this boat, if we go three ways."

"You do?" Burke asked, a skeptical note in his voice. "Last I looked you didn't have a job."

"I've been working for Uncle Kevin doing construction," Aiden replied, irritation in his eyes.

"And that's what you're going to do now? That's going to be your career? You're a firefighter, Aiden. If you don't want to be a smokejumper anymore, you can work here in the city."

"I don't know if I want to fight any kind of fire anymore," Aiden replied. "But let's put my career choices aside for the moment. I have the money. I think you both do as well."

"What about the rest of the family?" Drew asked. "Maybe someone else wants to go in—Sean, Emma."

"I think it would be simpler to keep it to the three of us. Of course, everyone else can be considered at a later date, and we'll share the boat. But it would be a nightmare to try to work with too many people on this."

"Now that I agree with," Burke said.

"Good. All I'm asking you to do today is take a look at the boat. I thought we could drive down to the marina after the party and check it out."

Burke sent him an enquiring look. "What do you think, Drew?"

"I'm not that into boats," he said.

"You're into anything that goes fast," Aiden reminded him.

That was true. He did like speed. "Does this boat go fast?"

"It will when we fix her up and get some new sails," Aiden said. "Look, there will always be reasons why we shouldn't do this, but the bottom line is that this is a great opportunity and something we can do together as brothers. How long has it been since we did anything together?"

"Probably at least ten years," Drew said. "Maybe longer." In fact, he couldn't remember the last time the three of them had teamed up to do anything.

"There you go," Aiden said.

"Maybe," Burke said with a nod. "I'll consider it after I see the boat."

"I will, too," Drew agreed.

"Great. This is going to be great," Aiden said, with a light in his eyes.

"We'll see," Burke said. "It's easy to think something will be good before you know all the facts."

"I'm optimistic," Aiden said.

"Or crazy," Burke suggested. "I'm going to see who else is here."

As Burke wandered into the living room, Drew said, "Is Sara really okay with you buying a boat, Aiden?"

"Sure, why wouldn't she be?"

"Time away from her."

"Sara can go on the boat, too. And she's not a clingy person. She's independent. She has her own life. One of the things I love about her."

"You got lucky when you met up with her again."

Aiden grinned. "I did." He grabbed a plate and perused the buffet table. "So what's good?"

"Everything," Drew said, reaching for another sandwich.

--→➤➤◄◄◄--

"Aiden wants to buy a boat?" Emma asked in surprise as Sara sat down on the carpet next to her. Across from them, Brandon was busy building some sort of fort with a huge bucket of blocks. He hadn't even looked up when Sara joined them. Nor had he done much to acknowledge Emma's presence in the attic playroom, but at least he wasn't playing alone.

"Yes," Sara said, drawing Emma's attention back to her. "It's your grandfather's boat."

"The *Eleanor*?" she asked with a frown. "He loves that boat. He used to take us out on it all the time when we were little."

"He doesn't think he'll have time to use it now that your grandmother's health is so fragile. Aiden is determined to keep the boat in the family. He's trying to talk Drew into going in on it with him."

"How do you feel about it?" Emma asked, seeing an odd look in Sara's eyes. Her friend seemed distracted. "Is everything okay with you two?" As the words left her mouth, she couldn't believe she was even asking the question, because Sara had been in love with Aiden since she was fifteen years old, and she'd been over the moon since Aiden had fallen in love with her last year.

"We're good," Sara said, her tone not at all convincing.

"Sara, come on. I know you. We've been best friends since we were kids, and we're soon to be sisters-in-law. What's going on?"

Sara stared back at her for a long moment, indecision in her brown eyes, then said, "I'm late."

Two words that every woman feared having to stay. Emma blew out a breath. "You're pregnant?"

"I don't know. Maybe. I shouldn't be. We've been careful. I mean, as careful as anyone can be with Aiden."

Emma put up her hand. "Please, I do not want to hear about your sex life with my brother."

"Sorry."

"How late?"

"Four days."

"That's not that long," Emma said slowly.

"It is considering I'm never late."

"You need to take a test."

"If I'm pregnant, it's going to mess up everything," Sara said. "Look how long it took us to set the date, to find a church and a reception venue that we both liked. And what about the dress I just spent several thousand dollars on? August is five months away. If I'm pregnant, I'll be too fat to wear it by then."

"So you'll get another dress. Or you can get married earlier."

"We wanted to do it together, Em."

Emma smiled. "I would love to get married on the same day as my best friend and my brother, but not if it doesn't work for you." She paused, seeing the tension in Sara's eyes and wondering if there was more going on. "It's not just the fact that you might not fit into your wedding dress, is it?"

Sara sighed. "There are a lot of reasons why this is a bad time for me to be pregnant. Aiden is still trying to figure out his career. He's been doing construction, but I don't know if that's what he wants to do long term, and he doesn't either. I've just started a new job. So asking for maternity leave will be tricky."

"That's all logistical stuff. What is really bothering you?"

"I don't know if I'll be a good mother. I thought my mom was good, but after her death, I discovered all the secrets she'd kept from me. What kind of mother keeps such big secrets? And God knows my father was a disaster as a parent. He was cold and judgmental and made me feel terrible most of the time. My house was not a happy place to grow up. What if I take after either or both of them?"

"Sara, stop. You are neither of your parents. You are the best of both of them. And even though your mom had her secrets, she loved you, and she tried to make up for your dad. But none of that matters. I know that you will make a great mother. You're smart and kind and you have a lot of love to give." She paused. "And before you completely freak out—"

"Too late," Sara said dryly.

Emma smiled. "You need to find out if you're actually

pregnant. Why haven't you taken a test?"

"I'm not sure I can handle the answer."

"Have you told Aiden?"

Sara shook her head. "I don't want to say anything until I'm certain."

"Maybe you should say something before he goes out and buys a boat he can't afford."

"He really wants that boat. He told me he has great memories of going out on the bay with his grandfather. I don't want him to miss that because—"

"Because you're having a baby?" Emma interrupted. "Trust me, Aiden will put family over a boat, but let's take it one step at a time. After the party, we'll go to the drugstore and get you a test. You can take it in my apartment. Max is working all day. We'll be alone."

Sara smiled, relief in her eyes. "Thanks, Em. Just talking to you makes me feel like everything will be okay."

"Of course it's going to be okay. It will be amazing. We could use another kid in the family. Give Brandon a little cousin." She glanced over at her nephew, whose attention was focused solely on the task in front of him. "I wonder if he's understood any part of our conversation."

"I don't know how Nicole deals with him. She's so strong."

"Mothers do what they have to do."

"Yeah, I'm hoping a lot of being a mother is instinctive." Sara paused. "I can stay with Brandon if you want to get some food."

"I'm not that hungry. I'll hang out here awhile longer."

"Okay," Sara said as she stood up. "See you later."

As Sara left, Drew came into the room. Emma was both surprised and happy to see him. Drew wasn't big on showing up for family parties.

"Hi Em."

"Drew."

"Happy birthday, Brandon," Drew said.

Brandon didn't lift his gaze. Drew gave her a questioning look, but she just shrugged. "What are you doing up here?" she asked.

"Looking for you and Brandon. How's it going?"

"Fine. We're hanging out. I'm doing a lot of talking. He's ignoring me." She smiled. "Kind of like the way you and I used to interact."

He laughed as he sat down on the carpet next to her. "I listened sometimes."

"I don't believe that for a second. Sara told me that you might be buying a boat with Aiden and Burke?"

"I just heard about it. I haven't agreed to anything. We're going to take a look at it later today."

"You'll agree," she said with confidence. "There's no way you'll let Burke and Aiden do this without you." She gave him a mischievous smile. "You always loved it when they let you play."

"I'm a little too old to worry about playing with my older brothers," he said dryly.

"Yeah, but it has to feel a little good to have them include you."

He shrugged. "I think it's my money they want."

"They're not that cold. Although, sometimes I think Burke put his heart into the freezer after Hailey's death, and I don't know what it will take to thaw him out."

"He has to grieve in his own time," Drew said quietly.

Drew knew a lot about grief. He'd lost a lot of friends in his eight years in the Navy, not that he ever talked about his time in the service, but it had taken a toll on him. She was glad he was home now; she just wished he'd open up a bit more. Maybe working on the boat with Aiden and Burke would help him reconnect with the family.

"I don't ordinarily like to encourage family activities that don't include me," she said. "But I think you should buy the boat. It would be good for all three of you. Actually, it would be nice if you could include Sean, but he's barely surviving as a musician. I'm sure he doesn't have extra cash. And Colton is perpetually broke. Shayla doesn't have time and Nicole has her hands full trying to save Brandon and her marriage."

"How is that going?"

She shook her head. "I have no idea. I don't think she and Ryan are even talking right now. They haven't officially filed for divorce, but someone is going to have to do something soon."

"I haven't seen Ryan in a few months," he murmured. "Maybe I can talk to him."

"It couldn't hurt."

Drew idly picked up a block, rolling it between his fingers as he watched Brandon. "What is he building?"

"I'm not sure, but Brandon has a good sense of structure. He loves to work with the blocks. It keeps his attention for hours."

"I used to love building stuff. Burke and I built almost an entire city in our bedroom one summer."

"I remember. Then Daisy knocked it over," she said, referring to their golden retriever.

He smiled. "I forgot about that."

"I'm pretty sure Aiden threw something into the room so that Daisy would go after it," Emma said dryly. "He was bored with you."

"I wouldn't doubt it. Good old Daisy."

"Maybe you should get a dog to keep you company."

"I have plenty of company."

"Do you?" she asked, arching an eyebrow.

"Yes. Speaking of company, where's your fiancé today?"

"Max is working."

"How are you two doing?"

"Still happy. Still engaged. Life is good," she said, which was really quite an understatement for how fabulous her life was now with Max.

"You deserve it after that douche bag you were with a few years ago."

"Don't remind me." She paused, giving her brother a thoughtful look. There was a familiar weariness in his eyes. She'd thought for a while he was just recovering from his years in the Navy, but there was something else going on. "What's wrong, Drew? You look tired."

"I haven't been sleeping well."

"Is it that woman again? The one you thought was dead? Did you see her again?"

He frowned. "I wish I'd never told you about her. And, no, I haven't seen her again."

"But you're still thinking about her."

"Mind your own business, Em."

"You're my business. You're my brother." She cocked her head to one side as she studied his expression. "She meant something to you, didn't she?"

"I don't know what she meant to me. She died before we had a chance to find out."

"You've never told me what happened. Was she someone you were trying to rescue?"

"I did try to save her, but I wasn't on duty. I was just nearby when she was involved in a boat accident."

"I'm sorry." Despite Drew's claim that he didn't know what the woman meant to him, Emma knew that there was some kind of strong connection. Drew had been in the search and rescue business for a decade. He was hardened to accidents and even to death. He'd spent years building a hard shell around his heart. While it saddened her to see, she suspected that wall was what kept him from losing his sanity.

"I don't want to talk about her," Drew said.

"If you change your mind, I'm here. And I might be able to help."

"How could you help?"

"Well, I could help you take your mind off this woman by setting you up with one of my hot, single girlfriends."

He groaned. "No setups. I can get my own dates."

"I know you *can*, but you don't," she said pointedly. "You haven't brought a woman around the family in a long time."

"For good reason. I don't need you scaring them off with the third degree."

"I wouldn't do that."

He laughed. "Sure you would."

"I care about you, Drew. You've had some rough years. I know you won't talk about them, so I'm not going to ask. But I want to see you happy, maybe even settle down with someone, have a long-term relationship."

"Just because you're engaged you want everyone else to be matched up."

"Okay, that's sort of true, but not completely."

"I'm fine. Don't worry about me."

"You always say that."

"Because it's true."

"Well, if you're not going to have a social life, then I guess you'll be one less sibling who needs to bring a guest to my wedding."

"No way. I'm not coming solo to your wedding. You'll put me at the singles table. I'll bring someone."

"Who?" she asked with a challenging smile.

"I don't know yet."

"Well, you have almost five months to figure it out," she said on her way out the door.

Four

———⇒⇒⇐⇐⇐—

Drew followed Aiden and Burke to the marina just after three o'clock in the afternoon. He'd opted to take his own car so he wouldn't have to drive all the way back to his parents' house. And he'd also wanted to have a few minutes to think about what he might be about to commit to.

It had been a long time since he'd done something with Burke and Aiden, and this would be a good opportunity to reconnect. But a boat? He'd always been about planes, then helicopters. He'd spent some time on carriers in the Navy, but that was just in between flights.

He'd certainly never thought of himself as a boat owner. But why not? It could be fun—something different, something to take his mind off the woman who haunted his dreams every night.

Shaking that thought out of his head, he turned into the crowded parking lot by the marina. The morning's storm had completely disappeared and the sun was bright in the sky, bringing out the locals and the tourists. After squeezing his black SUV into a compact parking spot, he got out of the car and walked toward the Bayview Yacht Club. Aiden and Burke were waiting for him on the sidewalk.

They walked down the dock together. The boat bobbed gently in the water in a slip at the far end of the marina, a beautifully proud and a little weathered thirty-foot sailboat.

They hopped on board and walked around. Drew hadn't been on the boat in years, but as he took a quick look downstairs at the galley and sleeping berth, he flashed back on some happy daytrips with his grandfather at the helm, and his dad showing him how to rig the sails.

"It's not in bad shape," Burke said, as Drew came up the stairs. "What does the interior look like?"

"Fine, a little aged," Drew said. "But not unacceptable."

"I agree," Aiden said, excitement in his eyes. "We have to do this." He waved his hand toward the bay, the majestic Golden Gate Bridge in the distance, Alcatraz and Angel Island. "Look where we are—in one of the most beautiful cities in the world. The Pacific Ocean is just beyond the bridge. We've all been working hard for a long time. Our jobs have big stakes, life and death. The pressure is tough. We need to relieve that tension every once in a while. This boat is the perfect solution. We can cruise, we can race." He paused. "We can entertain the ladies."

"You're getting married, that's lady singular to you," Drew said with a grin.

"Well, you and Burke can go crazy then. Look, I can do the dance and tell you all the reasons why we should do this. And then Burke can tell us all the reasons why we shouldn't. But bottom line—I'm buying this boat," Aiden said. "I want to partner with you both, but if you're not in, I'll keep looking. So what do you say? Are you in or are you out?"

"I'm considering it," Burke said. "Give me a minute."

As Burke went to check out the galley, Drew's attention turned to a small sailboat pulling into a slip two rows in front of them. As the woman got off the boat to secure the lines, his chest tightened, and his heart skipped a beat. She was slender, wearing jeans and a navy blue windbreaker. Her light brown hair was pulled back in a ponytail.

Two teenage kids got off the boat. They exchanged a few

words with the woman, and then took off. As she turned around, Drew saw her face.

"Oh, my God," he muttered.

"Drew?" Aiden asked. "What are you looking at?"

He heard the question but he didn't have time to answer. He had to get to her before she disappeared again.

He jumped off the boat and ran down the docks, hearing Aiden call after him. He didn't even glance back. He was not going to let Ria get away again.

But she was already walking down the dock toward the yacht club.

"Ria," he shouted as he ran after her.

She glanced back and stiffened, then turned around and quickened her pace.

What the hell?

He broke into a jog, catching up to her in the parking lot. "Ria, wait." He grabbed her arm, hoping he hadn't completely lost his mind and was about to scare the life out of a total stranger. But it wasn't a stranger staring back at him. It was Ria.

Her brown eyes widened, and she sucked in a quick breath of air.

"It is you," he said, feeling confused, relieved and amazed all at the same time. "You're alive."

Her hair might not be blonde anymore, but her brown eyes with the gold lights were the same, as well as her lightly sunburned cheeks, and her lips—her soft, full, pink lips that made his body tighten in memory.

He was suddenly slammed with a montage of images from the night they'd spent together. Every one of his senses came alive. He could smell the orange blossoms in her hair when he kissed her neck. He could taste the heat of her mouth. He could feel her breasts swell under his hands as he licked her nipples into peaks of pleasure. And the way she'd come apart under him, on top of him—he could still hear her soft cries of uninhibited pleasure.

Damn!

His breath came so fast he started to feel dizzy.

He'd wished a thousand times for people to come back from the dead, but it had never happened—until now.

"Drew," she said finally, biting down on her bottom lip, as she tried to come up with something else to say.

The silence went on far too long. He'd seen her in his dreams so many times he had to tell himself that he wasn't dreaming now. But he was holding her arm. He could feel the heat of her body. He could hear her voice. She wasn't a ghost.

"I don't understand," he said, shaking his head in confusion. "I thought you were dead. Everyone did."

"So you heard about the fire on the boat?" she asked slowly.

"Heard about it? I saw it. I was on the dock when the explosion almost knocked me off my feet." He could still hear the thunderous roar in his head and taste the terror that had run through him as he and Juan had sailed toward the destruction.

"You were on the dock?" Her eyes widened in surprise. "I thought you were on your way to the airport."

"I had a few more hours before my flight. I was down there looking for you."

She shook her head. "I didn't know."

He stared back at her. "How did you survive? The boat was blown to bits."

"I jumped off before it blew up." She licked her lips. "I swam away, and eventually I made it to one of the small islands nearby. I was there for several days before anyone found me."

Her words were logical, but there was something about her story that sounded practiced.

"What about the other people on board? Did they make it?"

"No, I don't think so."

He didn't understand why she was acting so guarded. There was fear in her eyes, but she hadn't been afraid of him on the island. Why was she now? Why wasn't she smiling, laughing, telling him about the adventure she'd had, the miraculous escape from death?

"Ria, what's going on?"

"Could you let go of my arm? You're hurting me."

He hesitated, then released his grip. "Sorry. Why did you run away from me just now? You heard me call your name."

"I didn't want to talk to you. It's—awkward."

"Why?"

"Because it is." She crossed her arms in front of her chest. "We had a one-night thing a long time ago. I don't know what you want me to say."

There were a lot of things he wanted her to say, and none of them were coming out of her mouth. "Your explanation of your escape doesn't make sense to me. Juan took me out to the scene of the explosion. There were dozens of people looking for you and your passenger. I was one of them. I was in the water searching for you. I don't see how you could have swum away."

Her face whitened. "I didn't know you were part of the search. Why were you out there?"

"Because I wanted to save your life."

"Oh. Well, that was generous of you."

"That's it?"

"I didn't know you looked for me. I'm touched."

"I waited on the island for two days. I know search parties went out in boats to the neighboring islands. They came back empty."

"I was on a really small island. It was very far away. I'm

sure most people wouldn't have thought I could swim that far. But I have strong survival instincts."

He gave her a long look. She avoided his eyes. "I don't believe you," he said. "Why are you lying to me?"

She stiffened. "I don't care if you believe me. You asked me what happened, and I told you. So we're done."

"Hold on," he said forcefully. "We are not done. I thought I saw you on Fisherman's Wharf right before Thanksgiving. And now I'm sure it was you."

"I don't remember seeing you."

She was lying again.

"After I saw you," he continued, "I called Juan at Sea Charters, and I asked him if you or anyone else on your boat had been rescued after I left. He said no and that the tragedy still haunted him."

She stiffened. "I wish you hadn't done that."

"Why?"

"Because it's complicated."

"The fact that you're alive when you're supposed to be dead is complicated? Yeah, that's an understatement."

"I didn't go back to the island after I was rescued. I wasn't particularly close to anyone there, and it was time to come back to the States." She paused. "Did you call anyone else besides Juan?"

"I also spoke to Martin at the bar. He said he'd made peace with the fact that you'd died doing something you love. I wonder how they'll both react when they find out you're alive."

"You can't tell them," she said quickly.

"Why not?"

"I have my reasons."

"Tell me what they are."

"I can't."

"Then I'll make some calls."

This time it was Ria who grabbed his arm. "Drew, you can't do that."

"I need to know why. Are you in trouble?"

"I'm trying to avoid being in trouble," she said pointedly.

"Maybe I can help."

"You can help by leaving me alone. Just go away and forget you ever knew me."

Considering the fact that he'd been dreaming about her nonstop for the last five months, and for the year before that, he doubted that would be possible. "I'm going to need more information." He glanced at her dark jacket, at the yacht club emblem on the chest pocket. "Do you work for the yacht club?"

She hesitated, then nodded, and said, "Yes. I give sailing lessons and run private boat charters."

"So being lost at sea didn't make you lose your love for the water?"

"The sea is the one place where I never feel scared. I trust the ocean to do what it's meant to. People are much more unpredictable."

Her cryptic words were tinged with pain and bitterness, maybe even a little anger, but he didn't think all of her emotions were about his unexpected appearance. "I can't just walk away, Ria. Not like this."

She let out a frustrated sigh. "Look, we had an incredible night together, Drew. I'll never forget it, but it's not going to happen again. I'm not that woman anymore, and I never will be again."

"Why not? What happened to you? What changed?"

"Everything," she said with a wave of her hand. "My whole world is different now. And there's no room for you in it. I'm sorry if that hurts your feelings, but that's the way it is."

"This isn't about hurt feelings. If you're not interested, I can take it."

"Then why are we still talking?" she challenged.

"Because your behavior is odd, and your explanations don't make sense. I feel like you're saying one thing with your words, but your eyes tell another story."

"That is crap," she said angrily. "You are reading way too much into my desire not to speak to you anymore. I'm leaving."

She spun on her heel, and he knew she was three seconds from disappearing out of his life for the third time.

"I have your necklace," he said abruptly.

Her step faltered. She turned slowly back to face him. "What did you say?"

"The gold chain with the heart entwined around an emerald. You said it belonged to your grandmother. I have it."

"Where did you find it?"

"In the sea, near the site of the explosion. It floated right past me when I was looking for you. For a few minutes, I had renewed hope that you were close by, but that hope eventually died."

She put a hand to her neck, as if she could still feel the chain. "It came off when I jumped overboard. I felt it slip away, but I couldn't stop to look for it. I had to get away from the boat."

"Do you want it back?"

"Yes."

"Then we'll have to meet again. When?"

"You could leave it for me at the yacht club."

"Do you really think you're going to get off that easy? You want the necklace, Ria, you'll have to talk to me. Can you meet me tonight?"

She shook her head. "No."

"What about tomorrow?"

She hesitated, indecision in her gaze. "I'm teaching most

of the day. Weekends are busy. But if you want to meet me here at five o'clock, I should be done by then."

"All right. I'll meet you at five. And just so you know—even though you're not happy to see me, I'm very happy to see you. I'm glad you're not dead."

"I *am* dead, Drew. Ria Hastings, the girl you met, died in an explosion off the Isla de los Sueños. I'm Tory Harper now. New name, new start, clean slate. After tomorrow, we say goodbye, and we move on. Okay?"

"Why do you need a fresh start?"

"I can't tell you why. But it's important. So do we have a deal?"

He could see impatience in her gaze, a need to lock him down, have him make a promise not to threaten her new life, but he wasn't quite ready to do that. "I'll let you know tomorrow."

It wasn't the answer she wanted. She bit back something, then turned and strode away, her body as stiff as a poker. She was furious, but more importantly, she was also scared. And it was the fear in her eyes that wouldn't let him say goodbye or promise not to ever bother her again. It was ingrained in him to help people who were in trouble. And Ria was in trouble.

"Drew?"

The irritated voice of his brother, Burke, drew his head around. Aiden and Burke were walking toward him. He'd forgotten all about them, all about the boat. He'd seen Ria and everything else had vanished.

"Where the hell did you go?" Burke demanded, anger in his blue eyes. "We've been waiting ten minutes for you."

"I saw someone I knew," he replied.

"Yeah, you almost broke your neck getting off the boat," Aiden put in. "Who was that woman?"

"Someone I thought was dead."

Enlightenment dawned in Aiden's eyes. "Wait a second. Is that the same woman you thought you saw before?"

He nodded. "Yeah, it turns out she survived. She's very much alive."

"Well, that's lucky."

"Yeah, lucky," Burke echoed, an odd look in his eyes. "What's her story?"

"Not sure yet. We're going to meet tomorrow, and she'll fill me in."

"Okay, so let's get back to the reason we came down here," Aiden interrupted. "Are you guys in or out?"

"I'm in," he said impulsively, trying to tell himself that the fact that Ria worked at the yacht club had nothing to do with his decision.

"Great," Aiden said with happy surprise. "Burke?"

"Why not? It's been too long since I let you talk me into something stupid, Aiden. I'm overdue."

Aiden grinned. "We're going to have a good time—we'll be the three amigos."

"If you call us that, I'm not going to do it," Burke said with a warning frown.

"Yeah, deal breaker for me, too," Drew agreed.

"Fine," Aiden said. "We should celebrate. Sara is tied up with Emma, so I'm free. Let's go to the bar at the yacht club. The first round is on me."

Five

Emma walked into the apartment she shared with her fiancé and yelled, "Max?" When there was no reply, she turned to Sara. "He's not here." She held up the bag they'd gotten from the drugstore. "Time for the moment of truth."

Sara looked less than thrilled. "I feel sick to my stomach."

"Could be nerves or morning sickness. Only one way to find out."

"I don't know if I'm ready," she said as she reluctantly took the bag.

"Come on, get it over with, so we know if our next move is a round of drinks or a gallon of ice cream."

"Okay, I'll do it. It's going to be fine, right?"

"Whatever happens," Emma reassured her. "It's not like you're sixteen and knocked up. You're an adult, an attorney, and you're engaged to the love of your life. Everything is good."

"Exactly. Everything is great, but I'm afraid a baby will mess things up. Aiden and I aren't married yet. And we weren't planning on having kids for a while. We wanted to figure out our career plans first. This is going to change everything, and I honestly don't know how Aiden will take it."

The fear in Sara's eyes reminded Emma of the little girl she'd grown up with, the kid who was afraid to do anything wrong for fear her father would hate her even more. Steven

Davidson had really done a number on his daughter, and Emma still disliked him for that.

"Aiden isn't your father," she said. "He loves you, and if you're pregnant, he's going to be stunned but thrilled. You always wanted a big family, Sara. Things are going to work out the way they're meant to work out. Now go take the test."

As Sara disappeared into the bathroom, Emma walked into the kitchen. She wanted to have wine and ice cream waiting. Depending on the outcome, they'd celebrate appropriately. As she passed by the kitchen counter, her gaze caught on the big binder she and Sara had put together for their double wedding.

Max and Aiden both joked about the size of that notebook, but she and Sara had had a lot of fun putting together ideas for flowers, cakes, reception sites, and wedding venues. In truth, they'd started planning their weddings when they were twelve years old. Now, the idea of doing it together seemed unbelievable but also a little magical. Last week, they'd finally set the date, picked the church and put down a deposit for a reception in the garden of an old Victorian hotel.

If Sara were pregnant, some, if not all, of their plans would change. It made her a little sad to think they might have to throw out the notebook and start over, but in the end she just wanted to marry Max. She could do that at City Hall and still be happy. Max had her heart, and she had his, and that's really all that mattered.

She moved to the refrigerator and pulled out a bottle of white wine. She opened the freezer next and grabbed a quart of ice cream. She set both items on the counter and waited.

A few minutes later Sara came out of the bathroom with a dazed but happy expression in her eyes.

"Well," Emma demanded impatiently. "Wine or ice cream?"

A smile bloomed across Sara's face. "Ice cream."

"Oh, my God. You're pregnant?"

Sara nodded. "It was positive."

Emma moved around the counter and gave Sara a big hug. "I am so happy for you. And don't start crying, or I'm going to cry, too."

"You never cry," Sara said.

"Well, I don't want to start now," she said with a sniff.

"I didn't think I was going to be this happy," Sara said, wonder still in her eyes. "But I am. I'm going to have a baby. I'm going to be a mother."

"It's fantastic. I cannot wait. You have to call Aiden."

Sara hesitated. "I'll tell him when I get home. I don't want to do it over the phone. And he's with Burke and Drew right now."

"Probably a good idea. He'll be overjoyed, but you still might want to tell him when he's sitting down. This kind of news can shake anyone up." She paused as the front door opened.

Max walked into the apartment. He looked tired. His tie hung loosely around his neck and the sleeves of his shirt were rolled up to the forearms. He'd been working a homicide case for two weeks that was giving him a lot of sleepless nights, but last night he'd made an arrest. Hopefully, that would be it. She walked over to give him a kiss. "Hi."

"Hi yourself," he said, giving her a loving look. Then he nodded to Sara. "How are you doing?"

"She's doing great," Emma said before Sara could answer. "Can we tell him? I know you want to tell Aiden first, but I'm not going to be able to keep it to myself for that long."

"Tell me what?" Max asked.

Sara held up the pregnancy test stick. "I'm pregnant."

"Well, that is great news." He crossed the room to give Sara a hug.

"I'm hoping Aiden will feel that way, too," Sara said. "He doesn't know yet, and it wasn't exactly planned."

"He'll be happy," Max said with confidence in his voice.

"I should go find him," Sara said, grabbing her bag. "Thank you, Emma, for forcing me to face my fears, the way you always do."

"Call me later and tell me what Aiden says. Maybe tomorrow we can go out and celebrate."

"Sounds good."

As Sara left the apartment, Emma glanced over at Max. He had an odd expression on his face. "Are you thinking about how you'd feel if I was unexpectedly pregnant?"

"You're not, are you?"

"Well, Sara and I do like to do things together," she joked. "But no, I'm not. If I were, how would you feel?"

"Terrified. A little girl with your blonde hair, blue eyes and stubborn personality would probably kill me."

She smiled back at him. "You're just as stubborn as I am."

"True." He paused. "Do you want to have a baby right now, Emma?"

She smiled and shook her head. "No. I want to marry you and start our lives. I want to be a little selfish and have you to myself for a while."

"I feel the same way," he said. "But one day…"

"One day," she agreed. "In the meantime, we need to be a little more careful than Aiden and Sara."

He laughed. "I'm always more careful than Aiden."

"True. I would really love to see his reaction when Sara tells him he's going to be a father."

→➔◄←

"I must admit this is one of your better ideas, Aiden," Drew told his brother as he raised his beer glass to his lips.

"The beer or the boat?" Aiden asked.

"Both," Drew said with a laugh. He set down his glass and glanced around the restaurant bar at the yacht club. The far wall was one large window that ran from floor to ceiling and overlooked the bay and the bridge. On the other two walls were television screens playing a variety of sporting events. A few men sat at the bar talking about the wind conditions out on the bay, and another larger group of people had commandeered one of the larger tables. "Nice place."

"We'll be spending a lot of time here," Aiden said.

"Unless we decide to dock the boat somewhere cheaper," Burke put in.

"The *Eleanor* has always been here," Aiden said.

"Because Grandpa had money, and this is the best spot in the city," Burke said. "But there are cheaper locations, I'm sure."

"We don't need to worry about that right now," Aiden said, dismissing Burke's concern. "When can you guys get me a check?"

"Monday for me," Burke said. "I need to move some things around."

"Monday works for me as well," Drew put in.

Aiden nodded. "I'll let Grandpa know. He's going to be thrilled that we're keeping the boat in the family. It's a sad situation for him and Grandma, but we're making it a little easier."

"Grandma didn't even recognize me at the party," Drew said, remembering the fearful look in her eyes when he'd approached her. "That's the first time she hasn't known who I was."

"There are a lot of us," Burke said quietly. "Don't take it personally."

"Hard not to take it personally when your grandmother forgets who you are."

"She usually thinks I'm Grandpa," Aiden said. "She talks to me about stuff as if I'm her husband, and I have no idea what she's talking about."

"Maybe we can get them both out on the boat again," Burke suggested. "One last ride around the bay."

"That's a good idea," Drew said.

"Absolutely," Aiden agreed. He turned his attention to Drew. "Now, let's get back to your mystery woman. Where did you meet her? What was the relationship?"

Drew took a sip of his beer, then said, "I met her about a year and a half ago, on Isla de los Sueños. I went there for a week with Tim right after I got out of the Navy. She was working at the beachside bar as a bartender."

"And you hooked up," Aiden said with a nod.

"Yeah. It was the last night I was there. It wasn't supposed to be anything, just a beautiful woman on a hot tropical night, but..." His voice drifted away as he searched for the right words. "It was more than I expected. *She* was more than I expected. The next morning, I woke up and she was gone. I later found out she was on a boat that caught fire and exploded. There were supposedly no survivors." He drew in a deep breath as the painful memory ran through him.

"So how did she survive?" Burke asked curiously.

"She said she swam for hours and ended up on some small deserted island. I don't know if I believe her. When we spoke just now, she was nervous, wary, evasive. And she mentioned that she wanted to start over, new name, new start."

"She changed her name?" Aiden asked, concern entering his eyes. "She sounds like trouble, Drew, and you don't usually go looking for trouble. That's my department."

"Well, you're getting married, so someone has to pick up the slack," he said lightly.

"She's on the run," Burke interjected. "No one changes

their name unless they're trying to hide."

"I agree," Drew said. "I'm hoping to get more information when I see her tomorrow."

"You're seeing her again?" Burke asked with a frown. "Is that smart?"

"Maybe not. But I have her necklace, and I want to give it back to her."

"You want to see her again, because you aren't ready to let her go," Aiden said. "You're hung up on her."

"I'm curious," he said, knowing that the word didn't begin to explain his complicated feelings towards Ria.

"My advice is to give her the necklace and say goodbye," Burke said.

"Or you could give her the necklace, sleep with her again, and then say goodbye," Aiden put in, a sparkle in his eyes. "Get her out of your system."

He liked Aiden's advice a lot better than Burke's, but he doubted Ria would get back into bed with him when at the moment she didn't even want to talk to him.

"I'm going to order some nachos; I'm hungry," Aiden said. "I'll be right back."

As Aiden walked over to the bar, Drew turned to Burke. His older brother seemed lost in thought. "Everything okay, Burke?"

His brother shifted in his seat. "Yeah."

Silence fell between them. Drew wanted to say something, but he'd always had a harder time connecting to Burke than to Aiden. Burke was so much more closed off. He kept everything inside. And he'd gotten more distant since he'd lost his fiancé in a fiery car wreck. And unlike Ria, Hailey couldn't come back from the dead.

"I'm sorry," he said.

"About what?" Burke asked.

"Hailey."

Burke drew in a sharp breath and his eyes darkened. "I don't want to talk about Hailey. Why would you bring her up now?"

"This situation I'm in, discovering someone isn't dead, must remind you—"

"Everything reminds me of Hailey," Burke said, cutting him off.

"I understand."

Silence followed his words, then Burke said, "You need to be careful, Drew. This woman didn't want to talk to you today, and she ran away from you the first time you saw her. You've never had any patience for liars or fakes, and she seems to be both."

He frowned at his brother's assessment. "You don't know her."

"It doesn't sound like you know her, either."

"I thought I did."

"After one night of sex?"

"I know it sounds crazy, but we had a connection that was more than physical. And I need to know what happened on the island. I haven't slept in a year and a half because of her. She's not out of my life until she answers my questions," he said with determination.

"All right. I hope you like the answers."

"So do I."

"Look what I got," Aiden said, appearing back at the table with a heaping plate of chips, cheese and peppers. "Dig in."

As they ate nachos and ordered another round of beers, the conversation drifted into other channels: the boat, the upcoming sailboat races, and finally to Aiden's wedding plans.

"Do you have a date yet?" Drew asked as he washed down the last chip with a swig of beer.

Aiden nodded. "August second, some church in the Presidio, and I forget where the reception is."

"Don't let Sara hear you say that," Burke said dryly.

"I won't," Aiden said with a grin. "Sara and Emma are having a fantastic time planning stuff, and the good thing about a double wedding is that I don't have to be involved. Sara goes to Em for advice on flowers and cakes. And vice versa. Max and I just sit back and say yes."

"Not bad," Drew said with a nod.

"Is Sara's dad happy about calling you his son-in-law?" Burke asked. "As I recall, he wasn't one of your bigger fans when you were growing up."

Drew was curious to hear Aiden's answer. It was no secret that Aiden's father-in-law- to-be, Steven Davidson, had never been friendly to any of the Callaways. The families had lived next door for two decades, but Steven had always kept to himself, even more so after Sara's mother died.

"He's surprisingly happy about it," Aiden said. "Although, I think that's partly due to the fact that I'm taking Sara off his hands."

"I thought they were getting along better," Drew said.

"They are. Steven is trying to be a father, which means a lot to Sara. She's always wanted more of a family."

"Well, she's going to get more family than she wants when she marries into the Callaways," Drew said dryly.

"Damn," Aiden said, his gaze now on the television screen. The Giants had just blown their chance in the bottom of the ninth. They were going into extra innings. "Miller can't hit for shit this season."

"He'll be back," Burke said, shifting his chair so he could get a better view of the game. "He hit .360 last year."

"What has he done for me lately?" Aiden asked.

"You always give up on people too fast," Burke said.

"And you'll ride a losing horse all the way back to the

stable."

Drew smiled to himself as Burke and Aiden jumped into an argument over the Giants' starting lineup. He'd mediated a lot of their battles, but today he was going to let them fight it out on their own. His mind was on Ria.

If she worked for the yacht club, maybe he could get some information about her from the office.

"I'll be right back," he muttered, although neither Aiden nor Burke were paying attention to him.

He left the restaurant and walked down the hall to the office. The receptionist gave him a friendly smile.

"Can I help you?" she asked.

"I was wondering about your sailing lessons."

"We have lessons to fit every ability level. Are you a beginner?"

"Intermediate. I think I saw a female instructor out on the docks…"

"That was probably Tory Harper. She's excellent and a seasoned sailor. She's sailed all over the world."

"Sounds perfect. Does she have any openings?"

The woman moved to her computer. "Let's see. When would you want to take the lesson?"

"What is the first available?"

"Tomorrow afternoon at four o'clock. It's an hour slot."

"I'll take it."

"Name?"

He paused, wondering if Ria would check the schedule. He decided to play it safe. Since she'd used a fake name, he would, too. "Tim Roberts," he said, adding his own cell number to the reservation.

"Great. Tory will meet you at the dock," the woman said with a smile. "Have fun."

"I intend to." He couldn't wait to see Ria's face when he showed up for his lesson.

Six

She'd handled Drew all wrong, Ria thought, as she got off the bus and walked down the street to her apartment building. She'd been so shocked to see him, she'd veered from the script she'd so carefully composed and instead lied like an amateur. He'd immediately seen through her, and she wasn't surprised. His intelligence and quick brain had been one of the things that had drawn him to her, not to mention his sexy smile and strong, masculine body.

She drew in a deep breath in an attempt to calm her racing heart. But the adrenaline rushing through her veins was overwhelming and her instinct to flee was taking over. Leaving San Francisco today was her best option, but there was no way Megan would leave before the prom. It was one week away, and it would break her heart to miss it. Megan had already had too much heartbreak, and the last thing Ria wanted to do was make her niece unhappy again.

So she would wait, at least until after the prom. Then she would reevaluate and have a long heart-to-heart talk with Megan, because she was coming to realize that the shy, terrified fifteen-year-old who'd come to live with her a year and a half ago was not the increasingly more confident sixteen-year-old who seemed to have locked her past away along with her old name. Megan wanted to be normal. And she was doing everything she could to forget that her life was anything but routine.

Ria knew it was probably a coping mechanism and a part of her wished she could compartmentalize so well, but she couldn't. Megan might be able to put away the fear, but she couldn't, because it was her job to protect Megan. She had to stay vigilant and get rid of any threats to their safety, which meant she had to get rid of Drew.

A little sigh escaped her lips at that thought. In any other time, any other place, she would have loved to see him again. She'd never forgotten their night together, and today she'd been reminded in glorious detail just how attractive he really was. His brown hair was longer now, and he'd lost the painful shadows in his eyes that had been so prevalent the night they'd met. He'd been getting out of the Navy then, leaving friends and memories behind to move forward. Apparently, that step forward had been a good one for him. Standing on the docks, he'd looked vibrant, alive, sexy as hell.

It had physically hurt to look at him, to lie to him, and then tell him to go. But she'd done what she had to do, and apparently she would have to do it again tomorrow. She could skip the meeting, but she wanted her necklace back, and he already knew where she worked. Her jacket had been a dead giveaway.

So her new plan was to meet him, get her necklace, try not to act so wary or scared, and hope that he would just accept that there was nothing wrong. She knew her story had triggered his protective instincts, and as much as she would like a protector, she couldn't do that to Drew. She would protect him by keeping him as far away as possible.

With that resolve, she walked up the steps to her apartment building and inserted her key in the lock. As usual, she glanced over her shoulder before making her way inside the building. There was no one else out on the quiet street, no one sitting in a car, no one who appeared to be watching her.

She paused in the lobby to open her mailbox. There were only a few pieces of junk mail, all addressed to previous tenants. She tossed them into a recycle bin. As she turned toward the elevator, the front door opened, and Amelia Barrows walked in. An attractive brunette in her mid-thirties, Amelia was her next-door neighbor and was a widow with a twelve-year-old daughter named Beth. Beth suffered from chronic asthma and respiratory infections, and Amelia worked two jobs to pay for all the medical bills.

While Ria had tried hard not to make friends, Amelia had been insistent on getting to know her and Megan. They'd bonded over the pressure of having to raise girls on their own. Ria had told Amelia that Megan was her younger sister, and that their parents were dead. It wasn't as big a lie as the others, but it was necessary. She didn't want anyone coming around asking about an aunt and a niece.

"You okay?" Amelia asked, her sharp gaze raking Tory's face. "You're pale. I hope you're not getting that stomach bug that's going around."

"No, I'm fine," she said, but as she closed the mailbox, her hand shook.

"You don't look fine." Amelia paused. "You can talk to me, Tory. I know that you like to lead a very private life, and I respect that, but if you ever need a friend, you have one. I hope you know that."

"Thanks," she said, seeing the kindness in Amelia's eyes. "I just ran into someone I wasn't expecting to see, but it's going to be fine."

"Is he the person you're running from?" Amelia asked.

Surprise shot through Tory. "What do you mean?"

"Okay, I know I just said I'd respect your privacy, but I've been thinking for a while that you're hiding out from someone. Maybe someone who hurt you or Megan."

Apparently, she wasn't as good a liar as she thought. "Why would you think that?"

"Because you're always looking over your shoulder. When we get coffee, you sit so you're facing the door. When your phone rings, you tense."

"This man didn't hurt me," she said, not addressing the rest of Amelia's statement.

"So what's the problem?"

She shrugged. "It wasn't the right time when we were together, and it's not the right time now. I was startled to see him, that's all."

"Did you love him?"

The question hit her hard. She'd been reluctant to analyze her feelings about the man who showed up in so many of her dreams. "I wouldn't go that far," she said slowly. "I liked him. I liked him a lot. But we really didn't know each other."

"Maybe it was love at first sight."

"I don't know if I believe in that."

"I do. When there's magic, you know it, right from the start." Amelia gave her a long look. "So why isn't it the right time now? You don't have anyone in your life that I've seen. And you deserve to be happy. Just because you're raising your little sister doesn't mean you can't have a man, too."

"A man would complicate things."

"Maybe in a good way. You haven't gone on a date since you moved in here."

"I'm off men for the moment." She pushed the button for the elevator.

"Well, I'm not. I had a great first date last night."

"Megan said you came home in a good mood." Megan had babysat for Beth the previous evening, which had been fun for both of the girls. Beth got to hang out with an older teenager, and Megan got to make a little of her own money and just be a normal teen for a few hours. Of course, Ria had kept a very close eye on both of them.

Amelia smiled. "It was easier than I expected. We didn't have any of those awkward silences. I probably talked way too much, but you know me. I can't shut up, especially when I'm nervous."

"I'm glad it went well," she said as they stepped on to the elevator.

"So well it scared me a little. It's been three years since Carl died, and I've only slept with one other guy in all that time, and that was a disaster. But when I was with Steve last night, I was—interested."

Ria smiled. "Interested is good, isn't it?"

"If he calls me again," Amelia said as they got off the elevator and walked down the hall.

"I'm confident that he will call." She stopped in front of her door. "I'll see you later."

"Sure. Can I just say one thing, Tory?"

"What's that?"

"There's never a right time to fall in love. Sometimes you just have to let it happen. Risk your heart."

Unfortunately, there was a lot more than her heart at risk.

———◆◆———

Ria spent Sunday trying to concentrate on her sailing lessons and not think about her upcoming meeting with Drew. For the most part, it worked. She loved sailing, and it was a beautiful day on a bay that was crowded with boats, so she had to pay attention. But as she prepared for her last lesson of the day, she couldn't seem to quiet the uneasy, nervous feeling of anticipation that ran through her every time she thought about Drew.

She grabbed her schedule and checked the name of her next student in an attempt to distract herself. It was a new student, which meant more time at the dock going over instructions and less time on the water. But new students turned into repeat customers, so she would make sure he had a great experience.

She glanced down the docks, seeing a man approaching. As he drew closer, her nerves tightened both in warning and in anticipation. It was Drew dressed in faded jeans, a gray t-shirt and a black jacket. He had on aviator glasses and damn if he wasn't the sexiest man she'd ever seen—a real heartbreaker.

He had the cocky, confident walk of a man who knew what he wanted and knew how to get it. Which was exactly what he'd said about her at their first meeting. He hadn't been wrong, but what she wanted to do with him and what she *needed* to do were two different things.

"You're early," she said, as he hopped aboard. "We're not meeting until five. I have a lesson now."

"I'm your next lesson."

"You're not Tim Roberts."

"I thought you might find a way to push me off on another teacher if you knew it was me, so I gave my friend's name."

She frowned. "What's this about, Drew? I said I would meet you at five."

"I wanted more time, so I bought an hour. I want to talk to you."

"I can't use this boat to talk. It belongs to the yacht club."

"Then I'll take a sailing lesson. It will probably come in handy anyway. My brothers and I are buying a sailboat, and it's been a long time since I sailed."

She frowned, considering her options. "Find another teacher."

"Why?" he challenged. "Aren't you good enough to teach me?"

"I'm a great teacher, but it will be awkward."

"You know what's awkward?" he asked, taking a step closer to her.

She had to fight the urge to back up. "What?"

"This conversation." He took off his sunglasses, and gave her a hard look. "Let's not pretend we're strangers, Ria."

"I agreed to meet you so you could give me my necklace. That's it."

"You get your necklace back after we talk. What's the big deal? You're here to give a lesson. I'm here to take one." He paused, cocking his head to the right as he gazed into her eyes. "Why are you afraid of me? We had a good time together. It was actually better than good; it was amazing."

"I'm not afraid of you. I've just moved on," she said, trying to force a casual note in her voice. She'd told herself she would play things differently today but cool and casual had gone out the window when Drew surprised her by showing up early. That was the problem with the man; he was always knocking her off balance.

"Okay, you've moved on," he said evenly. "Do we need to be enemies?"

"Do we need to be friends?" she countered. "We spent one night together. We barely know each other."

"I thought we got to know each other pretty well."

She swallowed hard as his gaze swept across her face and fell to her breasts. She couldn't help moving the clipboard in front of her chest. She needed some sort of barrier.

His eyes met hers. "Too late. I've seen every inch of your beautiful body."

Her cheeks warmed with remembered intimacy. "Don't make this so hard."

"You're the one who's doing that. So let's get this boat out on the water. I'm sure you don't want to tell your boss why you don't want to take me out."

She was cornered and they both knew it. "Fine. I'll give you the lesson, but for the next hour, I'm only answering questions about sailing. Take it or leave it."

"I'll take it."

⸻※⸻

Drew smiled with satisfaction as Ria gave in to his request. He'd just bought himself an hour of her time— literally, and he intended to make the most of every minute. Despite his agreement not to ask questions about the past, he wasn't leaving today without a better understanding of what had happened to her on the island, and why she'd needed to make a new start.

"So how much do you already know about sailing?" Ria asked.

"The basics. My grandfather used to take me out on his boat when I was a kid, the same boat my brothers and I are buying. He's decided his days on the bay are over."

"Why is that?"

"My grandmother has Alzheimer's, and my grandfather spends most of his time taking care of her."

"Oh, I'm sorry. That's too bad."

He heard the distracted note in her voice and knew she wasn't paying him any attention; she was still trying to come up with a way to get him off of her boat. "Are you?" he asked.

"What?" She gave him a confused look.

"Are you sorry? Are you even listening to me or are you planning your escape?"

Her gaze met his. "You mentioned something about your grandmother."

"Yeah, she's losing her mind. It's hard to watch."

This time he could see compassion in her eyes when she said, "That must be difficult."

"It's unimaginable. My grandparents have been devoted to each other for more than fifty years. They can finish each other's sentences. They're each a half of a whole. One without the other doesn't work." As he finished speaking, he realized how true his words were, and he was assailed by a feeling of overwhelming sadness. His grandfather was already sinking. What would happen when his grandmother was all the way gone?

"That's an amazing relationship," Ria said. "I've never known anyone who was married fifty years. That's quite an accomplishment."

"Neither one of them would ever walk away from their vows. It's not who they are."

"It doesn't sound like they were even tempted."

"Well, I don't know if I can go that far; my grandfather isn't the easiest man to be around, but she seems to handle his quick temper and demanding personality without a qualm. Anyway, I'm buying his boat with a couple of my brothers."

"What kind of boat is it?"

"It's a thirty-foot J boat. It has a sleeping berth, galley, and according to my brother made for cruising and racing."

"You're planning to race?"

"Possibly. Have you ever raced?"

"Lots of times," she said. "So your boat is much bigger than this one, but the basics are still the same. Let's start with the safety instructions. And don't try to tell me they're not necessary," she added, putting up a cautioning hand. "New students always get safety instructions. It's club policy."

"Instruct away," he said.

As Ria went through her safety talk, Drew's mind began to drift. He was distracted by her mouth, her eyes, and her curves. She'd taken off her jacket and wore a white polo shirt with the yacht club logo over a pair of soft jeans that clung to her hips. Seemed a little thinner than he remembered, but she still had curves in all the right places. Her breasts swelled against her shirt, and he could still feel the weight of them in his hands.

He drew in a quick breath as desire swept through him. He'd wanted Ria from the first second he saw her and that feeling was back.

He wished he could say he knew more about her now than he had before, but that wasn't true; he actually knew less. Because now he knew he couldn't take her at face value. She'd changed her name, but that begged the question— which name was really hers? Tory or Ria? Was who she'd been on the island a lie? Or was who she was now the pretense? Was she a victim or a villain?

Sighing, he felt like he was a treadmill; he kept going around and around, but he couldn't get anywhere, nor could he get off.

"If you're not going to take this seriously, then we can stop right now," Ria said abruptly. "You haven't heard a word I said."

"I was thinking about the last time we were together."

She caught her bottom lip between her teeth. "We're not talking about that now. So either pay attention or get off the boat."

"Fine. I'm paying attention."

"Good, because sailing in the bay can be tricky with the winds and the currents, and I don't feel like going for a swim."

"I know how dangerous sailing can be. I'm the one who pulls people out of the water."

"Right. I forgot about that," she murmured, her gaze narrowing. "You must have had some training on boats. You're in the Coast Guard, and you were in the Navy. Are you hustling me?"

"In the Navy, I landed helicopters on aircraft carriers in

the sea. I didn't pilot the ship," he said dryly. "And in the Coast Guard, I fly well above the waves. But yes I have some knowledge of boating, and I understand how wind and lift work together, so with your guidance, I should be able to master the sails fairly quickly."

"Then let's do it. The sooner we get out there, the sooner this lesson will be over." She tossed him a life jacket. "Put this on. No life jacket, no lesson."

He smiled at both her annoyance and her directness. Her candor was one of the qualities that had drawn him to her. He'd liked her behind the bar, seeing people for who they really were, not buying into half-assed pick-up lines. But she'd been a lot more free-spirited on the island, not nearly so tense or so wary. Hopefully, she'd let her guard down and trust him a little.

"The most important thing to sailing a boat like this is the wind," Ria said. "I know that sounds obvious, but it's important. This isn't a motorboat. You don't get to just sit back and relax. If you need to turn, you have to change the sails, same with going faster and slowing down. You want to be sitting on the side of the boat where the wind crosses."

"Got it," he said. "But I'm better at hands on learning, so can we get out there?"

"Untie the line, and we'll get started. I'll get us out of the harbor. Then I'll show you what to do."

Seven

It took about ten minutes to get past the harbor wall. Once in the bay, the real action started. For the next half hour, Drew wrestled with sails and the wind, feeling more than a little clumsy in his technique.

Being on the water seemed to ease Ria's nerves. She lost her attitude towards him and was both patient and encouraging as she taught him how to turn, how to go faster, and how to slow down.

As the wind and spray blew against his face, and the boat flew over the waves, he felt energized and excited to take on the sea. His competitive instincts kicked in, as well as his desire to impress Ria. He wanted to be good at this, as good as he was at flying, but logically he knew that might take some time.

Ria moved with agility and grace on the boat, no hesitation or doubt in any of her movements. She was in her element out here. Her cheeks were reddened from the sun and the wind, and there was a sparkle in her brown eyes. Her long brown hair was mostly pulled back in a ponytail, but every now and then a few more strands escaped the band to dance in the wind.

It was a great day for sailing—sunny and breezy with views from every angle. There were a lot of other boats out on the bay, and the sailors were quite friendly, waving, shouting hello, as they passed by. A few seemed to know Ria, or Tory, as they called her. And she was certainly friendly in acknowledging them. Her stiffness seemed to be reserved for him, and he knew that had something to do with the fact that he'd met her on the island under a different name. He needed to know more, but he was strangely reluctant to break the tentative truce between them.

When they reached the Golden Gate Bridge, Ria had him turn the boat back towards the bay. She suggested he loosen the sails so they could slow down and get a better look at the city skyline. He followed her instructions and then sat next to her on the bench as the boat slowed to a gentle, bobbing cruise.

"This is fun," he told her.

She smiled. "You're a natural. I had a feeling you would be."

"I like things that move: cars, planes, boats…"

"I just like boats," she said.

"You told me the sea was your escape."

"And yours was the sky."

"You remembered."

"I remember everything," she said.

Her gaze clung to his, and this time she wasn't trying to hide the shared memories. It was the most honest moment they'd had all day. He didn't want to ruin it, but he was on the clock, and he didn't know how long he would have her alone. "So do I. And the way you look now is the woman I remember. Your eyes are lit up, and your cheeks are pink, and you've got that reckless, fearless look in your eyes."

"That's because out here I'm not afraid."

"Another cryptic statement. What happened, Ria? Why the new name? Why the fear in your eyes? What's waiting for you back on land that makes you so guarded, so nervous?"

"That's a lot of questions."

"We can take them one at a time."

She let out a sigh. "If I let you into my life, I could put you in danger."

"So you're not talking to me for my own protection?" he asked, unable to keep the doubtful tone out of his voice. "I can take care of myself."

"I pissed off some very important and dangerous people on the island," she said. "I had to disappear."

"Did you blow up that boat?" As he asked the question, he realized he already knew the answer. "You did. That's the only way you could get off without being injured. Was it some sort of remote-controlled explosion? Did you have a life raft?"

"Does it matter how? I had to make it look like I was dead. So that's what I did." She licked her lips. "I honestly didn't know you would search for me. I thought you'd be long gone and that you'd never know anything."

"Would you have changed your plans if I wasn't leaving the island that day?"

She shook her head. "No. My plans were set. I had no other option."

"So when you came to my room that night, you knew you were going to disappear the next day."

"I told you that, Drew. I said it was only for that night. You didn't care."

He vaguely remembered her saying something about a night, but he'd been so caught up in her, he wouldn't have cared if she'd told him they had five minutes; he would have taken what he could get.

"I was honest with you," she said. "I never led you on."

"I think honesty might be a word you want to stay away from," he said dryly.

"Honest with you," she said pointedly. "I wasn't talking about anyone else."

"Then be honest with me now. Tell me why you had to fake your death, which is a pretty extreme measure."

"If I hadn't faked my death, I'd be dead for real, and if anyone were to connect me to you and to the island, it could be very bad, not just for me, but also for you. They might think you helped me get off the island." She took a breath, her gaze very serious. "This is even worse than I thought."

"Who are 'they'?"

"I can't tell you." She blew out a breath. "I wish you hadn't made those calls when you saw me a few months ago. You could have triggered something."

"Like what? The people I spoke to still thought you were dead."

"Yes, but you might have planted a seed of doubt."

"Were you running away from Juan or Martin?"

She immediately shook her head. "No. I actually liked both of them."

"Then I doubt you have anything to worry about."

"Believe me, there's always something to worry about. Juan is very closely connected with some of the people on the island that I want to avoid. And I'm not sure who Martin is connected to these days. He was only supposed to be on the island a few months. He was taking a break from school. He's been there over a year."

"I guess he likes the island lifestyle."

"Yeah," she muttered, obviously distracted.

"Ria—"

"Tory," she corrected, refocusing her attention on him. "That's my name now. Tory Harper. You have to remember to use it."

"Tory doesn't really fit you."

"Well, it is me," she snapped.

"Why don't you go to the police?"

"They can't help me. The threat is—international."

"Then what about the FBI?"

She shook her head. "Don't you think I've already considered every option? I'm not stupid, Drew."

"Believe me, I never thought you were. Maybe I can help you," he suggested. "I am with the Coast Guard, and I have friends in other areas of law enforcement."

Her frown only deepened at his words. "No," she said flatly. "If you want to help, stay away from me. Forget you ever met me. You do not want to be in the middle of this situation."

"Is there anyone who's helping you?" he asked. "Because I find it difficult to believe you could blow up a boat, escape from the middle of the ocean, start over with a new name without having anyone to help."

"I'm good at multitasking," she said lightly.

"I don't believe you."

"I had help with the I.D.," she said.

"What about your family? Where are they?"

"Let's talk about something else."

"Ria—"

"I've already said too much," she said, putting up a hand. "I'm handling things, and at the moment everything is fine. My only problem is you."

He stared back at her. "Why am I a problem?"

"I already told you. I can't have any connections to the island, and you are a link. People saw us talking in the bar that night, and you helped in the search. If anyone thinks you really saw me…" Her voice trailed away. And then she said. "I wouldn't be the only one in danger then, you would be, too, and I really don't want that."

Her gaze softened as she looked at him. "You don't deserve this kind of trouble, Drew. The night we met you were getting over something; I don't know exactly what. But there were shadows in your eyes, and you were tense when we first started talking. You told me you came to the island to rest and to forget, and I assumed you were referring to some dark moments in your Naval career. Maybe I was wrong about the reason, but there was pain in your eyes, and also loneliness." She frowned. "Maybe that's not the right word, but you seemed isolated from everyone in that bar. You weren't with your friend or his party. You didn't talk to anyone who approached you. You were your own island."

"And then you walked over," he said quietly, a little shaken that she'd read him so well.

"What were you trying to forget?" she asked.

"It wasn't any one thing, not a single moment or a single death; it was everything combined. I was tired, and even though I'd gone to the island to relax and blow off some steam, I couldn't get into the party mode. I couldn't waste time having meaningless conversation with people I didn't care about and couldn't relate to." He paused. "And then you walked down the bar."

"Because you were watching me."

"I couldn't take my eyes off of you."

"There were lots of pretty women in that bar," she said with a bit of a self-conscious smile.

"But you were more than that. You were smart and funny, and you didn't let me get away with my lame pickup lines."

"They were pretty bad," she agreed.

"I was out of practice."

"You said that at the time. I had a hard time believing it, because you know you're not bad looking."

He smiled. "Thanks."

"So how come you were out of practice?"

He knew she was using her questions to avoid his, but at the moment they were talking, and that was a good thing. "I was focused on my career in my early twenties, and then I was deployed for a long time. I lost some friends, and my life got a little dark for a while," he said, glossing over those bad years. "I didn't feel like I was in a position to start something with anyone."

"I'm sorry, Drew. I can't imagine what you went through, but I do know what it's like to lose people you care about."

"Who have you lost, Ria?"

"Well, I lost my grandfather. He's the one who taught me how to sail. From the time I could walk, he had me out on his boat. He was a commercial fisherman in his day job, and on the weekends we would go out in his sailboat." She paused. "We lived here in San Francisco at the time, so this bay feels a lot like home to me. And it did to him, too. His whole life was on the sea, which is probably why he ended up divorced. His wife said the sea was his mistress. And he used to tell me that my grandmother wasn't really wrong. He was always happiest on the water."

"Like you. It sounds like you were close."

"We were. My grandfather was my anchor. My parents didn't get along well. I'm not even sure why they got married in the first place. All I remember is them fighting. They got divorced when I was eleven. And the next year my grandfather died. That time was a little dark for me," she said, using his own words.

"But you still continued to sail after your grandfather passed."

"Yes, I joined some junior sailing clubs so I could get back on the water. No one else in the family had a boat, so that was my only option."

"And now you sail for a living. Not a bad job."

"I'm lucky to be able to do what I love. It doesn't pay a lot, but enough."

"Do you still bartend?"

"Sometimes. What about you, Drew? When did you

decide to become a pilot?"

"When I was fourteen. My dad's friend took us up in his small plane, and I was hooked. The first time I took the controls, I knew that's what I wanted to do for the rest of my life."

"And did you always have your eye on flying for the Navy?"

He smiled. "My first goal was to fly the fastest planes I could find. Fighter jets seemed the best option. But once I got in the Navy, there was more of a need for helicopter pilots so I changed directions. I liked the fact that helicopters require the pilot to really fly them, and the stealth factor was appealing. I could set down in remote locations. I could go where no one else could."

"You have an adventurous spirit."

"Yeah, kind of like you."

"Did you ever get shot at?"

"Lots of times. I only had one hard landing."

She gave him a knowing smile. "Is your idea of a hard landing equal to someone else's idea of a crash?"

"Possibly," he conceded.

"When you left the Navy, did you ever consider a civilian job, maybe flying tourists around Hawaii or something? You had certainly already done your duty."

He shook his head. "Way too boring. The Coast Guard is perfect for me. And it's a family tradition to serve the community or the world. My great-grandfather started it, and just about everyone since then has taken up a career that gives back in some way."

"That sounds like a burden."

"More of a guidepost. At least that's the way I looked at it. Some of my siblings have a different take. Did you grow up with any family traditions?"

"Not really. Although my grandfather used to tell me that

a pessimistic person complains about the wind, an optimist expects it to change, and the realist simply adjusts the sails. I think he stole the quote from someone, but it's the way he lived his life. And I try to live my life that way, too." She paused for a moment, giving him a long, thoughtful look. "Can I ask you something, Drew?"

"Shoot."

"Why are you so interested in me? Is it because I'm not interested in you? Do you want what you can't have? Is it the chase that makes me more exciting?"

He gazed back at her with a thoughtful expression. "First of all, I don't believe for a second that you're not interested in me. I know when a woman is attracted to me, even when she's pretending not to be."

"That's a cocky statement."

"It's true. And I don't need a chase to find you exciting, although I must admit I'm both intrigued and a little wary."

"You should be less intrigued and more wary," she said dryly. "Look, Drew, I had a great time with you on the island. But it's over. I'm not that woman anymore. And I can't be connected to you."

"Why don't you just let me help you, Ria?"

"I can't." She took a breath. "I'm not the only one involved and the secrets don't belong just to me." Glancing down at her watch, she added. "Your hour is up. Time to go back."

"We can't leave it like that."

"We have to. I know you're curious and frustrated and probably pissed off, but you have to let this go. You have to let *me* go."

A rough wave of disappointment ran through him. He wasn't ready to say goodbye yet, but she was already on her feet, adjusting the sails. "Let's see if we can find some of that speed you love so much," she said, giving him a bright smile that barely covered what looked like sadness. She might be determined to be alone and on her own, but she wasn't feeling that great about her decision. And neither was he. In fact, he was nowhere near done with her, but he'd save that statement for a later date.

The last thing he wanted her to do was run again. So he'd be patient, bide his time, and wait for his opportunity.

As they sailed back to the harbor, Ria let the boat run at full speed, and Drew reveled in the ride. All too soon, they were back at the dock.

After securing the lines, Ria held out her hand. "My necklace, please."

Drew pulled a baggie out of his pocket and handed it to her. As she took out her necklace, her eyes filled with moisture, and her hand trembled. "I never thought I'd see this again."

He was surprised by the show of emotion. "That necklace must mean a lot to you."

She nodded. "My sister gave it to me a very long time ago."

His nerves tingled. "You never mentioned a sister before."

Ria stiffened, as she realized she'd given something away. "It doesn't matter. Will you help me put it on?"

He took the necklace as she turned around and lifted her hair.

As he stepped behind her, the curve of her neck, the wisp of hairs around the sweet shell of her ear called out to him. He wanted to put his mouth on that soft skin and bury his face in her hair, and pull her body up hard against his, so she could feel how much he wanted her.

"Drew," she said. "Are you having trouble with the clasp?"

He was having trouble all right, but it had nothing to do

with the clasp.

He focused on getting the necklace hooked. Then he forced himself to step away. She turned to face him.

"Thanks for bringing it back, Drew."

He stared into her eyes. "I think I was meant to see you again, Ria."

"You don't believe in fate."

"Maybe I do. Do you know the odds of me being the one to find that necklace in the water? It has to be millions to one."

She licked her lips. "I'm just glad you found it."

Her cell phone rang, and she frowned, then pulled the phone out of the pocket of her jacket. Fear ran across her face as she saw the number. "Megan? Is something wrong? Where are you?" She paused. "You have to stop crying. I can't understand you." Another beat. "Okay, I'm coming right now. I'll be there as fast as I can." She hung up the phone. "I have to go."

"What's happened?" he asked, concerned by the worried light in her eyes.

"I have to go to the hospital."

He didn't like the sound of that. "I'll take you."

"No, I can get a cab," she said, as she hopped off the boat and walked briskly down the block.

"On a Sunday—in this area? It will take you a half hour. My car is in the lot."

She hesitated, her desire to get to the hospital obviously warring with her reluctance to spend any more time with him. Finally, she nodded. "All right. Thank you."

"No problem."

As they walked toward his car, he couldn't help thinking that maybe fate wasn't ready for them to say goodbye, either.

Eight

Ria tried to stay calm on the trip to the hospital. Megan was not in the hospital because of the danger that constantly surrounded them. In between sobs, she'd mentioned something about a softball hitting her in the face. So this incident was not life-threatening, nor connected to their past. It was just an accident.

Despite the mental pep talk, her heart was still beating too fast. Megan was her responsibility. She was supposed to protect her. She never should have let Megan go to the park with her friends, or at the very least she should have told her to stay in the outfield. Megan was not the most athletic kid on the planet.

But she was always saying no to her niece, so sometimes she forced herself to say yes just to avoid complete and utter rebellion.

"Do you know what happened?" Drew asked as he stopped at a light.

She shook her head.

"Is it someone in your family?"

She nodded, hoping the questions would stop there.

"Is it serious?" he asked.

"I don't think so," she said shortly. "I don't know. I just want to get there."

"We're almost there."

A few minutes later, he pulled into the circular lot by the emergency room of San Francisco General Hospital. "I'll wait for you."

"Don't," she said, her hand on the door. "It could be hours. You know how emergency rooms are. I'll get a cab." She stepped out onto the sidewalk. "Thanks," she added. Then she shut the door and hurried through double doors of the hospital.

Ria checked in with the nurse, who quickly found Megan's name on the computer and had someone take her to examination room three. When she walked into the small room, Megan was sitting up on the table, an ice pack to her face. There was blood on her shirt and jeans, but Ria didn't see any other injuries.

When Megan saw Ria, she burst into tears. She lowered the ice pack to reveal an incredibly swollen nose and two cheeks that were purple and black.

"My life is over," Megan said dramatically.

Ria put her arm around her niece's shoulders and patted her back. "It's going to be okay."

"It's not going to be okay," Megan wailed. "I look like a freak."

Ria stepped back. "It's not so bad," she said, trying to downplay the swelling. "What happened?"

"I was playing softball and the second baseman had to leave early, and they asked if I could do it. And I said yes," Megan ended her explanation with a sob. "I tried to field a grounder but it bounced off the dirt and hit me in the face. I think my nose is broken."

"Actually, there's just a small fracture," the doctor said as he came into the room holding an x-ray. He gave Megan an encouraging smile. "There's no displacement, so while your nose will be painful and swollen for a few days, I expect you to make a full recovery."

Ria felt an enormous rush of relief. "That's good news. Can I take her home?"

"Yes. The nurse will be in soon with the discharge papers. I gave Megan some pain medication, so she should take it easy for the rest of the day."

"I'll make sure of that," Ria promised.

He paused at the door and glanced back at Megan. "Maybe stick to the outfield in the future."

"I'm never playing again," Megan vowed as the doctor left the room.

"See, it's going to be all right," Ria said.

There was nothing but disbelief in Megan's eyes. "By next Saturday night? There's no way Eric is going to want to take me to the prom looking like a hideous monster."

"You are not a monster, and you'll look a lot better by then," she said, hoping that was the truth.

"I hate my life," Megan wailed.

Ria wasn't too thrilled with their lives, either, but at least the injury wasn't serious.

The nurse came in a moment later. Ria signed the appropriate forms, knowing with each signature that she was creating a paper trail, but that trail was tied to their new identities, so hopefully it wouldn't be an issue.

"Let's get you home," she said after the nurse left.

"I can't get on the bus like this. Everyone will look at me."

"We'll take a cab," she said. But as they walked out of the examining room into the waiting room, she saw Drew standing by the door. Her step faltered. She'd hoped he'd gone home.

Drew came forward, concern in his eyes.

"Everything okay?" he asked, his glance moving from her to Megan. "Hi," he said. "I'm Drew Callaway. I'm a friend of—Tory's," he said, stumbling over her name.

Ria appreciated the effort, even though the last thing she wanted to do was introduce him to Megan.

Megan shot him a suspicious look, and why wouldn't she? Megan knew better than anyone that Ria didn't have any friends.

"He is a friend," she told Megan. "This is my sister, Megan, Drew."

"Who's this?" Megan asked, a suspicious note in her voice.

"Your sister?" Drew echoed in surprise, shooting her a quick look. "The one who gave you the necklace?"

"No," she said quickly. "I need to get Megan home."

"That's why I waited. I thought you might need a ride." He glanced at Megan. "It's nice to meet you."

"Is it?" Megan asked grumpily. "I look like a freak."

"Can I ask what happened?" he questioned tentatively.

"Megan took a softball off her nose," Ria explained.

An understanding gleam entered his eyes. "I've been there. I took a hardball off my face in the tenth grade. Last time I was put at shortstop." He cocked his head to the right as he considered her injury. "Yours doesn't look so bad."

"How long did it take for the swelling to go down when you got hit?" Megan asked.

"About three days. I had a shiner for a while though."

"Great, that's just great," Megan said with a sigh.

"My car is not too far away," Drew said. "Shall I bring it around or—"

"We can walk," Ria said, wanting to get away from the hospital and home as quickly as possible.

She got into the front seat of Drew's SUV while Megan climbed into the back. When Drew asked for her address, Ria had another small panic attack. She would have preferred that he not know where they lived, but that was impossible now. She gave him the address and Drew started the engine.

"So you're a softball player, huh?" Drew asked Megan as he drove out of the parking lot.

"Not really. This was only my second time. Last time I was in the outfield. I should have stayed there," Megan said. "But Shari had to leave early and there was no one else who wanted to take her spot. I thought I could do it. Mom used to play softball, and she was really good."

Ria stiffened at the reference to Megan's mother. So far, Megan hadn't given away anything, but who knew what was coming next? The doctor had given her niece painkillers that had obviously loosened her already loose tongue. "Just rest," she told Megan. "Talking won't help the swelling."

Drew shot her a sideways glance that told her he knew exactly why she didn't want Megan to talk any more.

She ignored him and glanced out the window. It was after six now, and dusk had settled over the city, a beautiful purple pink glow along the skyline. It would be pretty out on the water now, the stillness of twilight.

But she couldn't escape to sea. She had to be a mom tonight, and even though she'd been in the role for a year and a half, it still didn't quite fit. She was only twelve years older than Megan, and sometimes it was difficult to be aunt, mom, sister and friend all at the same time, especially since Megan had started to push back. She was going through typically rebellious teenage years, which would have been hard enough to handle, but Ria had more than just Megan's hormones to worry about. She had to keep her niece alive. And whatever that required took precedent over teenage angst, at least most of the time.

"I'm hungry," Megan announced. "I didn't have lunch."

"I'll make something when we get home."

"But how am I going to eat anything? My jaw hurts, too."

"I'll make you a smoothie," she suggested.

"I already had a smoothie for breakfast. I could eat some

noodles. Can we stop at the Hot Wok on the way home?"

"I'll call in an order after we get home," Ria replied.

"It will take over an hour. They're super slow for delivery," Megan reminded her.

"I'm happy to stop," Drew offered.

"I'm sure you'd like to be on your way," she said.

"I have nowhere to be, and I'm hungry, too. Sailing worked up an appetite. Where is this place?"

Deciding that an argument would take longer than stopping for food, she said, "Turn left at the next corner. It's on the right side of the street." Megan was in pain, and getting her something she could eat was the least Ria could do. "It's hard to park, so if you want to wait in the car, I can run in and order. It usually doesn't take too long to pick up. Delivery is a different story."

"No problem." Drew pulled over to the side of the road in front of a loading zone.

"Is there something you like?" she asked.

"Whatever you order is fine with me."

As Ria opened the car door, she realized she was leaving Megan alone with Drew, and that probably wasn't a good idea. But Megan wasn't going to go in with her, and Drew had to stay with the car. She just needed to make this stop as fast as possible.

"Don't worry," Drew said, catching her eye. He gave her a knowing smile. "Megan and I will get better acquainted."

That's exactly what she was afraid of.

———⊰⊱———

Drew put the car into park, then turned in his seat so he could see Megan. The girl's face was swollen and bruised, but there was still beauty in her features. She had dark hair and dark eyes and an olive skin tone. She didn't look at all like

Ria. Half-sister, he wondered, or maybe even step-sister? Or was she a relative at all? At this point, he wasn't sure of anything where Ria was concerned.

He had a lot of questions he wanted to ask Megan, but seeing the hazy pain in her eyes, he couldn't bring himself to take advantage of her weakened state. Well, maybe he could just a little.

"How are you doing?" he asked.

She sighed, taking the ice pack away from her face. "My life sucks."

He bit back a smile. He'd heard those exact same words come out of his sisters' mouths a million times. "You're having a rough day."

"Not just today," she muttered. Before he could question that statement, she added, "How do you know Tory?"

He wasn't sure if it was wise to mention the island to Megan, so he said, "We met a while ago, and we ran into each other by the yacht club yesterday. Today she gave me a sailing lesson."

Megan gave him a suspicious look. "She never mentioned you to me."

"She never mentioned you to me, either."

Silence fell for a moment, and then Megan said. "So do you like her?"

He smiled. "Yeah, I do."

"She's not going to date you. She doesn't go out at all."

"Why is that?" he asked curiously.

"She just doesn't," Megan said. "She works a lot."

"Maybe she should take some time for fun."

"She's forgotten how to have fun." Megan sighed and settled back against the seat. "She used to laugh all the time. Now, I hardly ever see her smile."

"Why is that?"

Megan shrugged.

A moment of silence passed, then he said. "You two aren't very close in age. Do you have the same parents?"

Megan frowned, and then winced at the pain that followed. "That's a weird question," she said, a grumpy note in her voice. "I'm her sister. We would have the same parents, right?"

"I was thinking maybe there was a second marriage or a divorce or something."

"Oh. Well, you should ask Tory."

"She's not very talkative," Drew said.

Megan acknowledged his comment with a nod. "Trust me, I know. I talk all the time, way too much. It used to drive my mom crazy. She said I had an endless number of questions. And now it makes Tory crazy, too."

"Questions are good. It's the only way you learn anything."

"I think so, too. So what do you do?"

"I fly helicopters for the Coast Guard."

She sat up in her seat, new interest in her eyes. "Seriously? That's cool."

"It is cool," he agreed. "Have you ever been in a helicopter?"

"No, but I want to. My mom and dad took a helicopter tour in Hawaii, and they flew into a volcano. They said it was really exciting. Have you done that?"

"I haven't done that yet."

"You should," Megan said, ending her words with a yawn. "So where did you meet Tory?"

"In a bar." He figured he wasn't giving anything away with that answer.

"My mom met my dad in a bar," she said sleepily.

"Yeah?"

"My father told me that his heart literally stopped when he saw my mom; she was so beautiful. He knew right then that she was going to be his wife," Megan said, a dreamy note in her voice. "I want someone to fall in love with me like that."

Her words took him back to the island, to the moment that he'd set eyes on Ria. His heart had stopped, too. He hadn't called it love; he'd been much more comfortable with desire. Because physical attraction he understood and could handle. The emotional component had always eluded him.

"My mom said my dad swept her off her feet. She fell madly in love, just like they do in the fairytales." She took a breath. "But she didn't get her happily ever after."

Drew's gaze narrowed as Megan ended her words on a sniff and then quickly blinked away tears.

"Did something happen to your mom, Megan?"

"She died. So did my dad. It's just me now."

"You and Tory," he said.

"Right. It's just me and Tory, and I shouldn't talk about my parents."

Considering how many times Megan had already brought them up, Drew found her words to be a bit ironic. But he wasn't going to question a teenager about her dead parents.

After a moment of quiet, he said, "I lost my mother when I was five years old. She died of cancer. I don't have a lot of memories of her, but one that has always stuck with me is the lavender smell of her perfume. Whenever I smell lavender, I think of her."

Megan stared back at him. "My mom smelled like gardenias. She loved flowers. She'd spend hours in our greenhouse, and at night when she'd tuck me in, I'd smell gardenias in her hair." She paused, a guilty look flashing through her eyes. "Don't tell Tory I told you that."

"I won't. But can I ask why?"

"It makes her sad."

He nodded. "I can understand that."

"I missed my mom today," Megan confessed. "When I was waiting in the hospital by myself, I really wished she was still alive so that she could hug me and tell me everything would be okay." Megan sniffed again. "I can't cry because my nose is going to get all stuffy," she added, a desperate note in her voice.

"Don't cry," he said quickly. "It's going to be okay."

"My prom is on Saturday night. And I look like a monster. How is it going to be okay?"

He didn't know the answer to that question, but he felt a little more comfortable with the change of topic. "Makeup can hide a lot."

"How do you know that?" she asked suspiciously.

He smiled. "I have three sisters. And they all seemed to have facial emergencies before the prom. I remember when Emma got a big zit in the middle of her forehead. It looked like a volcano crater. She was going to call her date and tell him that she had the flu, but my sister, Nicole, talked her into some makeup rehab. By the time Nicole was done, you could hardly see it. Emma went to the prom and had a great time."

"You can't cover a nose the size of a grapefruit with makeup."

"The swelling will go down by then, and I'm sure you can hide the bruising."

"I hope so." She gave him a thoughtful look. "You're kind of cool. Maybe Tory should give you a chance."

"Maybe she should," he agreed with a smile.

The car door opened, and Ria got in with a large bag of food.

"That smells good," he said, his stomach starting to rumble.

"It is good." Ria gave him a wary look. "What were you two talking about?"

He smiled and decided to give her a taste of her own

medicine. "Wouldn't you like to know?"

"Drew—"

He saw the worry in her eyes. "Relax. Megan didn't give away any of your secrets."

"He's right. I didn't tell him anything," Megan added with way too much fervor.

Ria sighed. "I feel so much better."

Drew smiled. "I thought you would. Now, let's get to your house so we can eat. I'm starving."

Nine

"So this is your home," Drew said, as they walked into her apartment a few minutes later.

Ria nodded, knowing that Drew's sharp eyes wouldn't miss the fact that there was only one bedroom, and that room was decorated in typical teenage fashion. And if he missed that, the pillow and blanket on the back of the couch would no doubt suggest that at least one of them slept on the couch. The blank walls would reveal nothing about her past, but that would probably only reinforce the idea that she was in hiding.

There was nothing she could do about his assumptions. He was inside, and she had to deal with that fact.

She wasn't ashamed of the small one bedroom apartment. It was all she could afford. The neighborhood was safe, and no one could get into the building without being buzzed in— at least theoretically speaking. She hoped that her neighbors would never let anyone in without knowing who they were, but there were sixteen apartments in the building, and the only person she knew was her neighbor, Amelia.

"This is it," she said shortly, heading over to the secondhand table she'd put up next to the small galley-type kitchen. She set down the bag of food and then moved around the counter to grab plates and silverware.

"Not much on decorating, are you?" he said, as he took off his coat and tossed it over the back of a chair.

"I've been busy."

"How long have you lived here?"

"A while," she said, setting out plates. "Why don't you start opening up cartons?"

"And shut up?" he asked with a knowing smile.

"You said it; I didn't."

"We're so in sync, I can read your mind."

She rolled her eyes but refrained from making a comment as Megan slid into a chair at the table. Ria grabbed sodas and juice out of the fridge. Then she sat down next to Megan and across from Drew. It was surreal to be sharing a meal with him and Megan, she thought. In all the dreams she'd had about him, she'd never imagined this scenario, but ever since she'd run into him again, her day had been one surprise after another.

"This looks good," Drew said as he helped himself to the broccoli and beef dish.

"It's the best in the city," Megan said, as she carefully ate some noodles, wincing as she swallowed.

"How's the pain?" Ria asked.

"It's a little better," Megan said. "Do you think the swelling is starting to go down?"

Ria could see no change whatsoever, but that wasn't what Megan wanted to hear. "I think so." It was one lie she wouldn't feel guilty about. "Do you have homework tonight?"

"Not much. I did most of it already."

"That's good. You can get to bed early."

"I don't know if I can go to school tomorrow," Megan said doubtfully.

"We'll figure that out in the morning."

"It's not like school is that important," Megan added. "I'm not going to go to college."

"Why not?" Drew cut in, curiosity in his eyes.

Megan hesitated. "Well, it costs a lot. And we don't have

the money."

"There are scholarships," he pointed out. "A college education is important."

"Tory doesn't have one," Megan said.

That piece of news took him by surprise. Ria could see the discomfort in his eyes, but she wasn't about to make it easy for him. He'd butted in for no reason; now he could figure a way out.

"I didn't realize," he said slowly, turning to her. "Why didn't you go to college?"

"I was sailing around the world. I learned a lot more on my travels than I would have learned in school."

"And you have no regrets?"

"About skipping college?" She shook her head. "For me, no, but I think Megan should leave her options open. Certain jobs require degrees."

"Exactly," he said. "Until you know what you want to do, you should keep everything on the table." He glanced back at Megan. "Do you have any idea what you want to be when you grow up?"

Ria stiffened. While the question was one most high school juniors were asked over and over again by helpful relatives and school guidance counselors, for Megan, there was no simple answer.

"I don't know," Megan said. "I'd like to do something adventurous. But I don't like boats as much as Tory does. Maybe I could fly helicopters like you do."

"You could, but that would take some education."

"Are there a lot of female pilots?" Megan asked.

"Not a lot, but quite a few, and I've worked with some excellent female pilots," he answered. "I can introduce you to some of them if you ever want to know more about the job from a woman's point of view."

The last thing Ria wanted was for Megan and Drew to

start developing a relationship, but that relationship had obviously begun while she'd left them in the car alone together.

"Megan has a long time to decide what she wants to do," Ria interjected.

"Not that long. Doesn't she have to start applying for college in the fall?"

"Does she?" Ria asked in dismay. She hadn't realized college would be coming up so soon.

"Sure. And there are all the tests you have to take as a junior," Drew continued. "I'm sure Megan's counselor has gone over all that."

"She has," Megan said, taking a sip of juice. "She keeps bugging me to sign up or take a prep class."

"You didn't tell me that," Ria said, feeling like a bad parent for not making sure Megan was on the college track. She'd been so busy concentrating on their safety that she'd let a lot of other things slide.

"It's not a big deal."

"Maybe it is," she murmured, realizing she needed to focus a little more on the future as well as the present.

"I'm going to lay down," Megan said, pushing back her chair as she stood up. "I'm tired."

"I'll check on you in a while," Ria said.

"You don't have to check on me; I'm not six." Megan turned to Drew. "Maybe you could give me a ride in a helicopter some time."

"I could definitely do that," he agreed.

Megan took her plate to the sink then headed into her bedroom.

"Nice kid," Drew said when they were alone. "How come she gets the bedroom?"

"She needs privacy more than I do. She's a teenager. And, no, I couldn't afford a two-bedroom apartment."

He set down his fork. "Megan told me your parents are dead. Is that why you're raising her?"

She couldn't believe Megan had told him that, but at least he still thought Megan's parents and her parents were one and the same. "Yes, I'm raising Megan now, and as you've already noticed I'm not doing the greatest of jobs. I had no idea college applications started so early. I need to make sure Megan isn't missing any important dates."

"So you do want her to go to college and not follow in your wandering footsteps?"

"Megan and I are different people and my choices were very different than hers. Megan is smart, and I want her to have all the tools to do whatever she wants in life. And some of those tools can only be acquired with more formal education."

"Did your parents raise a fuss when you decided not to go to college?" he asked curiously.

"I'm not sure they even noticed."

He tilted his head to the left, his expression contemplative. She had a feeling he was putting things together, and they weren't making sense.

"So, I'm confused," he said. "You said your parents divorced when you were eleven. Megan told me her parents had the greatest love story of all time."

"Is that what you were talking about in the car?"

"Among other things. You have to be at least ten years older than Megan, maybe more. So I'm thinking you and Megan are not full siblings. Did one of your parents remarry? Is Megan the product of a second marriage?"

"Do you want some ice cream?" she asked, as she got to her feet to clear the table.

"You're going to ignore me?"

"I'm going to try."

"More mystery," he mused. "I'll figure it out, Ria. I don't

think it will be that difficult."

She set their empty plates on the counter, then said, "Megan and I aren't full siblings. But I love her and she loves me, and that's all that matters." She gave him a pointed look. "Satisfied?"

"For the moment. It's very generous of you to step in and raise her."

"We're family. End of story."

He smiled. "I'm sure you'd like that to be the end of the story, but we both know it's not. Is Megan the reason you needed a clean start?"

"Partly," she admitted. "I'm not going to tell you anything else, Drew. I think you should go home now."

"I thought you said something about ice cream."

"Really? You're still hungry?"

He nodded. "What kind do you have?"

She opened the freezer. "Cookie dough."

"My favorite."

She hated to admit it was her favorite, too. She was trying to find reasons why she and Drew didn't go together, not why they did, but ice cream was the least of her problems.

She scooped out ice cream for two bowls and then carried them to the table. Before she handed him his bowl, she said, "One condition."

"What's that?"

"No more prying questions for the duration of the ice cream."

"You're always setting boundaries for us, Ria. What happened to the free-spirited girl who sailed around the world instead of going to college? The one who lived on an island in the middle of nowhere, who took a chance on a stranger on a warm, tropical night?"

She knew he didn't intend to hurt her with the questions, but the reminder of who she used to be was more than a little painful.

"Can you agree to the rule or not?" she asked.

"Since you're holding my favorite ice cream hostage, I agree."

She pushed the bowl across the table. "Great."

"So," he began.

She sent him a pointed look.

"I wasn't going to ask about you," he said, as he spooned ice cream into his mouth. "Do you like Megan's boyfriend?"

"I wouldn't call Eric a boyfriend yet, but he seems like a good kid. He's a little shy, which I think is a good quality in a teenage boy. I'd be more worried about a cocky jock. They're always trouble."

"Are you speaking from experience?"

Although he'd once again veered into her personal territory, she decided to answer. "I dated one of the star football players junior year. He thought he was God's gift to girls, and most of us girls agreed. We went to the prom together. He got wasted, threw up on my shoes, and then got into a fight with one of his friends. It was a disaster. I'm hoping Megan's prom date is not as disappointing."

"So was that your type?" Drew asked. "The cocky jock?"

"Apparently I still have a weakness for that kind of man," she said pointedly.

"Hey don't put me in the same category as football vomit boy."

She didn't think he was anything like her prom date, but it was hard not to put him in the category of God's gift to women. He was very attractive with his thick wavy brown hair, intelligent eyes and strongly defined features. He was also intelligent and funny and he didn't take himself too seriously. He had a cocky edge, for sure, but that only made him more appealing. She liked a man who knew what he was doing, and Drew had already proven to her that he knew exactly what he was doing when it came to making a woman happy. She blushed at the thought and reached for her water glass.

"Getting hot in here?" he asked with a teasing smile. "I usually get cold when I eat ice cream."

"Let's talk about you for a change."

"What do you want to know?"

"Tell me about your prom date."

"I went with my girlfriend, Laurel. She was a runner. We were on the track team together. We were great pacing partners. Unfortunately, when we stopped running, we found that we didn't have a lot to talk about."

"And talking was important in a high school relationship?" she challenged.

"Maybe not so much," he admitted. "She was hot."

"I'll bet. How long were you together?"

"Until summer. She met someone else at a running camp, and I was happy to call it quits. I'd moved on from running to flying, and every spare minute I had went into flying lessons and getting enough hours so that I could get my license."

"When did you get that?"

"At sixteen. I got my driver's license and my pilot's license within three months of each other."

"Isn't it expensive to take flying lessons?"

He nodded. "Yes. I worked at the supermarket to help pay for it. But I also had a little help from my grandfather. He was a pilot, and he loved having someone to share his love of flying with. Kind of like your grandfather sharing his love of sailing."

"I thought you said your grandfather was a firefighter," she asked.

"Other grandfather. This was my biological mother's father."

"I need a family tree," she complained.

"It is a little complicated. I told you that my biological mom died when I was really young."

"I don't think you did," she said with a shake of her head.

"Oh, right. It was Megan I told."

"Why would you tell Megan that?"

"We were bonding," he said lightly. "Anyway, my mother's father was the pilot. He used to give me airplanes when I was little and talk about soaring into the sky. I loved listening to his stories."

"Do you still see him?"

"I try to stay in touch," Drew said. "There's a lot of family to keep happy."

"It sounds like it." She let out a breath, knowing she was getting too comfortable talking to Drew. "I should clean up."

"I'll help you."

"It's not a big deal. It will take me two seconds," she said, as she got to her feet. "You've done enough, and you should go home."

He stood up, blocking her way into the kitchen. "Every time I think about leaving you, I get the crazy feeling that I might never see you again, that you could disappear at any minute, without any explanation."

"That's not so crazy," she said meeting his gaze. "I have to protect Megan, Drew. And if that means I have to leave San Francisco, then that's exactly what I'll do." She paused. "But I'm not going anywhere soon. Megan couldn't possibly miss the prom."

"I want to help you, Ria," he said, a serious note in his voice. "Why don't you let me?"

His offer was tempting. She'd been carrying the burden for a long time. But she couldn't bring him into her mess. "There's nothing to do at the moment," she said, hoping the vague answer would be less challenging to him than an outright no.

"Are you sure?"

"Yes. Now can you move out of the way, so I can wash these bowls?"

He took the bowls out of her hand and set them on the counter. Then he put his hands on her waist. A shot of desire swept through her at the purposeful look in his eyes.

"What—what are you doing?" she asked, hating the breathless note in her voice. But with Drew holding onto her, with his body calling out to hers, with the memories of how good they were together flooding through her mind, she was feeling more than a little off balance.

"I'm going to kiss you, Ria."

"No."

"Yes. I've been thinking about it all day, and I think you've been thinking about it, too. We were good together."

"For one night a long time ago, and maybe it wasn't that good," she added desperately.

"Only one way to find out."

His deep, rich voice sent more shivers down her spine. And then his mouth came down on hers in a hot, demanding kiss that made her head spin. She felt like she was going back in time. She was on the island again. The tropical air smelled like flowers, and the heat of the night mixed with the heat between them. There was no yesterday, no tomorrow, just the moment, the night.

She opened her mouth for a much needed breath, and Drew took that opportunity to slip inside, his tongue sweeping against her teeth, as he took possession of her mouth in a way that made her entire body melt. Her mind made a feeble effort to resist the need rocketing through her, but her brain was no match for the strength of her desire.

She slipped her hands around his waist, under his shirt, letting her fingers roam the warm, rippled muscles of his back. He was a strong man, and she needed that strength supporting her, surrounding her, inside of her. The need to have him ran so deep she could feel the ache.

Drew groaned against her mouth, as if he could feel it, too. He pulled her up against his hard body as he devoured her mouth. And it still wasn't enough. They were wearing too many clothes. She wanted his skin against her skin, no more barriers between them.

Drew must have read her mind, because he was pushing her jacket off of her shoulders, his hands slipping under her knit shirt.

Her breasts felt heavy, full, tender, and as his fingers caressed her stomach, she ached for those hands on her breasts, all over her body.

A crash broke them apart. She stared at Drew, then her gaze moved to Megan's door. "Megan," she called.

Her niece popped her head out of the bedroom. "Sorry, I knocked my books off the shelf." She paused, giving them a curious look. "Everything okay out here?"

"It's fine," Ria said, hoping Megan couldn't see how rattled she was.

"All right," Megan said.

As the bedroom door closed again, Ria stepped back from Drew. Her face felt like it was on fire. A few hot kisses, and she'd forgotten everything, including where she was and what she was supposed to be doing.

"Don't say that was a mistake," Drew warned.

"It was a mistake." She crossed her arms in front of her chest, ignoring the tingling feeling in her breasts. "I can't do this with you. I have a kid now."

"Ria—"

"No more talking, please." She was holding on to her willpower by a thread. "Please go."

His lips drew into a tight line. "I'll go, but we both know we're going to end up right back here. One of these days you have to trust me."

"Trusting you is only a small part of it."

She slipped around him and walked over to the door. She opened it and waited. After a minute, he grabbed his jacket off the back of his chair and met her in the doorway.

"Just so you know," he said. "If you leave, I'll look for you. I'm not going to spend another year wondering where the hell you are, if you're dead or alive."

"I never asked you to wonder. You wanted one night. I gave it to you. That was supposed to be the end of our story."

"Well, it turns out it wasn't the end. It was just the beginning."

She pushed him into the hallway, shut the door, turned the deadbolt and fixed the chain. Then she leaned against the solid wood and drew in a deep breath, her heart still thudding against her chest. She put a hand to her mouth, her lips tender from the onslaught of his kiss. It had been exactly like the last time, fast, hot, intense, passionate…

But the last time she'd known she was leaving the next day. There would be no tomorrow, so she could live for the night.

Now she had to think about the future, about Megan, and about staying alive.

Ten

"Thanks for letting me stay home from school today," Megan said to Ria as they ate breakfast together on Monday morning.

Ria gave her niece a sympathetic smile. "Your face looks a hundred times better, but I do remember high school and mean girls. I think you can miss a day."

"My friends aren't mean. Well, Lizzie is a little mean," Megan amended. "But that's because she likes Eric, and Eric likes me."

Ria laughed at the smug expression on Megan's face. There was nothing like a little male attention to build a woman's ego.

"At least, he used to like me," Megan said, a little doubt in her voice. "He hasn't seen me yet. He asked me to text him a photo, but I said no."

"Good, because we have a rule about texting photos, don't we?"

Megan made a little face at her. "What does it matter if I send my friend a picture of me? He knows what I look like."

"Because, it's not that simple. I know you don't understand why I'm being so careful, but it's one thing to look at you and another to have a photo of you that could get into the wrong hands."

"Eric is just a kid. He's harmless. He's never even been

out of California."

"Did you tell him you've been out of California?"

"No, I'm not stupid," Megan retorted. "I even pretend not to understand what they're saying in Spanish class."

"Good, I'm glad to hear it. No photos, okay?"

"I already said no," Megan said grumpily. "Relax already."

Ria could barely remember what it felt like to be relaxed.

"And I was the one who was trapped on that island, not you," Megan reminded her. "So I know what's at stake. But it was a long time ago, and I don't want to live my whole life being afraid of every shadow."

"Then let me be afraid of the shadows. You just concentrate on your life." She paused. "I was thinking last night about college. I would like you to go, Megan. I'm sorry I wasn't paying attention. I hope you haven't missed some important admission tests."

"It doesn't matter, Ria. I won't be able to get into a university. My grades are okay this year, but we told them that I was home schooled, and we don't have transcripts for all of my high school years."

Ria frowned. Megan was right. She was a bright girl, but it would be difficult to create an educational background for her.

"It's fine," Megan continued. "I don't have to go to college. I should get a job anyway and help you pay for stuff."

"Maybe community college," Ria suggested. "It won't be a problem to get in there. You can do two years there, establish your educational credentials and then transfer."

"I suppose."

"We'll talk more about it. I want you to be able to do whatever you want in life."

"If I'm ever free to do it," Megan grumbled.

Ria wanted to tell her that she would be free one day, but how could she make that promise? Instead she said, "Your mom loved school. She was a straight-A student."

"But she didn't finish college. She met my dad, fell in love, and had me."

"And she was very happy about that choice. Don't ever doubt that Megan."

Megan sighed, her eyes filled with pain. "I miss her and Dad. Will it ever stop hurting?"

"Probably not, but you'll learn to live with it." She took a breath. "We can talk about her more, if it would help."

"Really? Because you don't usually like to talk about her."

"I just didn't want to make you sad. And maybe I didn't want to make myself sad."

"What happened between you?" Megan asked suddenly. "I didn't even know I had an aunt until I was ten years old. I didn't know I had a grandfather until we went to his funeral that same year. I asked Mom, but she said she wasn't close to her family. That's it. That's all she would say. But then suddenly she's calling you and telling you our problems and begging you to help."

"We were sisters, no matter the distance or the time."

"But what happened? And don't tell me nothing," Megan warned.

"I'll tell you the whole story, but not right this second." She ignored Megan's groan. "I have to go to work."

"It's Monday. Why are you working; it's your day off."

"I'm covering the office today. Janine has some personal business." She paused. "My family drama is not earth-shattering. It just involved a lot of angry people and hurt feelings and disappointment, and it happened a long time ago. I will tell you everything one day."

"Fine," Megan said, her sullen expression returning. "I

won't hold my breath."

Ria stood up. "Okay, you're going to hate what I'm about to say next, but I have to say it anyway. I don't want anyone here while I'm gone. You can stay home, but no one comes over until I'm back."

"Everyone is at school."

"Yeah, but you have open lunch, and I can see your friends coming over to say hello, so tell them that you're going to the doctor or something. Whatever excuse you want. But no visitors."

Megan sighed. "I don't know what the big deal is. They're my friends. I see them every day. And they've all been in this apartment before. There's nothing here that would make anyone suspicious."

"This is just another one of those rules you have to follow."

"Fine. But I still get to do the all-night party after the prom, right?"

Ria had been fighting that battle for a couple of weeks and had finally given in. Megan's group of friends was renting a hotel room for the night, because according to Megan and her best friend Lindsay, that's what everyone did. Finally, Ria had said yes rather than risk pushing Megan into doing something stupid and more dangerous.

"You can still do the after party," she agreed.

Megan looked relieved. "Good." A sparkle of mischief filled her eyes, "Maybe you should go out on a date Saturday night, too."

"I don't think so," she said, as she grabbed her keys and bag.

"Why not? Drew is hot."

"Drew and I are not dating."

"He wants to date you. He told me so in the car."

She frowned. "What else did he tell you?"

"Not much. How come you never told me about him?"

"There was nothing to tell," she said quickly.

"He's the guy, isn't he?" Megan asked with a gleam in her eyes. "You said you started something with someone that you couldn't finish. It was him, wasn't it?"

"Yes," she admitted. "But I'm no longer interested in Drew."

"Are you sure? I thought I interrupted something last night."

"Megan, please, let it go," Ria said, feeling uncomfortable with the conversation. "I don't want to talk about Drew, especially with you."

"I'm the only one you can talk to, and I don't see why you can't go on a date. It's been over a year and a half. We're supposed to be living a normal life. I hate that you're always working or staying home because of me."

"Don't worry about me, Megan."

"You gave up a lot for me. I want you to be happy, too."

"Maybe I could go out with someone new, someone that I meet now. But Drew is part of my past, and I've told him so many lies, there's no way I can untangle them all. Plus, I can't risk a connection to the island and that's where I met Drew."

"You met him on the island?" Megan asked in surprise.

"Yes, right before we left." She held up her hand to stop any further questions. "I'm leaving now. Remember, no visitors."

Megan made a face at her and tossed her crumpled napkin in her direction. "Go to work."

"Don't forget to—"

"Lock the door after you. I've got it."

Ria left the apartment, pausing in the hall until she heard the dead bolt slide into place, then she headed to work.

—→»≪←—

Drew worked seven a.m. to four p.m. on Monday, flying shore patrol, searching for disabled vessels and possible threats to homeland security. As he flew over the bay, he was reminded of his sailing lesson with Ria, and how different the view of the city had looked from the water. Ria had been different on the boat, too. She'd been relaxed, happy, two emotions that had quickly vanished with the urgent phone call from Megan.

He still couldn't believe Ria was now raising a sixteen-year-old, but he was beginning to understand that her situation was much more complicated than he had initially imagined. He wasn't sure what he was going to do about her, but after their kiss at the end of the night, he knew there was no way in hell he was going to just walk away, not with so many unanswered questions.

After work, he headed down to the marina, to meet up with Aiden and Burke, and to drop off his check for his share of the boat.

He couldn't help looking for Ria when he got to the docks, but she was nowhere in sight, and the boat she'd used the day before was in its slip. No surprise, really, it was almost five o'clock on Monday; there were few boats left on the bay.

When he hopped onto the *Eleanor*, he found Aiden alone on the boat. He was sitting on the bench and seemed to be lost in thought.

He hadn't seen his brother this contemplative in a long time. "Hey. Is everything okay?" he asked, sitting across from him.

Aiden straightened. "Yeah, it's all good. Or it will be if you brought your share of the money."

"I've got it. Where's Burke?"

"He gave me his check earlier today. One of his crew fell through the roof on a fire last night and ended up in the hospital with a broken leg. Burke wanted to spend some time at the hospital."

"Understandable."

"Sure."

"Okay, what's wrong?" Drew asked, as Aiden once again seemed to lose track of their conversation. "You're never this quiet. Are you having second thoughts?"

"Not exactly."

"What does that mean?"

Aiden met his gaze. "Sara is pregnant. She told me last night. It wasn't planned, but it's great news."

"Okay," he said, not sure what else to say since Aiden's words didn't match his expression. "That's wonderful. You're going to be a father."

"What the hell do I know about being a father? I spent most of my own life trying not to follow my father's lead."

"I think something locks in when you have a kid. You just do what you have to do. You're going to make a great dad. But what's even better is that you're going to have a kid with the woman you love. You're starting a family."

"I do love Sara. Sometimes, I can't believe I didn't see how phenomenally great she was at fifteen."

"Sara was shy, and she always had her nose in a book back then. I remember her sitting on her porch reading while the rest of us were playing tag in the street. You two were universes apart back then."

Aiden ran a hand through his hair and let out a sigh. "Am I crazy to buy a boat when Sara is pregnant?"

He shrugged. "Without knowing your finances, I can't answer that."

"It won't kill my bank account, but it will take a hit. I thought we would have more time, but we weren't careful enough."

He grinned. "Big surprise."

Aiden smiled back. "What can I say—Sara is hot."

Drew conceded that point. "Look, about the boat, if you don't want to do this now—"

"We have to do it. I told Grandpa last night and that grumpy old man got all choked up when he knew the boat would stay in the family. I don't want to let him down."

"I might be able to kick in a little more cash," Drew suggested. He didn't have a wife or kids to worry about.

"No, it should be equal partners. It will be fine. I'll figure it out," he said. "I just have a lot to figure out."

"Are you definitely done with smokejumping?"

"I thought I was, but maybe I should reconsider. Or I should think about Burke's offer to join the department here in the city."

Drew didn't know what Aiden had gone through in his job, but he did know that smokejumping was dangerous and grueling work, and he could totally understand why his brother would want a change. "What about construction?" he asked.

"Uncle Kevin has been great, but he has a lot of people on his crew. I don't know if there's enough work." He paused. "Sara has a good job, but she'll probably want to be home with the baby. And I want her to be able to do that if she wants to. I'm supposed to be the provider."

"You'll make it work," Drew said, having every confidence in his brother. Aiden might be a rebel and a little on the reckless side, but he also had a strong work ethic and was extremely loyal to family and friends. "You won't let Sara down."

"I hope not."

As Aiden finished speaking, his phone rang. "It's Sara." He answered the phone. "Hey, babe." His expression paled as he listened. "That doesn't sound good. I'll be right there."

It was the second time in two days that Drew watched

someone take what was obviously a disturbing call. "What's wrong?" he asked.

"Sara isn't feeling well. Apparently, the baby is making her nauseous." He frowned. "Damn. I'm supposed to take the checks to Grandpa tonight."

"I'll do it for you."

"That would be great." Aiden handed over his check and Burke's. He glanced around the boat. "I still think this will be a good investment in the long term."

"So do I. And your kid is going to love it, too."

Aiden smiled. "My kid—never thought I'd use those words."

"How do they feel?"

"They're not sounding as terrifying as they were a few minutes ago."

"Tell Sara, congratulations," Drew added as Aiden headed off down the dock.

He followed more slowly, deciding to stop in at the yacht club before heading home. Once inside the building, he headed down the hall to the main office. He saw Ria locking the door, and his heart skipped a beat. Every time he saw her, he felt like he took a punch to the stomach.

Surprise flashed in her eyes. "What are you doing here, Drew?"

"I had to meet my brother at the boat. But I figured I'd stop in here before I left and see if you were around."

"I'm just heading home."

"How's Megan? Has the swelling gone down?"

"It was better this morning. Hopefully by tonight there will be even more improvement."

"Is she still in pain?"

"Not too bad. She stayed home from school, but that was because she didn't want anyone to see her face. I checked in with her at lunch, and she felt well enough to babysit for our neighbor tonight, so I think she's on the mend."

"I'm surprised you let Megan babysit." From what he'd seen Ria kept a tight hold on Megan.

"It's just next door and only until eight."

"It sounds like you're free then," he said, latching on to an impulsive idea. "Why don't I give you a ride home?"

She hesitated. "Drew, we can't keep doing this."

"Doing what?"

"I told you I didn't want to see you again."

"Well, too late for that. I'm here. You're here. And I'm saving you from the bus. It's just a ride."

She stared back at him. "If I take the bus, are you going to be waiting at my building when I get home?"

"There is that possibility," he conceded.

"Fine, I'll take the ride."

"Great." As they walked out to the parking lot, he said, "How was your day on the bay?"

"I wasn't on the bay today. We don't offer lessons on Mondays or Tuesdays. They're usually my days off, but the receptionist in the office is away, so I agreed to fill in and pick up some money."

"Office work doesn't sound like your style."

"It's not my first choice, but whatever pays the bills."

He opened the car door for her and was surprised when she gave him an odd look. "What?" he asked.

"Nothing." She slid into the seat.

He shut the door and walked around to the driver's side. As he fastened his seatbelt, she said, "I can't remember the last time anyone opened a door for me."

"My father drilled manners into me at an early age. Always open a door for a lady. Always pull out her chair. I don't even think about it; I just do it."

"It's nice. Your dad sounds like a good role model."

"He is. He's bigger than life. A hard act to follow."

"Really? Even for a daredevil helicopter pilot?"

"I'm not a firefighter. He would have preferred I follow in the family tradition."

"Why didn't you?"

"My heart was in flying," he said simply.

"How did your dad take it when you told him?"

"He tried to hide his disappointment. It helped that both Burke and Aiden were already firefighters. And Emma was also on her way to becoming a firefighter and then a fire investigator, so he gave me his guarded blessing."

"I'm sure he was proud of your service, Drew."

"Yeah, he was." As he drove down the street, he added, "By the way, we have to make one quick stop."

"Where?"

"My grandfather's house. It will take less than two minutes."

"I don't want to meet your grandparents," she said, her brows knitting together in a frown.

"Why not? They're nice people."

"I'm sure they are, but my goal is to get you out of my life, not to get myself into yours."

"My goal is to get you to trust me. Once you meet my grandparents, and you see the kind of solid stock I come from, you'll have no choice but to trust me."

She sighed. "I told you it wasn't just about trust."

"That's the first step."

"Is it really only going to take two minutes?"

"Five minutes at the most," he assured her.

Eleven

Five minutes had turned into ten, with no end in sight, as Ria and Drew waited for his grandmother to appear. A middle-aged woman named Doris had let them into the two-story, three-bedroom condo on Lake Street and explained that Patrick had run to the store. Eleanor was just getting up from a nap and would be with them shortly.

Doris had left them in the living room, and up until now, Ria had been sitting patiently on the couch. But she was starting to wonder just how long this quick stop was actually going to take.

"Drew—"

"I know. I'm sorry," he said apologetically. "My grandfather should be home soon. He doesn't like to leave my grandmother alone for long. Just to warn you, she drifts in and out of reality. Sometimes she makes sense, and sometimes she doesn't. She might not even know who I am."

She saw the pain in his eyes and felt a wave of compassion. She hadn't lost anyone to Alzheimer's, but she did know what it felt like to lose family.

"We were very close when I was growing up," he added. "She was always there when we came home from school. There were so many of us kids around that my mom couldn't give everyone the attention they needed, so Grandma filled in the gaps. She had a great sense of humor. She was always smiling, laughing, and she never let the little stuff bother her. I remember one time when she was babysitting, she let us put up a tent in the attic. We got our sleeping bags and pretended to have a campout. I think she even made s'mores." He smiled at the memory.

"She sounds wonderful."

"But she doesn't smile like she used to, and she's often confused or scared. When I saw her the other day, she acted like she was afraid of me." He got up and paced restlessly around the room. "I want to help her, but I don't know what to do."

Ria was beginning to realize that Drew couldn't stand by when something was broken and not try to fix it. "It doesn't sound like there's anything anyone can do," she commented. She stood up and walked across the room. Since they weren't going anywhere soon, she might as well learn a little more about the Callaways.

On the mantel were several framed photographs. "Who are all these people?" she asked.

"Callaways," Drew said, coming over to join her. He pointed to an old black and white photo. "Those are my grandparents, and their six kids. My father Jack is right there. He's the second oldest in the family." He paused and pointed to the next photo, which was in color and appeared to have been taken by a lake. "That was the last family reunion, two years ago up in Lake Tahoe."

"I don't see you anywhere."

"I was still deployed. I don't think they missed me. There were at least seventy-five people there."

"Huge family."

"Everyone in my dad's generation had a bunch of kids, and some of their kids had kids, so it's a crowd. We rent four houses on the lake now. Actually, one of them belongs to my grandfather, so that's the home base, and we try to snap up anything else that's close by."

As she looked at the family pictures, she was struck by the feeling that she'd come up really short in the draw for family. "It looks like fun," she said, unable to keep the wistful note out of her voice.

Drew gave her a speculative look. "You sound sad."

"Do I? I'm just tired."

"And maybe a little lonely," he suggested.

"I'm not lonely. I have Megan."

"Who else do you have?"

She was saved from having to answer by the arrival of Drew's grandmother.

Eleanor was a petite and pretty white-haired blonde with beautiful light blue eyes. She wore gray slacks and a pink sweater, both of which hung loosely on her thin frame. Doris helped her to the couch, then left them alone.

"Hello, Grandma," Drew said. He sat down on the couch next to her. "How are you today?"

"I'm fine, Drew. Who's your friend?"

Drew seemed to visibly relax when she called him by name. "This is Ria," he said.

She inwardly sighed at the use of her old name, but there was no one in this living room who cared.

"Ria, that's a pretty name for a pretty woman," Eleanor said with a friendly smile. "Are you Drew's girlfriend?"

"No, we're just friends," she said quickly, taking a seat in the chair next to the couch.

Eleanor laughed. "Oh, I can't believe that's true."

"I'm working on changing her mind," Drew said.

"I suspect so," Eleanor said. "What brings you here tonight, honey?"

"I have to talk to Grandfather. He went to the store, I guess."

"He loves to go to the store. It gives him a reason to get

out of the house. Sometimes I make him as crazy as I am," she said.

Eleanor's disarming candor was very appealing, Ria thought. Maybe she wasn't always lucid, but when she was, she seemed to at least know that something was wrong.

"You're not crazy," Drew said quietly.

She patted his leg. "You're a sweet boy to lie to me, but I know I'm losing my mind. I wish it wasn't so, but I can't seem to stop it. The doctor says it's going to be worse on Patrick than on me. I'm not going to know when I'm out of it, but he will. That's what I hate the most. I don't want to think about him looking at me like I'm a stranger, even if that's how I'm looking at him. That man is the love of my life, and I'm his. I never thought we might end up not knowing each other."

"Grandpa is a strong man. And he loves you," Drew said with a fierce note in his voice. "He'll help you through this, and you'll never be a stranger to him, Grandma."

"Time is so fleeting, Drew. You think it's going too slowly at times. I remember when I was a young mother, and I was stuck at home with six babies. I was changing diapers every other minute and helping kids with multiplication problems and breaking up fights over the last Oreo cookie, and I used to think—will they ever grow up? Will it ever get easier? And then one day, I looked around, and everyone was gone. The house was so quiet. Some days I'd give anything to go back to those loud, noisy, exhausting years."

"If you want loud noise, you know where to find it, Grandma," Drew said. "You're always welcome at our house."

She smiled. "Even your house is getting quiet now. And that little Brandon; he's such a gentle soul, but so lost. I worry about Nicole. She thinks she can pull off a miracle, but I don't know if that's possible. We seem to be in short supply of miracles these days. Although, I'd give up my mind if it would mean Brandon could get his back."

"My nephew has autism," Drew said to Ria. "He was diagnosed when he was three; he's six now."

She nodded. "I'm sorry to hear that." The Callaways might be a big, loving and close family, but they still had their problems.

"Nicole reminds me of myself," Eleanor said. She paused for a moment, the sparkle in her eyes growing dim. "I know what it's like to worry about your child. I remember when Jack came home with a bloody nose, two black eyes and a broken hand. I wanted to kill the guys who had hurt my boy."

Drew's brows knit together. "When did Dad get beat up?"

She gave him a startled look. "What did you say?"

"I asked when Dad got beat up," he repeated.

"Your dad? Jack?" she asked in confusion.

Drew nodded. "Yes, Jack. When did he get hurt?"

"I'm not supposed to talk about it." Panic entered her voice. "Patrick says we must never talk about that day. It's dangerous. If Patrick doesn't do what they say, then next time it's going to be worse. It won't just be a warning. Someone is going to die."

"What?" Drew asked sharply.

Eleanor grabbed Drew's arm. "I told him to go to the police, but he says he can't. He says I don't understand. You won't let anything happen to Jack, will you?"

"I won't," he said.

"Do you promise?"

"I promise."

Drew shot Ria a pained look, and her heart went out to him. She'd never seen anyone go from perfect clarity to confused fear.

"Can I get you some water, Grandma?" Drew asked.

She blinked a few times and then said. "What did you say?"

"Would you like something to drink?"

"No, I'm fine. Tell me how you and your friend met," she said, glancing over at Ria, then back at Drew. "Was it love at first sight?"

Ria was curious to hear Drew's reply, and she had to admit to being a little amused by how his grandmother's question had shaken him up. Drew had her off balance the last two days. Now he was the one who had to find his feet.

As he searched for an answer, Ria decided to help. "Was it love at first sight, Drew?"

He gave her a wry smile. "Was it for you?"

"I think your grandmother asked you the question."

He glanced back at his grandmother, who also seemed amused and back in perfect control of her senses. "You're trying to get me into trouble, aren't you?"

"You've never brought a girl to meet me. I'm curious."

"I like her," he said. "A lot," he added, turning his gaze on Ria. "And I think she feels the same way. Don't you, Ria?"

Shivers ran down her spine at the look in his eyes. She'd tried to turn the tables on him, but he'd flipped them right back at her.

Before she had a chance to answer, the front door opened and closed, then a tall, gray-haired man walked into the living room. He had a ruddy complexion and blue eyes, that weren't as light or as bright as his wife's but were penetrating and intelligent.

"Drew, what are you doing here?" he asked.

"Grandpa," Drew said, getting to his feet. "Aiden couldn't make it, so he sent me. This is my friend, Ria, my grandfather, Patrick Callaway."

"It's nice to meet you," Ria said, inwardly adding yet another person who now knew her name was Ria.

"You, too," Patrick said. "Why don't we go into the kitchen, Drew? Maybe your friend could chat with Ellie?"

"It's fine," she said, in answer to Drew's unspoken question.

As Drew and his grandfather left, she smiled at Eleanor. "You made Drew very uncomfortable."

"I know," Eleanor said with a smile. "He's always so private, I have to tease him now and then, or I'll never get any information."

"Was he always that way?" she asked. "Even when he was a child?"

"Oh, yes. Drew keeps everything inside. I've tried to tell him that's not healthy, but he always says that's just the way it is. I know he went through some hard times in the Navy. I could see the shadows in his eyes, the grief in his expression when he thought no one was watching. There was a heaviness about him when he first came home, as if he had the weight of the world on his shoulders." She paused. "But today he seems lighter, more relaxed. Maybe that's because of you, dear."

"I doubt that. We're really not together."

"Why not? You like him. He likes you."

"It's complicated."

"The best things always are," Eleanor said. "And it's fine to make Drew work for it. Then you'll know if he's serious. The Callaway men have too much charm for their own good. Sometimes they get caught up in their hype, if you know what I mean. When Patrick first asked me out, I said no. And I kept saying no for the next month. Finally, I agreed to have coffee with him." She smiled. "You would have thought he'd won the lottery. Do you know what I told him on our first date?"

"I can't imagine."

"I said I'm not *playing* hard to get, Patrick, I *am* hard to get. And if you want me, you're going to have to work for it."

"I'll bet he took that as a challenge."

Eleanor's eyes twinkled. "He absolutely did. He went out

of his way to prove that he was the one and only man for me."

Ria smiled. "I think Drew has a lot of his grandfather in him."

"He definitely has his stubbornness. But Drew is more of a thinker, and he guards his heart like it's made of pure gold."

"Why do you think that is?"

"I've never been sure. Maybe losing his mom when he was a small child made him a little wary of love. Or maybe it was a broken heart somewhere along the way. Like I said, Drew doesn't confide in me. But there's something about Drew that sneaks up on you. If you're not careful, you'll wake up one day and realize you're in love with him."

Her nerves tingled at Eleanor's words. "I better be careful then."

Eleanor laughed. "I like you, Ria."

"I like you, too," she said.

"You know I may not remember you five minutes from now."

"I know. But I'll remember you."

"That's what keeps me going," she said. "Knowing that my family will remember the woman I used to be."

"I think the woman you are now is pretty great, too," Ria said.

Eleanor met her gaze. "You'd make a fine Callaway."

"I told you—"

"I know what you said, but my grandson is very good at getting what he wants."

Where was her grandson? Ria wondered. Drew's five minutes had now turned into half an hour.

"Are you sure you want to sell the boat?" Drew asked his grandfather as they sat at the kitchen table together.

"Positive." Patrick took out his reading glasses. He looked at the checks and then nodded. "You boys are going to have a great time with that boat. I know I did."

"You can still come out on it," Drew said.

"Those days are long gone."

"Grandma seems pretty good tonight. She's making sense. At least most of the time."

"Don't worry about what she says, Drew. Random thoughts pop into her head, and she gets things mixed up."

"She told me about some time where Dad got beat up. She implied that it was some form of blackmail. That someone wanted you to do something." As he finished his statement, his grandfather's jaw tightened and anger filled his eyes.

"She has Alzheimer's, Drew. I can't unravel every story she tells you. And I'm damn tired of trying. You and your brothers and sisters need to stop trying to make sense of things that don't make sense."

"Okay, sorry," he said, seeing the weariness in his grandfather's eyes. "Is there anything I can do to help?"

"No." He pulled off his glasses and rubbed his eyes. "I just want to savor the good moments now, let everything else go. Because one day there won't be any more good moments."

Drew hated to think about that day.

"I'll put these checks in the bank in the morning. But here are the ownership papers and the maintenance log," Patrick said, pushing a binder across the table. "I kept track of everything. A few of my friends have used the boat in the past few months and said everything was in good shape, but you should get it checked out from top to bottom. I probably should have dry-docked the boat, but I kept thinking that I'd get Ellie back out there. She always loved to sail."

"It's not too late. Any time you want to go out, you can."

"I couldn't take the risk that she'd get confused or scared out there and put herself in danger."

"Do you really think that would happen?"

"Anything is possible. Sometimes she gets combative. It's just fear, and I know that, but it's hard to see the woman I love jerking away from me as if I was going to hit her."

"Is there any treatment?"

"The drugs she's on now seem to be working better, but I don't know. Anyway, you don't need to worry about it." Patrick stood up. "We better get back in there. Lord only knows what Ellie has told your friend."

"What did you and my grandmother talk about?" Drew asked, as he drove Ria back to her apartment.

Ria smiled. "She said you're a charmer like your grandfather. Personally, I had a little trouble seeing your grandfather's charm behind his gruff exterior, but I guess I'll take her word for it."

"These days, I'm not sure you should take her word for anything."

"She seemed focused most of the time, except for those few minutes when she was talking about your father getting beat up. Do you know what that was about?"

"I have no idea. I asked Grandpa, and he just blew me off. My dad has never mentioned anything, and he's big on sharing stories of his life. I can't imagine why he'd leave something like that out."

"Maybe there's a reason he didn't tell you. Your grandmother made it sound like it was some sort of warning or form of retribution."

"She might have made the whole thing up, Ria." His hands tightened on the wheel.

"Or not. Every family has secrets."

"Are we talking about your family or mine?"

"Just saying you may not know everything there is to know about your father or your grandfather."

"I know both of them pretty well," Drew said defensively. But this wasn't the first time that his grandmother had made vague references to some secret event in the past. Emma and Aiden had both come to him with similar stories.

As he turned down Ria's street, he saw a parking spot near her building, so he grabbed it.

"You don't have to park," she said quickly.

"It's almost seven. I was hoping I could bum some food off of you." He gave her a pleading smile.

"I doubt I have much in the fridge."

"I'll have whatever you're having."

"That's a risky statement. I could be having peanut butter and jelly."

"I love peanut butter and jelly," he said, as they got out of the car.

As they walked down the block, he caught Ria taking several glances over her shoulder, and before she inserted her key into the front door of the building, she took another look around.

"We're alone," he said. "No one is following us."

"Not this time," she said. "But I have to be careful."

They walked into the building and Ria pushed the button for the elevator. "Your grandmother told me that she loves to sail. I guess she doesn't know that Patrick is selling her boat to her grandchildren."

"He doesn't want her to know. He doesn't think it's safe for her to be out on it anymore. I really wish I could do something to make things easier."

"You're lucky to have had your grandparents for so long," Ria said as they got on the elevator. "But I know it's never long enough."

"You said your grandfather died and your parents and your sister," Drew said, his gaze narrowing on each word. "That's a lot of death for anyone to handle."

"It is," she said tightly.

"Is there anyone else left in the family?"

"No, it's just me and Megan."

They stepped off the elevator and walked down the hall. Ria opened the door and set down her bag. "I'm going to check on Megan next door. Then I'll see if I can find some food for dinner."

"We can always order take-out. My treat," he said.

"I think I can find something to make if you're not too picky."

As she left the apartment, Drew walked around the living room, noting the contrast to his grandmother's place. There were no personal photographs anywhere. A few fashion magazines were on the coffee table, but he didn't see any books anywhere. No personal or sentimental-type items. He doubted there was anything in the apartment that Ria couldn't leave behind at a second's notice, and that thought bothered him.

A cell phone began to ring, and it took him a moment to realize it wasn't his phone. He walked over to Ria's bag and grabbed her cell phone. As he thought about taking it to her, the phone stopped ringing. It was a cheap throwaway phone. He was almost surprised that she had a phone; she was so secretive. Then again, she had a kid to stay in contact with.

The voice mail lit up with a message, and he battled a very strong urge to see who was calling Ria.

It was a total invasion of her privacy. But damn...

His curiosity overrode his conscience, and he played back the message.

A female voice said, *"It's your mother. Call me."*

His gut tightened. *Her mother?* She'd told him her mother was dead. Megan had said the same. He was staring at the phone when Ria re-entered the apartment.

She turned white when she saw him holding her phone. "What the hell are you doing?"

"I thought you said you didn't have any family. So do you want to tell me why your mother just left you a message?"

Twelve

"You had no business answering my phone," Ria said, fury and fear running through her at the same time.

"I didn't answer it. I just listened to the voicemail."

She grabbed the phone out of his hand. "And that's supposed to be better? Get out, Drew."

"No. Not until you tell me why you lied about your mother."

"I don't have to tell you anything. What is wrong with you? Do you really think it's all right to listen to someone's phone messages?"

"You're what's wrong with me, Ria—you and your secrets. I can't stop thinking about you. And now when I think about you, I worry about you. I wonder why you had to change your name, why you let people think you were dead, why you look over your shoulder every three minutes."

"I never asked you to worry about me."

"You didn't have to ask. You and I have been connected since our night together on the island. Maybe if you hadn't *died* so suddenly, what was between us would have run its natural course. But the shock and tragedy of your death hit me hard. You were so alive, so passionate, so vibrant, and then you were gone. What was I supposed to do with that? Did you really think I could just forget you?"

"I told you I didn't know you thought I was dead."

"Well, you know now."

"Yes, I do."

They stared at each other for a long minute.

There was a depth of caring in Drew's words and in his gaze. She felt herself weakening, wanting to let him in on her secrets, but how could she do that?

"You still had no business listening to my messages," she said.

"I know. You should call your mother back. It sounded important."

She could not call her mom back with Drew in the room. "I'll do it later."

"Where is your mother, Ria? Why did you tell me she was dead?" He paused. "Is anyone actually dead? Or do people in your world just start over with new names?"

Before she could answer, the front door opened, and Megan walked in. "Hey, Drew," she said with a welcoming smile. "I didn't know you were coming over."

Drew forced a tight smile on to his face as he gazed at Megan. "How are you feeling? Your face looks better."

"Except for the black eyes that make me look like a raccoon." She paused, looking from Ria to Drew and back again. "What did I miss?"

"Nothing," Ria said.

"Only the fact that your mom called," Drew said.

Megan gasped. She sent Ria a shocked, questioning look, and Ria knew that Megan was about to give away something, if not everything.

"My mom," she told Megan. "Drew listened to my phone messages."

"That's not cool." Megan gave Drew a wary look. "Why did you do that?"

"Because I'm worried about you and your sister, and no one will tell me anything." He turned to Ria. "Why did you just say *my mom* when you and Megan are sisters? Why don't you have the same mother?"

"Because we don't." She took a breath, glancing over at Megan. "Would you give us a minute?"

"Sure." Megan stopped by her bedroom door. "If you trust him, I trust him," she said.

"Thanks. I'll get dinner going soon," Ria promised.

"Okay."

As Megan disappeared into her bedroom, Ria knew she was facing a pivotal moment. Whatever decision she made now could be the difference between life and death, maybe for all of them. But Drew wasn't going away, and she was out of lies.

"Megan is my niece," she said finally. "Her mother, Kate, was my sister. Kate died two years ago in a car accident."

Drew's gaze was dark, unreadable. "Is that the truth?"

"Yes. My mother is still alive. That's who called me."

"Where does she live?"

"Massachusetts, and no, I can't be more specific. She's remarried, has a second family, and is far removed from anything going on with me and Megan."

"Not that removed if she has the phone number to what I'm sure is a disposable phone."

He had her there. Drew didn't miss a thing. "I update her periodically. Megan is her grandchild."

"What about Megan's father? Your father? Where are the men?"

"They are both dead. My father died of cancer when I was twenty-one, and Megan's father was killed in the same accident that took Kate's life."

Drew paced around the room and then sat down on the couch, kicking up his feet on the coffee table. "Go on."

She sat down in the chair across from him. "What else do you want to know?"

"Why are you and Megan living like you're in the underground?"

"Megan's mother, Kate, was involved with some dangerous people. Before she died, she made me promise to take care of Megan. I'm trying to keep that promise."

Drew blew out a breath that was filled with frustration. "Dammit, Ria. Do we have to play twenty questions? I'm tired of going around in circles. Tell me what's going on."

"I just did, Drew."

"You said before you couldn't go to the police. But nothing you've just told me explains that comment."

She thought for a long moment, debating how best to phrase her answer. "In order to save Megan, I had to break the law. If I tell you what I did, you might feel compelled to turn us in, and I can't take that chance."

He stared back at her with shock in his eyes. Whatever he'd been expecting her to say, it hadn't been that.

"You're a man who's used to defending right against wrong," she continued. "You've spent the last decade living by a code of ethics and honor. I can't believe you would throw all that away for a woman you met in a bar one night."

Silence followed her words. Apparently, she had finally found a way to halt Drew's endless list of questions.

"You're more than a woman I met in a bar, Ria," he said slowly. "If you weren't, I wouldn't be here right now. And you know it."

The intense look in his eyes made her swallow hard. "And you're more than a man I just had a one-night stand with, which is why I think you should go home and forget we ever met again. You may not believe me, but I'm not just trying to protect myself, I'm also trying to protect you."

"I can take care of myself."

"When I tell you the same thing, you don't believe me," she said dryly.

The tension in his jaw eased. "I know," he admitted. "But that's different."

She sighed, then got to her feet. "I should get dinner started. Megan is probably hungry."

"I'd like to stay."

"Why?"

"Because we're not done yet."

"I'm done answering questions for now. If you want to stay for dinner, fine, but it won't be much."

"I don't need much."

"I have to call my mother back first." She picked up the television remote and handed it to him.

"Ria—I'm sorry I listened to your message. That was wrong."

"Thank you, but I probably would have done the same if our positions were reversed," she admitted. She took her phone into the bedroom and closed the door.

Megan was sitting on the bed with her computer in front of her and headphones on. She pulled out the earpieces and gave Ria a questioning look.

"I told Drew that you're my niece, that your parents were killed in an accident, nothing else," she said.

"That's a lot," Megan said, surprise in her eyes.

"I had to say something. He's relentless."

"He likes you. And he seems like a good guy." Megan frowned. "Although, he did spy on your phone, which is weird."

"I made him way too curious." Ria sat down on the edge of the bed. "I don't know what I'm going to do about him. I know you don't want to hear this, but the best thing for us to do would be to disappear."

Megan immediately shook her head. "No way."

"After the prom," she said.

"No. I'm not leaving San Francisco. I want to stay with

my friends and with Eric. I want to graduate from the school I'm in now. I don't want to start over again from scratch. We have a life here, and I don't think Drew would do anything to hurt you or me."

"He's a link to my past. And even if he didn't do anything intentionally, if anyone put us together—"

"Who would do that?" Megan challenged.

"I don't know," she admitted, but she couldn't shake the feeling that keeping Drew in her life was a dangerous idea.

"Maybe you're just afraid you're going to like him too much," Megan suggested. "Maybe that's the real reason you want to run."

Her niece had a point.

"Would it really be so bad if you let yourself care about someone?" Megan asked.

"We may not be able to stay here, Megan. I know you don't want to face that fact, but it's there. And while I want you to have as normal a life as possible, I need to stay vigilant, and I might not be able to do that if I let myself get distracted."

"Drew is distracting," Megan said with a smile. "I mean, seriously, Ria, have you ever dated someone that attractive before?"

"He would be at the top of the list, but that's beside the point."

"I think you should give him a chance." She paused. "Is he gone?"

"No, I had promised him dinner before he picked up my phone. So I'm going to keep my promise. But I need to call my mother back, so can you entertain him for a few minutes? Preferably without any stories from the past?"

"Sure. What do you think your mom wants?"

Ria heard the edge of bitterness in Megan's voice when she emphasized the word *your*, and she couldn't blame her niece for having hard feelings towards her grandmother. Megan had never met her grandmother, but obviously Kate had filled her daughter's head with long lists of her mother's flaws. Kate had picked sides in their family a long time ago, and her sister's side had always been with their father, not their mother.

"I don't know what she wants, but we agreed to speak only every three months, so I need to make sure nothing is wrong."

"I'd tell you to say hello for me, but I don't think she'd care."

"She does care, Megan, and the fact that you've never met her is not all her fault."

"I don't want to talk about it." Megan slid off the bed and left the room.

After she closed the door, Ria punched in her mother's number. "It's me," she said when her mom answered. "Is everything okay?"

"I'm not sure," her mother said. "I might just be being paranoid."

Her stomach tightened. "Tell me."

"I've seen a car a couple of times in the neighborhood. This afternoon there was a man in the front seat and he was talking on the phone. I got a license number, and I asked a friend of mine's husband if he could check it out for me."

"What friend is that?"

"A woman I play tennis with. Her second husband is a police officer. I told her I'm part of a neighborhood watch group, and I'm trying to be vigilant."

"I hate to get the police involved."

"Well, I have other children to worry about, and I need to make sure this car is not connected to you."

"I understand. Let me know what you find out."

"How's Megan?"

"She's doing well," Ria said, realizing it was true. Megan had really begun to blossom in San Francisco. She was finally living the kind of life she was supposed to live. "She's going to the prom on Saturday."

"Really?" her mother asked in surprise. "You're letting her go out?"

"I don't have a choice. She's trying to be normal, and normal kids go to the prom. We bought a dress the other day, and she looked gorgeous. She has Kate's smile. I just wish Kate could see her."

"I do, too," her mom said with a sigh. "I remember when Kate went to the prom. It was right before your dad left, before everything turned upside down, and she decided that she hated me. It seems like a different life now."

"It is a different life. I can barely remember when it was the four of us together. And now it's just me and Megan."

"You've acted with great courage, Ria. You're saving Megan's life. I'm very proud of you."

Ria was shocked at her mother's complimentary words. She didn't think she'd ever made her mother proud. Most of her decisions, like not going to college, had filled her mother's eyes with disappointment. "Thank you," she said slowly.

"I know we haven't been close in a long time, and a lot of that is my fault. But I do love you, Ria. And I love Megan, too, even though I don't even know her."

Her mom paused, and Ria could hear her talking to someone, telling them they couldn't have ice cream unless they ate their green beans. One of her half-siblings, Ria thought, feeling both connected and disconnected to the woman on the other end of the phone.

"I have to go," her mom said.

"Call me if you find out anything."

"I will."

Ria closed her phone and returned to the living room. She'd expected to find Megan talking Drew's ear off, but instead the two of them were on their feet playing an interactive videogame called Street Fighter. Drew seemed to be frustrated with the game, which didn't surprise her. Megan was an expert player.

After they'd first left the island, they'd had to stay out of sight for weeks at a time, and videogames had been their sole entertainment. At first Ria had shied away from the battle games, but she'd soon come to realize that Megan gained confidence and strength by defending herself, even if it was only in the virtual fighting world.

"What the hell," Drew muttered, looking down at his controller. "Mine is broken."

"It's not broken. I'm kicking your ass," Megan said.

"Don't feel bad," Ria interjected. "She kicks my ass on a regular basis."

As Megan gave Drew a few tips to improve his performance, Ria moved into the kitchen and opened the refrigerator. She had eggs and vegetables, so it was going to be omelets for dinner. Megan would appreciate not having anything tough to chew, and if Drew didn't like it, he could certainly find his own dinner somewhere else.

She sautéed vegetables in a pan, then whipped up the eggs and folded in the vegetables. She cut up some fruit, made toast, and set out plates on the small table. "Dinner is ready," she said a few moments later.

"Gotcha again," Megan said, a triumphant note in her voice. Then she set down her controller and headed to the table.

Drew followed more slowly. "Well, that was fun," he said dryly. "I used to be good at videogames."

"Really?" Megan asked doubtfully.

"Yeah, really," he said. "I used to beat all my brothers."

"How many do you have?" Megan asked.

"Four brothers and three sisters," he replied.

"That's crazy," Megan said.

"That's the way I'd describe it."

"Are you the oldest?" Megan asked.

"No, I'm right in the middle. And my family is getting bigger every day. My sister Emma and my brother Aiden are both engaged. Emma and Aiden's fiancé, Sara, were childhood friends, so they're planning a double wedding in August. And I just found out today that Sara is expecting a baby. I'm not sure how that will affect the double wedding, but there's certainly a lot of action in the Callaway family."

"Weddings and babies," Ria murmured, thinking how lovely it all sounded. How nice to be in a family with no bigger problems than that.

"A double wedding is so romantic," Megan said. "I would love to get married on the same day as my best friend, Lindsay."

"You wouldn't want your own day?" Ria asked.

Megan shook her head. "Double the wedding, double the fun, double the presents."

"I guess that's true," Ria said with a laugh.

"Good eggs," Drew murmured as he quickly worked his way through his omelet.

"I told you it would be nothing fancy."

"I'm not picky when it comes to food. Growing up in a big family, you learn early to eat whatever is there and eat it quickly."

"I always wanted a brother or a sister," Megan said, a sad note in her voice. "I don't know why my parents didn't have more children."

Ria didn't know why, either. Kate had always talked about having more than one, but that was probably before she realized just what kind of family she had married into.

"So where is this double wedding?" Ria asked, wanting to get off the subject of Megan's parents.

"I have no idea. I try not to pay attention when the women start talking weddings," Drew said. "I don't know why anyone wants to spend so much money and time on a party."

"It's not a party; it's a wedding," Megan said. "It's the most important day of your life."

"Don't argue with a sixteen-year-old," Ria advised. "Especially when it comes to romance and love. You will lose."

He smiled. "Are you speaking from experience?"

"Absolutely."

Megan rolled her eyes, then took her empty plate to the sink. "Can Lindsay come over for a while? We want to work on our English project together."

"Sure."

As Megan left the room, Ria glanced over at Drew and caught him staring at her with a more serious and thoughtful expression than their recent conversation should have elicited. "What?"

"You don't like it when Megan talks about her parents. Are you afraid she's going to give away your big secret?"

"It's painful to talk about my sister, and, yes, I'm always afraid that Megan will give something away. She thinks that we're safe now."

"You've allowed her to think that way. You don't want her to live in fear. So you take it all on," he said. "I admire that, Ria. But don't you ever want to share that burden?"

She shrugged. "I'd only be making someone else's life as difficult as mine."

"What did your mother want?"

"She was just checking in."

"And..."

"She noticed an odd car in her neighborhood. She's going to check it out with the local police."

"So your mother can go to the police, but you can't?"

"She can talk to the police about an odd car in her neighborhood. That has nothing to do with me."

"Obviously, she thinks it might. Why doesn't she have Megan?"

"My mother has another family. She has young children to worry about."

"Your family is getting bigger by the minute, too," he said with a wry smile. "So much for it's just me and Megan."

"It is me and Megan. I honestly don't think of my mother's second family as mine."

"How many kids in her second family?"

"Two boys; they're eleven and twelve."

"Not much younger than Megan," he commented.

"Kate was nineteen when she had Megan. And my mother was forty when she had my brother. It's weird. We're quite the dysfunctional group."

"Not that weird. I have a blended family, too. My father had four boys. My stepmother had two girls. Together they had twins. I know what it's like to merge two families."

"We didn't merge, Drew. My mom got remarried and started a new life that didn't include me. She met her second husband when I was thirteen. I had agreed to live with her instead of my dad, because I didn't want her to be alone. Two years later she wasn't alone. She was in love. And I was the third wheel. They got married and started having babies when I was in high school. As soon as I graduated, they wanted me out of the house so they could have more room."

"That's when you decided to sail around the world."

"I had some friends who were crewing on some luxury yachts. I decided to sign on, and from there I jumped from one gig to the next. I rarely made it home for anything, and it didn't seem to bother anyone that I was gone. I think in some ways I was a reminder to my mother of her first failure. It was easier when I was away."

He frowned. "I'm not getting a great vibe on your mom."

"She's not a bad person. She loves me. She just doesn't show it much."

"How does she treat Megan?"

"She doesn't have contact with Megan, but she cares about her in an abstract way. And that is enough about my family," she said decisively, as she got to her feet. "You've had dinner. Time to go home."

He rose, blocking her way, and she had the feeling they were about to repeat last night's goodbye kiss.

"Drew, I can't do it again."

"Do what?" he asked with mock innocence.

"You know," she said, wishing his smile didn't melt her resolve every single time.

"One kiss," he glanced towards Megan's door. "A quick one."

She doubted that would be the case, since time ceased to exist whenever he put his mouth on hers. "Lindsay is on her way over."

"Well, that's a new excuse."

"I don't need an excuse. I'm saying no." She couldn't help the little sigh that punctuated the end of her sentence.

"I feel the same way," he said quietly, and before she could react he pressed his mouth against hers in a warm, tender and brief kiss. "See, that wasn't so bad."

No, it wasn't bad. It was a tempting little appetizer, and she wanted more. But she couldn't have more. "Goodnight, Drew."

"Ria, before I go—"

"No more questions tonight. You need to understand that I've told you all I can. I don't want to put you in danger, and I don't want to put you in a position where you have to compromise your ethics or your integrity."

"That's my choice, Ria. But I think your main concern is whether I'm going to turn you in for whatever it is you did."

"Yes, it is. I don't know what you're going to do next. You're a wildcard and that bothers me."

He gave her a long look. "Honestly, I don't know what I'm going to do next, either. It occurs to me that maybe you're just trying to find another way to get me out of your life by playing the *I've done something horrible* card. Or you could be doing exactly what you said, trying to keep me away from a bad situation. Or—"

"There's another scenario?" she asked wearily.

"Or," he emphasized. "The truth lies somewhere in between. I don't have enough facts to come to a logical conclusion."

"You're not going to get any more facts until you can promise whatever I tell you stays between us."

"Would you believe that promise if I made it?" he challenged.

She nodded. "Yes. I believe you're a man who keeps his promises. And I think the reason you haven't pressed me for the rest of my story is that you're not sure you can make the promise I'm asking of you."

He frowned. "I feel like we're talking in circles."

She felt much the same way. "I never asked you to get on this treadmill with me. You jumped on, and so far I can't seem to get you off. I don't know what the problem is. Most men would have run for the hills by now."

"You don't know what the problem is?" He moved over and framed her face with his hands, his heat burning through her skin. "The problem is you. You're sexy, beautiful, intriguing, irresistible." His gaze fell to her mouth. "I want to kiss you. I want to strip these clothes off of you and make love to you the way I did before. I want to know if it was as good as I remember or if it's better."

Her heart started to race. "Drew——"

He shook his head, cutting her off. "I know. I need to stop. Megan is in the next room."

"Even if she wasn't, we couldn't—we shouldn't. It was a mistake the first time."

"No, it wasn't." He paused for a long moment, his fingers sliding through her hair. "I like you, Ria, and I'm concerned about you. I think you're into something way over your head. I suspect it involves Megan, and knowing the threat is international, I can't help noticing the fact that Megan's looks are not exactly all-American. She has an exotic beauty, one that reminds me of some of the native women I met on the island."

She swallowed hard, Drew's words reminding her that the very intelligence she liked about him could unravel everything.

"Nothing to say?" he asked.

She shook her head and stepped away from him. "No. I can't tell you anything more without your promise. Can you make it?"

The length of time it took for him to answer was her answer.

"That's what I thought," she said, feeling suddenly sad.

"Hold on."

Before he could say anything more, Megan opened the bedroom door and came back into the living room, her dark eyes sparkling with excitement. "I just had the greatest idea."

Ria had the distinct feeling that whatever was coming next was not going to be *great* at all.

"I have to write an essay on someone who makes a difference in the world, and I couldn't really think of anyone I could actually talk to, and then I thought, wait a second—

Drew works for the Coast Guard. He saves lives. That's making a difference in the world. What do you think?"

"Uh, sure," Drew said distractedly. "You can interview me if you want."

"I need more than an interview. I need photos, too. Maybe of you in your helicopter." She gave him a hopeful smile. "Could I come to the Coast Guard Station and see you at work, maybe take a ride in a helicopter?"

"You can definitely get a tour of the station, and you can sit in the helo, but I can't take you up, unfortunately. We only take civilians up for very special reasons."

"It would still be cool," Megan said.

"I'll check my schedule tomorrow and see if I can set it up."

"That would be awesome. The paper is due on Monday, so this week maybe?"

"Got it."

"Great." Megan skipped back into her bedroom.

"Sorry about that, Drew," Ria apologized. "Megan put you on the spot. You don't have to do it. It's too much trouble."

"It's not too much trouble. I'd like to show Megan around the Air Station. As I said before, you need to stop trying to make decisions for me, Ria."

"Fine."

He stared back at her. "Are you going to come with Megan?"

The last thing she wanted to do was set up another date with Drew, and she had a feeling that Megan's request for a tour was not just based on her need for an essay subject. She was determined to get them together.

"If you can do it tomorrow afternoon, I can make it," she said. "The rest of the week will be busy with work."

"Then let's plan on tomorrow afternoon. I get off at four,

so come then." He paused. "How are you going to get there?"

"We'll take a bus or a cab. Don't worry about that."

"I'll give you a ride home afterwards."

"All right," she said, knowing it was pointless to argue.

"Give me your number in case something changes," he said.

As she rattled off her number, she couldn't help thinking that the more she tried to push Drew away, the closer he seemed to get.

Drew slid his phone into his pocket and grabbed his coat. "I heard what you said, Ria. I need to think about everything you've told me. Because you're right; I won't make a promise I can't keep." He gave her a long look. "Just give me a little time, all right? Don't disappear on me."

She stared back at him. "I won't make a promise I can't keep, either."

Thirteen

—➤➤❮❮◄—

Ria and Megan arrived at the San Francisco Coast Guard Air Station just after four o'clock on Tuesday. The sight of a security gate and armed guards sent a little chill through Ria's body. She hadn't really thought of Drew as law enforcement, but rather as a pilot. In truth, he was both. She'd been crazy to tell him she'd broken a law. He wouldn't be able to forget that, and he probably also wouldn't be able to commit to keeping her secrets. With any luck, he'd come to realize that the less he knew, the better.

The Air Station was located just north of San Francisco Airport, and Drew met them just outside the main building. He was in uniform, wearing a navy blue shirt and matching slacks. On the chest pocket was his name: Commander Drew Callaway.

Ria had a hard enough time not finding him sexy in normal clothing; the uniform put her over the top, and she couldn't help but feel a bit of pride to be with him.

"Perfect timing," Drew said. "I just got back."

"Did you rescue someone?" Megan asked, her brown eyes lit up with excitement.

"Not today. We flew a training mission. We practice a lot to keep our skills up." He paused, glancing at Megan. "Your bruises are almost gone."

"I know. I'm so happy," she said with a big smile. "I can

cover a lot with makeup now. So what are we going to see today?"

"I'll give you the grand tour, starting right here." He waved his hand toward a bright red helicopter sitting on the tarmac. "That's an H-65 helicopter, what we call the Dolphin," he said. "It can fly in any weather, night or day. A typical crew includes two pilots, a flight mechanic and a rescue swimmer. I'll take you inside the hangar so you can actually sit in the helicopter."

"This is so cool," Megan said. "You have the best job."

"I love what I do. It's not only a great job; it's an important job."

"What else do you do besides rescue people from the water?" Megan asked as they walked toward the large helicopter hangar.

"I'm glad you asked," he said with a smile. "We do a lot more than most people realize. The objectives of the Coast Guard are not only search and rescue missions, but also homeland security, maritime enforcement, which includes drug smuggling, and we also get involved with environmental protection." He paused, glancing over at Ria. "You've probably had some dealings with the Coast Guard during your sailing days."

She nodded. "Yes. For most boaters, the arrival of the Coast Guard is a welcome sight."

"Unless you're doing something wrong," he said dryly.

"Right," she said, meeting his gaze.

He opened the door and waved them into the large hangar. "This is the helicopter hangar. The building next door houses our fixed wing aircraft." He took them over to the helicopter and allowed Megan to hop into the left seat. Then he proceeded to explain the console and controls, talking briefly about the basics of flight.

Ria was surprised at how interested Megan was in Drew's

talk. Even when he got technical, Megan seemed to follow along, often asking very intelligent questions. Her niece had never shown that much interest in boats. But apparently helicopters were more exciting to her.

"Do you ever get scared?" Megan asked. "Have you crashed?"

"I've had a few harrowing moments," he admitted. "A few months ago we were looking for a boat in trouble off Bodega Bay. The fog layer was below a hundred feet, and we need to hover around fifty feet. We were completely blinded on the way down, and the ship's mast was about thirty feet tall on pitching waves. If we missed by just a little, we could hit the mast and take everyone down."

"What happened?" Ria asked, caught up in his story.

"We made it through the fog, rescued the fishermen, and headed for home."

"Do you ever have to abort?" Megan asked. "Leave someone behind, because it's just too dangerous?"

"We try not to. The motto of the Coast Guard is *Semper Paratus*, which means *Always Ready*. And the Coast Guard's Rescue Swimmer motto is *So Others May Live*." He paused, his gaze somber. "I can't lie and say we haven't lost people, but we save everyone we can save. As a pilot, I have to protect my crew as well as the people who are in trouble. Sometimes it's a tough call."

Ria thought that call would be extremely difficult for Drew to make. He wasn't a man who was comfortable with failure. He set high standards for himself and probably everyone around him.

Drew took them through the engine and prop room next, then gave them a peek into the operations center and dispatch. As he exchanged hellos and introduced them to his coworkers, Ria could see how well liked Drew was and how well respected.

"So that's it," Drew said as they completed their tour. "I wish I could take you up for a ride, give you the true experience."

"This has been more than enough," Ria said. "I'm sure Megan has lots of material for her report."

"I do," Megan said. "But I might have some questions when I start writing."

"I'm always available."

"I need to change clothes, then I'll give you a ride home," Drew said. "You can wait here. There's water, coffee, a restroom."

"We'll be fine," Ria assured him.

As Drew left, she and Megan moved into the lounge. One wall was covered with grouped photographs, each group showing a different decade in Coast Guard history that started around World War II and ended with the present.

"This is seriously more interesting than I thought it would be," Megan commented.

Ria appreciated the interest in Megan's eyes. While her first priority with Megan was keeping her safe, her long-term goal was to give Megan what she needed to live a happy life.

Megan paused in front of the most recent group of photos. "There's Drew," she said. "It looks like he's getting some kind of award."

Ria took a closer look. Drew was in full dress uniform, and he was shaking hands with the Mayor of San Francisco. The accompanying article talked about the bravery displayed by Drew Callaway during a search and rescue mission. His rescue swimmer and another male were trapped in a sinking vessel. With no other available swimmers, Drew turned over command of his helo and went into the water to save both people.

"Wow," Megan murmured, reading the article over Ria's shoulder.

Ria met her niece's gaze. "Wow," she echoed.

"Do you really think you're going to find someone better than Drew?" Megan asked. "He's like a superhero."

Ria smiled. She couldn't argue with that.

"You're like a superhero, too," Megan added. "You saved my life. I think you and Drew would be perfect together. And you're crazy if you don't think so, too."

—➤➤◄◄—

Ria was still thinking about Megan's words when they piled into Drew's car and headed back to the city. She didn't think she could do better than Drew, but she thought he could probably do much better than her. Another time, another place, another lifetime—maybe they could have finished what they started, because she liked him so much. But it was ridiculous to think that they could have a future in the life she was living now. Maybe Megan could let herself get caught up in the romance of it all, but Ria didn't have that luxury. She had to guard everything, and that included her heart.

"Did you have a good time?" Drew asked.

She nodded. "I'm very impressed."

"Well, that is partly why I became a pilot—I figured it was a good way to get girls," he said with a smile.

"It definitely is," Megan put in from the back seat.

Ria laughed. "Sixteen-year-old girls," she said.

"I know. You're a tougher nut to crack, Ria."

"I'm impressed, too. Megan and I read an article about one of your rescues."

"I forgot that was still on the wall. No big deal," he said with a shrug. "It's what anyone on the crew would do when faced with a similar situation."

"Did the other pilot want to make the rescue attempt?" she asked.

"I was in the right seat that day. Tim was in control of the helo."

She stiffened at the mention of Tim. The name set off warning bells from a long time ago. "Tim," she muttered. "He was the guy on the island with you, wasn't he?"

He shot her a quick look. "Yes."

"And he works with you now?" Her stomach turned over. "Was he there this afternoon? Did he see me? Did he see us?" She didn't remember seeing the attractive blond from the island, but there had been a lot of men milling about the air station.

"Relax. He left at four. He didn't see you."

She blew out a breath. "You should have told me that I might run into him."

"I knew you wouldn't. That's why I didn't tell you."

"But someone might tell him we were there."

"I introduced you as Tory," he reminded her. "And what would anyone say? That I showed a woman and a teenager around? That's hardly big news."

"Who's Tim?" Megan asked.

She glanced back at her niece's curious face. "He was with Drew on the island when we met."

"He thinks you're dead, Ria," Drew said, drawing her attention back to him. He placed his hand on her thigh. "There really isn't anything to worry about."

She looked into his eyes and felt reassured by the confidence she saw there. "I hope not."

"So I'd like to treat you to dinner," he said, as he turned onto the freeway.

"I'm starving," Megan immediately put in. "So I'm in."

"What about you, Ria?" he asked.

"I could eat. What did you have in mind?"

"The best spaghetti in the city."

"I like spaghetti," she admitted. "Is it on the way?"

"It is."

There was something about the way he wouldn't look at her that made her think there was something else about to happen besides a meal out. Ten minutes later she knew she was right when he turned into a residential neighborhood.

"Drew?" she questioned.

He parked in front of a two-story house. "It's spaghetti night at the Callaways."

"This is your house?"

"It's my parents' house. We're celebrating Aiden and Sara's big news tonight."

"Then you should go. Megan and I can catch a bus home."

"Don't be silly. I want you to meet my family. And my mom really does make the best spaghetti in town."

"It's a private celebration. Megan and I will be intruding," she protested.

"At the Callaways, it's always the more the merrier."

Ria glanced back at Megan. "What do you think?"

"It sounds good to me," Megan said with a shrug. "Drew's family sounds cool."

Everything having to do with Drew seemed to be *cool* in Megan's eyes.

"Well, I survived meeting your grandparents, so I guess I can survive this, too," she said with a sigh.

He laughed. "I'm thrilled you're so enthusiastic. You'll have fun. Trust me."

Midway through the spaghetti feast, Ria realized she was having fun, and so was Megan. The Callaways had welcomed them like family. In fact, Drew's mother and two of his sisters had given her big hugs upon arrival. She'd been so closed off from people the last two years; she'd almost forgotten the pleasure that came from a simple hug.

And Drew was right; there were no strangers in the Callaway house. After an initial round of introductions, in which Drew absentmindedly called her Ria instead of Tory, it was a free-for-all as far as conversation was concerned. While Ria wasn't happy with his slip on her name, she was pleased that he'd made no mention of their previous encounter on the island and had simply referred to them both as friends.

While Drew got caught up in a conversation with his brothers, Ria was more than happy to sit back and observe. Megan also seemed a bit in awe of the big, loving family, but when Drew's younger cousin asked Megan if she wanted to watch a video upstairs with her, Megan went right along.

Ria glanced up as Sara joined her in a corner of the living room.

"How are you doing?" Sara asked, giving her a warm smile.

"I'm great. Congratulations on the baby."

"Thanks. It still doesn't feel quite real. Actually, I take that back. It feels very real when I'm throwing up in the morning."

"Morning sickness?"

"And afternoon and evening," Sara said. "Just looking at the spaghetti made me queasy. But it was really nice of the Callaways to have a party for us." She paused. "You look a little overwhelmed."

"That's because I am," she admitted. "I come from a very small family."

"Me, too. I grew up next door, and my house was as quiet as a church. I'd come over here to hang out with Emma and feel like I'd landed in the middle of a tornado. But it was nice to have a second family."

"And now you're an official Callaway," Ria commented.

"Another fact I still can't quite believe. I had a mad crush on Aiden as a teenager. He actually broke my heart back then. We didn't see each other for a decade, and then last fall I came back to see my father, and there was Aiden. It was finally the right time for both of us. And I'm glad that we had our time apart. We both needed to grow up," she added with endearing honesty. "So tell me about you and Drew."

"We're friends."

"Just friends? Because the way Drew looks at you—"

"It's complicated," she said, her cheeks burning at the knowing gleam in Sara's eyes.

"Love is always complicated."

"I don't know if you'd call it love," she said immediately, but then she wondered if that wasn't exactly what she'd call it. Neither one of them had said *I love you*, but she couldn't deny that there were deeper feelings brewing below the surface, at least on her side. "I'm raising a sixteen-year-old," she added, seeing the curiosity in Sara's eyes. "I'm sure Drew could find any number of women not carrying around that kind of baggage."

"I could see Drew as a father," Sara said. "Growing up, he was always nice to the little kids in the neighborhood. Burke was always demanding, impatient. He was the leader. Aiden wanted to win at all costs, but Drew tried to make sure everyone played—everyone got a chance. I always liked that about him."

"Are you talking about Drew?" Emma interrupted. "Because I have lots of stories."

Ria smiled at the mischievous sparkle in Emma's eyes. From what she'd seen so far, Emma was a firecracker, pretty, funny, and outspoken. She also seemed to be in everyone's business.

"Don't scare her off," Sara said.

"Yeah, don't scare her off," Drew echoed, coming up behind Ria. He slung a casual arm about her shoulders and gave her a smile. "What have my sister and sister-to-be told you?"

"We were just getting started," she said, feeling both very comfortable and a little awkward with Drew's arm around her. So much for trying to look like just friends.

And she wasn't used to being part of a couple. It had been years since she'd met anyone's family. In fact, she couldn't even remember the last time. Her relationships had been brief and very transient from the end of high school on. She'd never stayed in one place long enough to get serious about anyone. Nor had she met anyone who'd made her want to stay. Funny, Drew had said pretty much the same thing about his romantic past. In some ways, they were a lot alike.

"I could tell you about the time Drew threw my doll off the roof," Emma said.

"She had a cape. I thought she could fly," Drew put in.

"He was always trying to make things fly," Emma said with a laugh. "You don't know how many paper airplanes hit me in the back of the head."

Drew laughed. "That's true. You were a good target. Where's your better half tonight?"

"Max is working," she said. "And I think I'm his better half."

"Of course you do," Drew said.

Ria smiled at the teasing conversation, her normal tension dissipating as Emma and Sara shared stories about Drew. It was so nice not to have to guard every word, to just be normal for a while. She was beginning to realize how addicting that sense of normalcy was and she could understand better why Megan didn't want to leave her friends. It was much more tempting to believe that the danger was over, and they were free now, but was that true? She couldn't quite bring herself to believe that.

A half hour later, Drew asked her if she was ready to

leave, and she reluctantly said yes. Spending time with his family had been a nice respite. But she had to get back to her real life, a life that didn't include Drew by her side, acting very much like her boyfriend.

After driving them home, Drew insisted on walking her and Megan upstairs. Even though there wasn't the constant threat of danger, she doubted he would have acted any differently. And now, having met his family, she could see the influence they'd had on him.

Once inside the apartment, Megan mumbled a quick goodbye and headed into the bedroom.

Ria lingered at the door. "Thanks," she said. "For everything."

"You're welcome. It was fun."

"It was fun," she agreed. "Your family is amazing. You're very lucky."

"They didn't scare you off with their stories?" he asked, taking a step closer to her.

"Unfortunately, no," she said, drinking in his warm, musky scent as he put his hands around her. She wanted what was coming, wanted it more than her next breath. "Kiss me," she whispered.

He answered with his mouth, with a sensuous kiss that went on for several long minutes, their lips clinging together, tasting, touching, wanting…

Finally, he lifted his head, his breath coming fast. "I really want to get you alone, Ria. Any chance that could happen any time soon?"

She hesitated for a long moment, then said, "Saturday is the prom. Megan will be gone all night."

Desire flashed through his eyes. "I like the sound of that. But Saturday is too far away."

"Only four days."

"Feels like a lifetime."

She had to admit it felt that way to her, too. On the other hand, she should probably use the time in between to come up with a reason not to see him again. Nothing was resolved. There was still a big secret hanging between them.

"I'll see you Saturday," he said. "Don't come up with a way to ditch me."

"I might have to try. I feel like we're too close."

"Really? Because I feel like we're not close enough." He gave her a kiss. Then left her with tingling lips and an aching heart.

Fourteen

The rest of the week passed both slowly and also too quickly, Ria thought, as Saturday dawned. But she had no time during the day to worry about her date with Drew. She was too busy getting Megan and Lindsay manicures, hairstyles and makeovers. By the time four o'clock came, Ria was more than ready to send the two incredibly primped girls on their way.

A knock came at her door at half past four. It was her neighbor, Amelia, and her daughter, Beth, wanting to see Megan in her prom dress. While Beth went into the bedroom to join the girls, Ria gave Amelia a tired smile. "Getting beautiful is exhausting."

Amelia laughed. "I'm sure it is. Big night for Megan."

"I just hope it won't be a letdown. She's built it up so much in her mind, that anything short of fantastic might be a disappointment."

"She'll have a great time. She's really come out of her shell the past few months. I remember how quiet she was when you first moved in. Now she's very outgoing."

"And never shuts up," Ria said. "But she's happy, and that makes me happy."

"Is Megan's improved mood the only thing making you happy?" Amelia asked with a gleam in her eyes. "I saw a very good-looking man leaving your apartment last night."

"That was Drew."

"And Drew is…"

"I'm not sure. We're figuring that out."

"I hope you're having fun doing the figuring."

"We're going out tonight," Ria admitted.

Amelia gave an approving nod. "Good. It's about time you thought about yourself for a change. Not that I don't admire what you're doing for Megan, because I do. I just know it's difficult to be a single mom. And you have to take care of yourself, too. Megan will be happier if you're happier. So suck it up, let down your hair, and have some fun."

"Well, if I have to," Ria said with a smile.

"I know, it's going to be a real hardship," Amelia returned. "If you don't want him, send him my way."

"I want him," she said, surprising both herself and Amelia with her candor. "I just wish I didn't."

"Why?"

She could have fallen back on her usual answer—that her life was too complicated for a relationship—but for the first time in a long time the truth slipped through her lips. "I'm afraid he could break my heart."

Amelia gave her a sympathetic look. "Love is always a risk. That's why they call it *falling* in love. You never know where you're going to land. But if you pick the right guy, he'll catch you, and together the ride will be amazing."

⟶⟫⟪⟵

Ria was still thinking about Amelia's words when she opened the door for Drew a half hour later. Amelia and Beth had left, and Megan and Lindsay were breathlessly awaiting the arrival of their dates.

But when she saw Drew, the furthest thing from her mind was the upcoming prom. He wore tan slacks and a dark brown knit shirt, and he must have recently stepped out of a shower, because his brown hair was damp, and his cheeks were cleanly shaven. He looked good enough to kiss, and her heart speeded up at the thought of the evening ahead. They were finally going to have some time alone together, and she was both terrified and exhilarated by the thought.

But first she had to get Megan and her friend off.

As Drew stepped into the room, he waved his hand in the air and coughed at the thick smell of perfume.

"Did you break a bottle or something?" he asked.

Ria laughed. "Or something. Try two teenaged girls and two battling scents of seduction."

"They want to dance with these guys, not kill them, right?"

"Drew," Megan squealed as she came out of her bedroom. She struck a model pose. "What do you think of my dress?"

"You're beautiful."

She blushed under his compliment. "I wouldn't go that far."

"I would. Your date is going to be knocked out. And yours, too," he added, turning to Lindsay, who was standing in the doorway. "You must be Lindsay."

"And you must be the pilot," Lindsay said, a touch of awe in her voice. She glanced at Megan. "I see what you mean."

Megan nodded. "Told you."

As the girls returned to the bedroom, Drew turned a quizzical eye in Ria's direction. "Do I want to know?"

"All you need to know is that you're a hit with the teen crowd."

"I'm more interested in being a hit with you." He gave her a quick kiss. "How soon are they leaving?"

Before she could answer, the buzzer pealed.

"Right now," Ria said, then buzzed in the boys.

The next few minutes were a blur of corsages and boutonnieres and lots of pictures. Every time Megan smiled for the camera, Ria felt a twinge of fear, but she told herself she was being foolish. And since there was no way she could stop it, she needed to just let the worry go.

Eventually, the kids made their way downstairs where a limo was waiting. Eric's father had paid for their ride to the prom. Ria stood at the window, watching as they got into the car. She felt suddenly emotional, wishing Kate could be here to see her daughter.

Drew peered over her shoulder. "Megan looks happy," he said.

"So far it's the perfect night." She blinked the tears out of her eyes and glanced back at him. "I hope it ends up that way."

"And no one throws up on her shoes," he said.

She smiled. "Exactly. So what now?"

He smiled back at her. "I'd really like to take advantage of this empty apartment, but I've made plans for us."

"You have," she said, a little surprised.

"I asked you on a date. That usually requires a plan."

"What are we going to do?"

"Grab your jacket, and you'll find out."

"I'm not dressed up." She'd put on her nicest sweater and her best pair of jeans, but they were still jeans.

"You're dressed perfectly. But it's going to get cold later, so bring a warm jacket."

She moved over to the closet and grabbed her coat, wondering where they were headed. Drew looked smug and a little too proud of his plans. She had a feeling he had more in mind than dinner and a movie.

"When is Megan expected back from the prom?" he asked as they walked out to his car.

"Tomorrow morning," she admitted, suspecting Drew was going to like her answer.

His face lit up. "Really? You're actually going to let her stay out all night?"

"Yes. I fought the battle, but I lost. They're staying at a hotel about six blocks from here. There are three couples, one room, so hopefully not a lot of—you know."

"Oh, I know," he said. "And are you that sure you've been given the right information?"

"Megan wouldn't lie about it to me."

"I lied to my parents," he said with a frank smile.

"Yeah, I did, too," she said. "But Megan knows that she can't treat this like the other kids. I have to know where she is. And she has to tell me the truth."

His expression grew more somber, but all he said was, "Okay."

She was surprised he'd let the subject drop so easily, but perhaps that was another hint that he still wasn't ready to know everything just yet. That was fine with her. She wanted time off from the worry and the danger. She just wanted to have some fun and be with Drew. Like Megan, she would pretend for a night that her life was perfectly normal.

—⟫⟪—

"Where are we going?" Ria asked.

"You'll see," Drew replied as he drove past the marina, the yacht club, and eventually over the Golden Gate Bridge. He couldn't wait to see her reaction when she realized what they were going to do.

"Are we going far?" she asked.

"That depends on your definition of far."

"And that's not an answer."

"Now, you know how I feel when you won't answer any

of my questions," he retorted.

"Funny."

"Relax, we're almost there. You're going to love it."

"You're awfully confident considering you don't really know what I love."

"I have a good idea about some things," he said pointedly. "Although, I might need a refresher course later on."

"We'll see how well the first part of this evening goes."

A moment later, he took the first exit into Sausalito and drove down a winding road to the bay. At the end of the road stood a small building and a helicopter pad. A bright red four-seater helicopter awaited, along with his friend, Randy Cruz.

"Oh, my God, we're taking a helicopter ride, aren't we?" she said.

"You're riding. I'm flying."

"That's your helicopter?"

"No, it belongs to my friend. He flies helicopter tours over the bay, and he was happy to let me use his helo for our date." He paused. "You're not scared, are you?"

"I've never been up in one, but I'm game."

He'd known she would be. Ria wasn't one to shrink from a challenge.

They got out of the car and headed over to the helicopter. Randy had it gassed up and ready to go. After introducing Ria to Randy, his friend handed her a two-way headset and helped her into the right front seat while Drew got in on the left. He adjusted his headset and said, "Everything okay?"

"I'm trusting you to let me know if it's not okay."

"You don't have anything to worry about. You showed me your world. I want to show you mine, and there's nothing like flying over the city when the night lights start coming on."

"What are we waiting for?" she asked.

And on that note, he took off. Ria gasped as the helo left the pad, and she seemed to have a good grip on her armrests for a minute or two, but as they gained altitude, she started to relax.

"What do you think of the city from up here?" he asked her.

"Beautiful," she said, her gaze on the lighted skyline.

He flew her around the city, past the skyscrapers and the Bay Bridge, around by the new Giants' Ballpark and McCovey Cove, and then he reversed the route, flying past the various islands in the bay—Treasure Island, Angel Island and Alcatraz.

"I thought it would be louder," Ria said. "But it's quiet. It's like we're alone in the sky. Just you and me."

"Just you and me," he echoed, a warm feeling rushing through him as the words left his mouth. "And now for the grand finale."

"It's over already?" Ria asked with disappointment.

"Unfortunately, Randy could only give me thirty minutes," he said. "But no trip over the bay is complete without a fly under the Golden Gate Bridge."

"Fly under?" she echoed.

He took the helicopter down, hearing her catch her breath again, and then flew her under the magnificent bridge, out towards the ocean. The skyline was a dark purple as twilight fell over the city, the fog bank miles off shore.

He wanted to keep going. He wanted to stay in the air forever with Ria at his side, but reality forced him to turn back toward Sausalito.

A few minutes later they were back on the ground.

They got out of the helicopter and handed their headsets to Randy who asked Ria how she'd enjoyed the ride.

"It was awesome," she said, her face lit up with pleasure. "I only wish it was longer."

"We'll do it again," Drew said. "Thanks, Randy."

"Anytime," Randy said.

When they reached the car, Drew moved to open the door for Ria, but she caught him by the arm. He gave her a questioning look. "What's wrong?"

"Nothing," she said with a smile. "Everything is perfect. The ride was perfect. And this is going to be perfect."

She kissed him, her mouth warm in the cool evening breeze. He wanted to deepen the kiss, but she was already moving away.

"Thank you," she said. "That was an amazing experience. I can see why you love flying."

"That was just a taste. Next time we'll do it in the daytime. We can fly up to the Napa Valley or over to Lake Tahoe, really see the landscape."

"I'd like that." She paused, a question in her eyes. "So back to my place, or..."

"Not yet. The evening is just beginning."

"Really?" she asked with an arch of her eyebrow. "What's next?"

"You'll see."

"You're enjoying being the man of mystery, aren't you?"

"Every second," he said. "But mostly I'm enjoying being with you."

She met his gaze and gave a nod. "Me, too."

Ria had been in sole control of her and Megan's life for the last year and a half, so it was refreshing to let Drew take the lead. After the breathtaking helicopter ride, she was already prepared to call the date a success. Anything more would just be icing on the cake. As they drove back over the bridge to the city, they were quiet, and it was the kind of quiet that felt right. They didn't need words to fill the space. They could just breathe and be, and Ria let everything else go.

After getting off the bridge, Drew drove them back to the marina, parking by the yacht club. "Your turn," he said.

"I can't take the boat out now," she said, hating to disappoint him. But she could only use the sailboat when the yacht club was open.

"We don't need your boat. I have one."

"That's right, you do," she said, following him down the docks to the *Eleanor*.

The large boat was beautiful, older, but well taken care of, and having met the original Eleanor, Ria could imagine all the wonderful times she and Patrick had had on this boat. She checked out the boat, the galley and sleeping berth, and thought Drew and his brothers were going to have a lot of fun in the upcoming years.

"What do you think?" Drew asked.

"It looks to be in pretty good shape."

"How do you feel about a moonlit sail?"

"Pretty good," she said with a smile. "Do you want to do the honors?"

"I'm happy to put you in charge."

"Okay."

It was a nice change to be at the helm of a bigger boat, and Ria enjoyed sailing the *Eleanor* out into the bay. "How far do you want to go?" she asked Drew as they passed Alcatraz.

"This is good for me," he said. "I think it's time for dinner."

"Out here?"

"Can you think of a more romantic restaurant?"

She really couldn't. "You put some thought into tonight."

"I put thought into everything I do."

That didn't surprise her. Drew might like to fly into the

wind, but he wasn't the kind of man to take off without some sort of plan.

He held up two wine bottles. "White or red?"

"White. What's for dinner?"

"Crab salad, fresh rolls, and strawberries."

"Impressive."

"Since you love the sea, I was hoping you liked seafood."

"How could I not? My grandfather was a fisherman."

"What about your dad?" he asked, as he handed her a glass of wine. "You've never really told me about him, except to say that he died, and that your parents didn't get along. What was your relationship like?"

"I adored my dad when I was little. But he didn't turn out to be the hero I imagined that he was."

Drew gave her an understanding look. "Most people don't. What did he do?"

"He cheated on my mom. It went on for over a year. He worked in sales and traveled a lot for his job. The affair was with his assistant, a lovely woman named Gwen. I really liked her until I found out she was screwing my Dad." She sipped her wine. "My father said that my mother froze him out, that after she had me she didn't want to have sex anymore. That he'd spent ten years watching her roll over to her side of the bed, and he couldn't stand looking at her back anymore. So they divorced. I went to live with my mom."

"Why did your sister stay with your father? It sounds like he was the one to blame for the divorce."

"I thought it was pretty clear-cut, and I was only eleven. But Kate adored my father, and she was six years older than me. She said I didn't understand, that she'd heard the way my mother spoke to my father, and she didn't blame him. She put it all on my mom. She said my mother broke up the family because she wasn't willing to try." Ria paused. "My mom pretty much said exactly the opposite. Anyway, Kate was almost done with high school, and she didn't want to move, so that was part of why she stayed with my father.. I went to San Diego with my mother and then we eventually moved to the East Coast. I didn't see my father or sister again for a very long time."

"Why?" he asked.

"There was always a reason. Kate got pregnant young and had a baby, so her life totally changed. And my father just couldn't seem to work out any kind of visitation plan with my mother."

"Doesn't sound like he tried that hard." He stopped abruptly. "I'm sorry. I shouldn't have said that."

"No, it's true. He didn't try that hard, and my mom didn't, either. I think they both wanted to move on, and I was the person who dragged them back to that time in their lives they wanted to forget. My mother told me once that she got pregnant with me to try to save the marriage."

"Why would she tell you that?"

"It just came out one night when she had too much wine. It actually made sense to me. But I'm making her sound worse than she is. She does love me, and we did have a relationship, just not the greatest one. It was a long time ago."

"I'm beginning to understand why you took to the sea."

"I wasn't just running away from family. I've always had wanderlust, always wanted to travel, and so I did."

"I always wanted to travel, too, one of the reasons I joined the Navy. I just didn't expect to see so much hot desert."

"I can't imagine living in a landlocked country or state. I'd go crazy in the middle of the country."

He smiled. "I think you would."

"So where's that salad you were bragging about?"

"It's in the galley. Do you want to eat down there or up here?"

"Up here. It's a beautiful night. And the stars are just coming out." Besides that, close proximity to the sleeping berth below was only going to put ideas in her head that she didn't want to think about right now.

While Drew pulled dinner together, she gazed out at the water, thinking of a different sea on the other side of the world, of how many miles she'd traveled, how many lies she'd told, how lonely and scared she'd felt. But tonight, back in the city where she was born, and with a man who had freed her soul once before, she felt like she'd finally come all the way home again.

Drew came up the stairs, juggling a couple of plates. While she set up a picnic on the bench, he went back down for the rest of the items.

The crab salad was delicious and flavorful, and the freshly baked bread made a nice accompaniment to the meal. They ate quickly and quietly and finished off with a fresh fruit medley of berries, melon and orange slices.

"That was perfect," she said, wiping her mouth with a napkin.

"I picked it up at Giancomo's on Fisherman's Wharf."

"Then I guess you weren't bragging when you said you do good take-out."

"I know what I'm good at." He gave her a thoughtful look. "There's something I've been wanting to ask you."

"What's that?" she asked, feeling wary about his tone.

"Where are your friends, Ria?"

"What do you mean?"

"It's not a difficult question. You must have had friends in your life."

"I've lost track of most people, but sure, I have friends. They're around."

"Not around here that I've seen."

"No, most of them are still working on boats at various

ports around the world. And now I don't have time for friends, and even if I did what would I have in common with other twenty-eight-year-olds when I'm raising a teenager? They're hitting up clubs on the weekends, and I'm helping Megan get ready for the prom."

"You're sacrificing a lot for her."

"It's not a sacrifice. I love her. She's my family. And I'd give up on a lot more than friends for her."

He nodded. "I know you would." He looked up at the stars. "It's a clear night."

"And this is a great view," she said. "Although, we'd see more stars if we were further away from the city."

"Did you ever get scared out in the middle of the ocean?"

"I've been through some bad storms, and I have a healthy respect for Mother Nature, but I never came close to being in real trouble."

"I guess you're not counting the boat that blew up."

She stared back at him. "Do you want to talk about that now?"

"No. Not tonight." He took a breath. "I don't want to talk anymore at all."

"Neither do I."

"I want to kiss you, Ria. And I don't want to stop there."

"Neither do I," she repeated, smiling.

He smiled back at her. "You're beautiful."

"Thank you. But I thought we weren't going to talk." She'd barely gotten the words out when he bridged the space between them and crushed his mouth against hers.

Fifteen

The remnants of their dinner fell to the floor as Drew pushed her back against the cushioned bench. She went willingly, wanting everything he had to give. His tongue tangled with hers as he angled his head, making the kiss deeper, hotter, and hungrier. His passion set off the sparks that had been smoldering for weeks, months, more than a year. Every one of her nerve endings was on fire, each one calling out for a touch, a kiss, a caress. The time apart faded away. There was no yesterday, no tomorrow, just now. And now was all she needed.

She thought she could kiss him for hours and still want more, so when Drew raised his head to look at her, she uttered a small protest.

"Downstairs. Bed."

"Up here. Stars," she countered. She liked looking at him in the moonlight, the beams throwing shadows on his strong and handsome face, the desire sparking like gold in his brown eyes. "There's no one else around. Just you and me and the night sky."

She put a hand on the back of his neck and pulled him back to her. She took the initiative this time, sliding her tongue across the seam of his lips, nipping at the corners of his mouth until he groaned with pleasure and urged her inside. He tasted like wine and strawberries, a delicious mix of heat and sweet.

"You're killing me," he said, with a gasp for air.

"Are you complaining?" she teased.

"Not for a second. But let's get more comfortable."

He grabbed the cushions off the opposite seat and laid them on the deck of the boat, making a soft bed between the benches. Then he pulled her down next to him. She fell on to her knees, facing him. The look he gave her was dark, intense, filled with need, and it was all for her. She'd never felt so wanted.

She took off her jacket and tossed it aside, then pulled her shirt over her head and placed it over the jacket.

Drew's gaze moved to her breasts and the lacy black bra that barely covered them. Her nipples hardened, calling out for a touch, a stroke, and Drew answered that call, cupping both of her breasts with his hands, as he kissed her neck and slid his mouth down along her collarbone and the valley of her breasts. It seemed to take forever for his fingers to flick aside the scrap of lace. And then his tongue touched her nipple, and a shot of desire ran through her body. He lifted his head and looked into her eyes.

She answered his silent question by unhooking her bra and taking it off. There might be secrets between them, but at least some of the barriers were coming down. She might not be able to give him the truth of her life, but she could give her body and maybe what was left of her heart.

"Beautiful Ria," he murmured. "I've dreamed about this moment for a long time."

"You don't have to dream anymore." She reached for the hem of his shirt and helped him pull it over his head. His chest was broad with a smattering of dark hair that tapered down his muscled abs. She caught her breath at the male perfection. "Now, I'm the one who's dreaming."

He laughed. "I like your chest better."

She smiled as they fell onto the cushions of their makeshift bed. It wasn't long before they stripped off the rest of their clothes and there, under a starry sky, they kissed and caressed and drove each other into a frenzy of need that could only be satisfied by the other. Drew filled the empty spaces in her heart and her soul, making her whole again, and when the climax came, she felt like she'd finally found what she'd searched the globe for, the place that was home. It wasn't a city or a country or a house. It wasn't even the sea. It was Drew. And she was going to hang on to him as long as she could.

———»»«———

An hour later, the breeze kicked up a notch and Drew went downstairs to grab some blankets. When he came back, he stretched out next to Ria and pulled her into his arms, wrapping the blankets around both of them.

Ria put her head on his chest, and he could smell the shampoo in her hair, the scent that had haunted him for over a year. "Orange blossoms," he said.

"What?" she asked lazily, tracing circles on his chest with her finger.

"Your hair smells like orange blossoms. When I woke up on the island, I could smell it on my pillow.

She lifted her head. "I didn't know it was that strong. Sorry."

"Don't apologize. It's enticing—seductive. It suits you."

"I like enticing and seductive."

"So do I," he replied with a smile.

"You look happy right now, Drew."

"Well, that's because I *am* happy. How about you?"

"Deliciously exhausted."

"It was better than the last time," he said. "Better than all the memories."

"Was it? It seems good every time to me." She paused.
"When I'm with you, I'm myself. I felt like that on the island,
and I feel like that tonight. Somehow you strip away all my
barriers, all my fears. In your arms, I'm young, fun, and free.
It's like you release something inside of me."

Her words touched him deeply and scared him a little,
too, because he felt much the same way. With Ria, he didn't
seem to have his usual defenses in place. And he wasn't quite
sure how to handle something serious. But he was going to
have to learn quickly, because what he felt for Ria was
serious and intense. He might bring out her fun side, but she
brought out the side of him that wanted more than just a fling.

"Nothing to say?" she teased. "I can hardly believe I've
rendered you speechless."

"Just thinking," he said. "When I first met you on the
island, I felt like I'd just walked into the sun after a long time
in the dark."

"That's because I was blonde then."

"It wasn't just your hair color. It was you. Your sparkling
eyes, teasing smile, your smart mouth—"

"What?" she interrupted.

"You gave me a hard time, Ria."

"You asked me to go to bed with you, and I didn't even
know you."

"But I wanted to know you. I *had* to know you," he
corrected. "That night, a feeling of desperation ran through
me. I was afraid I would have to leave the island before I had
a chance to talk to you, to touch you. Thank God you came to
my cottage."

"I'm not sure you should be grateful about that." She
sighed and put her head back down on his chest.

He tightened his arm around her shoulders, loving her
soft curves alongside his body. "It was the best night of my
life."

"Mine, too," she murmured.

She'd no sooner finished speaking when a spray of water hit him in the face. "What was that?" he sputtered.

Ria sat up, wiping water off of her face. She glanced at the tall ship passing not too far away from them and smiled. "We caught some of the wake. Maybe it's a sign that we should go back to the harbor."

"It's gone now."

"But the wind is picking up."

"That's a good thing," he said.

"Why?"

"Because I'm in the mood for a wild ride. What about you?"

"Absolutely," she said, throwing one leg over his hips. "And this time I'm going to be on top."

"Honey, you can be wherever you want to be."

Ria woke up to the early morning sun on her face. A glance at her watch said it was just after six. She wrapped the blanket around her as she stood up, knowing there would be fishing boats going out for the day. Then she grabbed her clothes and went downstairs to use the restroom and get dressed.

There were no supplies in the galley, so coffee would have to wait until they got back to the harbor.

Drew came down the stairs with a blanket wrapped loosely around his hips. "There you are," he said, swooping in for a kiss. "I was getting lonely."

"You were asleep when I left."

"Yeah, and you really have to stop leaving before I wake up."

Despite his smile, there was an edge to his words, and

she realized that he was thinking about the first time she'd left him.

"I never wanted to hurt you, Drew. If you can't believe anything else I say, I hope you'll believe that."

"I know you didn't leave because of me. I just can't forget the ground moving beneath my feet when your boat blew up and the terror that followed me all the way out there. You weren't supposed to mean anything to me, Ria. I was shocked at how shattered I felt."

"You weren't supposed to mean anything to me, either." She put her hand on his face, caressing the rough stubble along his jawline. "But you do—mean something. I just don't know what I have to offer you."

He put his finger against her lips. "Hush. It's too early for this conversation."

She wondered if it wasn't too late.

"I need coffee," he added.

"We should get back," she agreed. "Megan will be home in a few hours. I'll get the boat going while you get dressed."

Twenty minutes later, the *Eleanor* was back in dock. Ria felt sorry that the night was over, but as the sun moved higher in the sky, she could no longer live in the world of beautiful illusion that she'd felt the night before. Her real life was about to get started again.

When they got back to her apartment, Ria made coffee and pancakes while Drew flipped through the Sunday morning news programs. She knew she should tell him to leave, but she kept putting it off. They wouldn't have too many more minutes together, and she wanted to make the most of each one.

As she flipped pancakes on to a plate, she got a text from Megan.

"Eric's dad's car got a flat tire. We're waiting for roadside service. Home soon. Had a great time!"

Ria blew out a breath of relief. Megan was fine. The prom was over, and so was the all-night party—one less problem to worry about.

"Everything all right?" Drew asked, as he turned off the television and joined her at the table.

"Megan is running late. Eric's father's car got a flat tire."

"But she's safe."

"Yeah. I'll be happy when I see her face though. She said the prom was great."

"You both had a good night," he said with a grin.

"Well, I hope she wasn't doing what I was doing," she said dryly. "I don't even want to think about that."

"She's sixteen and quite the romantic."

"She's smart, too," Ria said. "And we've been open with each other. I guess I have to trust her."

"Trust is hard for you."

"Yes," she admitted.

"And not just because of this situation," he added. "I think your trust issues go back to your father and maybe your mother, too."

"Are you my shrink now?"

"Sorry. Those pancakes smell good."

"Sit down. They're ready."

"Wonderful," he said between mouthfuls. "There's no end to your talents."

She smiled. "Don't I know it."

"There's that smart mouth I like so much." He leaned across the table and kissed her. "Maple syrup," he said, licking his lips. "I like it. I could think of a few other places I might like to drizzle that syrup."

Her face warmed at his sexy words. "Stop that, Drew. Megan is going to be home any second, and I don't need either one of us to be hot and bothered."

He grinned. "When you're around I'm always hot and

bothered."

She popped the last bite of pancake into her mouth and then said, "I'm going to take a shower. You can do the dishes."

"Or I could take a shower with you," he suggested.

"Not going to happen," she said, tossing her napkin at him, and then she went into the bedroom and shut the door.

When she got into the bathroom, she caught sight of her face in the mirror, and she was actually surprised at her reflection. She couldn't remember the last time she'd looked so alive, so happy. Actually, she could remember the last time. It was a year and a half ago, right after she'd climbed out of Drew's bed.

Moving away from the mirror, she turned on the shower and didn't wait for the water to heat up. She could use a little cold water on her face. She needed to get her head together. Today was a new day.

—◦➤➤◄◄◦—

Drew cleaned up the breakfast dishes and tried not to think about Ria naked in the shower. The ringing of his cell phone provided a welcome distraction.

"Tim," he said in surprise. "You're up early on a Sunday."

"I picked up a shift last night for John. His wife went into labor."

"That's great news. What did she have?"

"Don't know yet. Apparently, the labor is still going on. Anyway, I wanted to let you know that I spoke to my friend on Isla de los Sueños."

His stomach turned over. He'd forgotten all about Tim's offer to look into Ria's boat accident. And Tim didn't know that he'd met up with Ria again. He'd thought about mentioning it, but Ria was so afraid he'd reveal her whereabouts that he'd kept quiet.

"Drew? Did you hear me?"

"Yeah. What did you find out?"

"Your bartender wasn't the only one to die in that explosion. Apparently, the niece of Enrique Valdez was also on that boat as well. Her bodyguard was supposed to be with her, but he overslept and didn't make the trip. He ended up dead two weeks later. Valdez blamed him for his niece's death." Tim paused. "Valdez is rumored to be the head of a large criminal organization. Most people on the island speak his name in hushed tones."

Drew sat down at the kitchen table, the pieces falling into place. Valdez's niece had to be Megan. "What was the girl's name?" he asked.

"Marguerite Valdez. My friend said that no bodies have ever been found, but that he's sure he would have heard something if your friend or Valdez's niece had turned out to be alive. Many, many people spent days looking for them because of Valdez's money and power. Everyone wanted to be the hero, the one to bring his niece home."

"Okay," Drew said, wanting to end the call before he said too much.

"I can keep asking questions," Tim said. "In fact, I might be headed down there in a week or two. They're having a poker tournament on the island. Maybe you'd like to go with me."

"I don't think so."

"Yeah, I figured you'd say that. Sorry I don't have better information."

"It's fine. And you don't need to ask any more questions. I'm going to move on."

"Well, that's good news. Do you think you can finally let her go, stop trying to save her?"

That was a million dollar question, Drew thought, and he still didn't have an answer. "I'll see you next week, Tim."

"Yeah, see you then."

Drew hung up the phone, his pulse pounding way too fast. He'd been afraid to push Ria to the end of her story, worried that whatever line she'd crossed would be one too many for him to overlook. Now he knew exactly what she'd done. It was so clear he couldn't believe he hadn't realized it before.

Ria walked back into the living room, her hair wet from her shower. When she saw his face and the phone in his hand, she stopped abruptly, giving him a wary look. "What's wrong?"

He got to his feet and walked over to her. "I'm going to ask you a question, and I want the truth." His gaze locked with hers. "Did you kidnap Megan?"

Sixteen

Ria stared at Drew, her blood pounding through her veins. Apparently, he'd made his decision, and now she had to make hers. She would tell him her story, but she wouldn't necessarily wait around to see what he would do with the information. The prom was over. If she had to leave, she would.

"Megan came with me willingly," she said. "Does that sound like a kidnapping?"

"But you don't have custody of her, do you?"

"No, I don't. Her uncle has custody, but he is a dangerous criminal. Megan was not safe with him. So I stepped in."

"Start at the beginning," he said.

"That's going to take some time. Megan will be home soon."

"And I assume she already knows the story." He walked back over to the kitchen table and sat down. "Talk."

A moment later, she took the seat across from him. "I've told you a lot of it already, but here's the rest. Kate was eighteen when she went to study abroad in Spain. Like me, she also had wanderlust in her soul; she just didn't care to see the world by boat." Ria took a breath, trying not to get sidetracked by sad thoughts of her sister.

"Anyway," Ria continued, "Kate was only in Spain for six weeks when she met Reynoldo Valdez. He was twenty-five years old and a young lawyer, very handsome, sophisticated. He'd been educated in the U.S., so he spoke perfect English. They fell in love. When her semester of study was over, Kate couldn't bring herself to leave. She signed up for another year. A few months later, she became pregnant. She dropped out of school and married Reynoldo."

"And your family had nothing to say about that?" he asked.

"My family was scattered to the winds. My mother was having her own love affair. I was fourteen and trying to make my way through my first year of high school. My dad was doing his thing, whatever that was. Everyone was thinking about themselves."

"At least two of those people should have been thinking about you," he said quietly.

"Well, this story isn't about me, at least not yet. Both of my parents tried to talk to Kate, but she was headstrong and in love. She was still angry with my mother, so she didn't give a damn what my mother had to say. Kate convinced my father that she was having the time of her life with her rich, handsome husband. After Megan was born, Kate sent me a picture of the two of them. She looked happy, and the baby had all this beautiful dark hair. I really wanted to see them both, but I was a kid. I couldn't get myself to Spain. Kate had no interest in returning to the States."

Ria cleared her throat. "For the next several years, I had little contact with Kate," she continued. "I wrote to her a few times, but she rarely wrote back. Then one day she sent me an email and asked me to stop writing her. She said she would be in touch with me when she could. I thought that was weird, but our relationship was so distant by then, I didn't care anymore."

"I doubt that you didn't care, Ria."

"Well, I tried not to care. After I left home and started

traveling, I didn't really think about Kate. When I was twenty-two, my father got really sick. He was dying, and he wanted to see me. I could hardly believe it," she said, thinking about how shocked she had been at the time. "I was angry that ten years had passed since our last visit, but I was also touched that he remembered me at all. So against my mother's wishes, I flew to his house. He was living in Texas at the time with some woman I didn't know. That's when I saw Kate again. She had Megan with her. Megan was ten years old. She was the cutest thing. We were together a week before my dad passed away."

"Ria, are we getting to the kidnapping part soon?" he asked impatiently.

"You wanted the story from the beginning, so sit back and be quiet."

"Fine."

"During that week Kate and I bonded again as sisters. She confided in me that her husband's family was not what she had thought. She loved Reynoldo, and he was an honorable man, but she believed that many of the family businesses were fronts for organized crime and that his brother Enrique was the ringleader. She was fearful for Reynoldo and also for herself, because people who challenged Enrique tended to disappear." Ria thought back to that long ago conversation that had changed so many lives. "I didn't completely believe her. Kate loved drama. I should have taken her more seriously."

"It's always easier to see things when you're looking back," Drew said. "What happened next?"

"Nothing happened for a while. Kate told me that the reason she'd asked me not to contact her was because she didn't want anyone to know about me. After my father passed away, the Valdez family thought she was an orphan. She'd apparently told Reynoldo at their first meeting that her mother was dead, because to all intents and purposes she was dead to Kate. The next time I saw my sister was three years later—in France. I was in a sailboat race, and she and Megan came to see me. I guess she had a friend who lived in the area, so she was able to get away from the family without anyone knowing she was coming to see me. Megan was thirteen, and I could see the changes in both of them."

"Like what?"

"They were tense, quiet, nervous. Kate told me she thought Enrique was having her followed. He'd taken charge of the family a few months earlier when Reynoldo's father died. Kate was afraid that Reynoldo was standing in Enrique's way. She was planning an escape. She'd already gotten fake papers set up for her and Megan and Reynoldo, but she had yet to convince Reynoldo to leave his family and his home. He thought he could handle his brother, but Kate didn't believe that. She said her husband was too kind; he saw the good in people instead of the evil. She made me promise that if anything happened to her, I would find Megan, and I would get her away from the Valdez family."

"What did you think at that point?" Drew asked curiously.

"I believed her. She showed me evidence that Enrique wasn't just a criminal; he was also cruel. He'd hurt people. He'd hurt women especially. And she said that for some reason he seemed to think she was his property, even though she was married to his brother."

"If she and Megan were away from the family at that point, why didn't they stay away?"

"Because Kate loved Reynoldo, and she didn't want to take Megan away from her father. Reynoldo wasn't ready to admit defeat yet."

"Over the next few months Kate would use random phones to call me to let me know about the plans she was making. She was a few weeks away from her escape when she and Reynoldo were in a car accident. They were driving down the steep hills by their house when the brakes failed. They were killed instantly. Megan was put under the guardianship of Enrique."

Drew let out a breath. "And that's where you came in."

"It took me a while to find Megan. Enrique moved her to the island. I guess he was afraid that she would talk to the wrong people and he wanted to keep her under his thumb."

"So you went to the island to get her."

"Yes, but I couldn't do anything right away. I had to build an identity that wasn't suspicious, and then I had to find a way to contact Megan. She was rarely out of the house, and when she was, she had bodyguards with her. After a few months, Enrique rarely came to the island, and the guard grew more complacent. Megan began to be seen in town more often. One day I followed her into a ladies' room in the back of a restaurant. That's when we saw each other again."

"How did she react?"

"She started crying. She said she'd been waiting for me to come for her. That her mother had told her I would save her. She cried harder when I told her we were going to have to take our time, come up with a plan. She was scared of Enrique and tired of being a prisoner. We set up a way to meet once a week for a few minutes. Eventually, we put the plan in motion. Megan would convince her handlers to let her take a sailing lesson." She let out a weary breath and waved her hand in the air. "You know the rest."

"Not exactly. How did you get explosives to blow up the boat?"

"I saved fireworks from the Fourth of July. I went on the Internet and learned how to make a timer. It was rough, and I wasn't sure it would work, but it did. I had a life raft on board, and I used that to get us to another boat that I'd stashed on a nearby island. For days I thought someone would catch us. I knew Valdez would have an army out looking for Megan, but we managed to get away."

"Where did you go?"

"We moved around a lot the first few months. Megan was pretty shaken up. It took a while for her to start breathing more freely. We took some self-defense classes, so she'd feel like she wasn't so vulnerable. I even learned how to shoot a gun, but I was afraid to keep one in the house, so that didn't do much good. I knew I wasn't going to win in a gun battle against Megan's uncle, so I concentrated on staying hidden." She paused, trying to get a read on what Drew was thinking, but he wasn't giving much away. "I couldn't go to the cops, because Enrique is Megan's guardian, and to answer your original question, in the eyes of the law, I kidnapped her."

Drew sat back in his seat, his gaze reflective, thoughtful. "Did Enrique hurt Megan?"

"Not physically. She told me that he scared her, that he threatened her. He said if she didn't want to end up like her mother, she needed to be loyal to him." She paused. "I forgot to mention that Megan saw her parents' car go off the road. She was looking out her bedroom window, watching them leave. I guess Kate had decided at the last minute to go with Reynoldo to meet his brother. But, of course, they didn't make it. Megan said she started screaming and went running down the hill, but no one would let her get to her parents. I thank God for that. I wouldn't have wanted her to see them like that."

He shook his head, his jaw tight. "That's too much for a kid to see."

"Yes. And for a long time she had nightmares, but she's better now."

"She speaks perfect English without a trace of an accent. Surprising for a kid who grew up in Spain, in what I assume was a Spanish-speaking household."

She nodded. "Kate wanted Megan to speak perfect English and perfect Spanish. She worked a lot with her. She felt certain that at some point they would be back in the States, and she wanted to be sure that Megan could fit in. Megan hasn't spoken Spanish since the day we left the island. Sometimes, I forget that's her first language. And since she's been spending so much time with kids her own age, I only occasionally notice a trace of an accent."

"What did you do to the bodyguard so that he wouldn't show up on the boat?" Drew asked, returning to the events that occurred on the island.

"Megan put sleeping pills in his coffee."

"You should have killed him. You would have saved Valdez the trouble."

Her eyes widened. "Wait. What do you mean I would have saved Valdez the trouble?"

"The bodyguard was stabbed to death two weeks after you left the island."

"Juan told you that? You didn't mention it before," she said, suddenly suspicious about his new information.

"It wasn't Juan; it was Tim. I just got off the phone with him."

Anxiety shot through her as she stood up. "Your friend? You told Tim about Megan and me? You said you didn't."

"It was last week before you and I reconnected. I mentioned to Tim that you were haunting my dreams. It wasn't a surprise to him, because I was distracted on the job. He said he had some friends on the island, and he could ask them if any new information had come to light in the last few years. I forgot all about our conversation until he called this morning."

"So Tim called his friends on the island and asked about me?" Her stomach turned over. "I have to go. I have to pack.

As soon as Megan comes home, we'll get out of here. She won't want to go, but she'll have to. The prom is over. The fairytale of normality is done. The clock struck midnight."

He put his hands on her shoulders and gave her a little shake to stop her ramble. "Ria, don't panic. Tim doesn't know you're alive. And I told him to drop it. Nothing has changed."

His words took a little of the edge off, but she still hated the idea that someone else had called people on the island to ask about her. If anyone started hearing rumors that a woman who looked just like her had been spotted in San Francisco, it could get back to Valdez. "What exactly did he tell you when he called just now?" she asked.

"He said Valdez's niece was on the boat. I knew there was supposedly another passenger, but I never really asked who that was, or if I did, it didn't matter to me. I was only focused on you." Drew paused. "He also told me about the bodyguard. But he reconfirmed that everyone thinks that both of you are dead."

She walked over to the window and glanced outside. Everything looked normal on the street below. So why did she feel like her entire world had just been spun on its axis?

"It's going to be all right, Ria."

She turned back to face him. "I'd like to believe that's true, but I can't afford to be wrong." She swallowed hard. "What are you going to do now, Drew, now that you know the whole story? Are you going to turn us in?"

"Of course not."

A wave of relief followed his words. "Now that you know, you're an accessory to my crime."

"I'm not worried about that. I'm more worried about the long-term plan. You're playing defense, Ria, and you can't do that forever. You need to find a way to attack Valdez, to beat him. Hiding out forever isn't a reasonable solution."

"And attacking and beating a crime lord doesn't seem too

reasonable either," she said, unable to keep the sarcasm out of her voice.

"We need to think."

"No. *We* don't need to do anything," she said pointedly. "I told you my story, but I'm not asking you for help. I'm handling this."

"You're in over your head."

"I'm a strong swimmer."

"So am I. And there's no way in hell I'm walking away from you or Megan. If you pack up and disappear, I will hunt you to the ends of the earth. And I will find you."

She wanted to ask him why he would go to that much trouble, but she couldn't get the words out. Fortunately, their conversation was over for the minute. She could hear Megan's voice in the hall.

"They're back," she said. "Let's not talk about any of this in front of Megan, all right?"

He nodded.

She checked the peephole by habit, then opened the door. Megan and Eric walked into the apartment. Megan had exchanged her prom dress for leggings and a tank top, and Eric now wore jeans and a t-shirt. They looked happy and tired.

"Sorry, we're late," Megan said. "It took forever for the tow truck to come."

"Yeah, my dad said to apologize," Eric said.

"It's fine. Did you have fun?"

"We had a great time." Megan's smile went from ear to ear. "But I need a long nap."

"I'll text you later," Eric said.

"Okay," Megan replied.

There was an awkward kiss between them, and then Eric left the apartment. Megan closed the door behind him and said, "The most amazing night of my life."

Megan's words filled Ria with happiness. "It was that good?"

"The best. Eric wants me to be his girlfriend." She paused, looking over at Drew. "Sorry, I didn't even say hi to you."

"No problem," Drew said. "I'm glad you had fun."

"What did you tell Eric?" Ria asked.

"I said yes, of course," Megan said. "He's such a cool guy. I have to tell Lindsay I have a boyfriend now."

"Didn't you just see her?" Ria asked.

"An hour ago. Eric asked me to be his girlfriend when we were in the car," Megan said, as she texted Lindsay with rapid-fire fingers. When she was done, she added. "I'm going to take a nap."

"I figured," Ria said. "I have some lessons this afternoon. So you'll be in the apartment the rest of the day?"

Megan rolled her eyes. "Yes, I won't leave the apartment." She grabbed a banana out of the fruit bowl and paused, a light of curiosity in her eyes. "So what did you two do last night?"

"We went for a helicopter ride," Ria said, feeling as if last night was now already a distant dream."

"Don't forget the sail that followed," Drew added.

"Wow. You got to go up in his helicopter? No fair. I thought you said you couldn't take us up," Megan complained.

"It was my friend's helo," Drew said. "And I'd be happy to get you a ride sometime."

"You better. It sounds like you had the perfect night," she added, giving Ria a smile.

"It was good. I'll tell you more about it later." After Megan left, she turned back to Drew. "It's your turn to answer *my* question."

"What's that?"

"What are you going to do now?"

"Who said I was going to do anything?"

"You're a man of action. And you like to solve problems. I'm fairly certain you're going to do something, and I don't want you to. This is my problem, not yours."

"We'll talk later, Ria."

"That's not an answer."

"It's all I have right now." He walked over to her. "I need to think. What you told me is a lot to take in."

"I know."

"But I'm not going to hurt you, Ria. And I'm not going to let anyone else hurt you or Megan." He kissed her hard on the lips, then left.

As she closed the door behind him, she couldn't help thinking that she should have run when she had the chance. While having Drew on her side was wonderful and somewhat reassuring, she now had to worry about him, too, and there was no way she was going to let anyone hurt him, either.

Seventeen

After leaving Ria's apartment, Drew drove home. He took a shower, changed his clothes and debated his next move. The night had certainly been incredible. Being with Ria again had been even better than the first time. But with the morning had come reality and revelations. His mind was still spinning from Ria's story. One thing was clear; he needed more information on Enrique Valdez. And he needed to get that information from someone who wasn't involved or biased. While Ria might trust her sister implicitly, he needed to be sure that Kate hadn't spun Ria a tale just to get Megan away from the Valdez family. Although, Kate's death certainly lent credence to her earlier assumption that her life was in danger.

Drew ran his fingers through his damp hair as he considered his options. He had friends in the Coast Guard's drug enforcement unit that he could call on. If Enrique Valdez was an international drug smuggler, he would no doubt be on their radar. He could also talk to Max and Emma, see if they could tap into Valdez's criminal activities. But he had to be careful. If he asked the wrong person, he could put Ria in danger, which was exactly what she was afraid of. He didn't want to blow her trust in him, but he also couldn't stand by and do nothing.

Which left him with the two people he knew he could trust—Emma, and her homicide detective fiancé, Max

Harrison.

He pulled out his phone and texted Emma to see if she and Max were home. She told him to come on over, so he grabbed his keys and headed out the door.

Ria might not want his protection, but he would give it anyway, because he cared about her. She was an amazing woman, beautiful, strong, and brave. He still couldn't believe how daring she'd been to rig explosives to a boat and fake their deaths in order to escape from a criminal overlord. And it had worked. Everyone thought she was dead. If he hadn't seen her on the wharf months earlier, he'd still be haunted by dreams of a beautiful woman lost at sea.

Ria was definitely one of a kind—a survivor. She'd lived through the divorce of her parents, her mother's remarriage, the death of her father and her sister, and now she was raising her teenage niece, a generous and unselfish act that made him admire her even more.

It was clear that she and Megan adored each other. They were clinging together like the last two survivors on a life raft.

But it wasn't just them anymore. He was involved, and he was not going to let anything bad happen to either one of them.

A few minutes later, he pulled up in front of Emma's building. She lived in a ground floor flat with a backyard garden that was rare in the city, and as he walked into her apartment, he was impressed by the charm of her home. It wasn't super girly; that wasn't Emma's style, but there were fresh flowers and paintings on the wall, and the décor was a mix of male and female, oversized furniture and a big screen TV contrasted by soft pillows and throw blankets.

"You finished decorating," he murmured with approval. The last time he'd been in her apartment she'd just been moving in.

"Almost," she said, sipping on a smoothie.

"Did you just work out?" he asked, noting her yoga pants and workout top.

"Yes, I had to work off some stress this morning."

"Wedding stress?"

"No. Work stress. I've got an arsonist torching cars in the Sunset District, and it's pissing me off that I can't find him."

"You will," he said confidently. Emma was like a bulldog when it came to catching firebugs. She didn't quit, even when the odds were stacked against her. In some ways she reminded him of Ria. They were both ready to battle whenever they had to.

"So, what brings you to my apartment on a Sunday morning?" she asked, sitting down on the bar stool in front of the island in her kitchen.

"I have a question. I was hoping to talk to Max, too. Is he here?" He glanced toward the bedroom where he thought he could hear the sound of running water.

"Taking a shower," Emma said. "He should be done in a sec. He's not one for long showers, unless, of course, we're taking one together."

He groaned. "I do not want to hear about that."

She laughed. "I know. I just love to make you uncomfortable. You're so easy." She paused. "So, does this have something to do with Ria?"

"Yes."

"I thought so. I liked her. She's a little on the quiet side, but you two looked good together." Emma paused, speculation in her eyes. "When you introduced her to the family, you didn't mention it, but is she the woman from your past—the one you thought was dead?"

"Smart girl," he said.

She sipped her smoothie, then shot him a cocky smile. "I'll take that as a yes. So what's her story?"

"I'd rather tell both you and Max at the same time."

"That sounds intriguing. And maybe a little worrisome," she added, concern filling her gaze.

"Hey, Drew," Max said, as he came out of the bedroom wearing jeans and a t-shirt. "I didn't know you were coming over."

"Max," he said with a nod. "Sorry to intrude on your Sunday."

"We're not doing anything."

"Drew has a question for both of us," Emma put in. "I think it's serious."

"I'm right here. I can speak for myself," Drew said with annoyance.

"So talk," she told him.

"I need to get some information on someone. I'm pretty sure he's a successful international criminal. And I'm wondering if you can help me."

"An international criminal?" Emma echoed. "What on earth is Ria mixed up in?"

"Who's Ria?" Max asked.

"She's the woman Drew brought to the house the other night," Emma told her fiancé. "I mentioned her to you."

"Emma," Drew interrupted. "Can I talk now?"

"Sorry," Emma said. "Go on."

"I can't go on until I ask you if this is something you'd be willing to do for me on an unofficial basis. It does involve Ria, and I don't want to put her in danger. And I can't say anything more without your agreement. I know it's a lot to ask."

"If she's in danger, then you could be in danger," Emma said, a frown pulling her brows together. "I don't like the sound of that. Of course we'll help. Won't we, Max?"

"If you have any reservations, just say no," Drew said.

"I can ask some questions without making it official,"

Max said. "What's the name?"

"Enrique Valdez. I don't know much about him, except that he allegedly runs a criminal organization with a home base possibly in Spain, and that he also has a private estate on an island called Isla de los Sueños. I'd like to know what exactly he's involved in and how close anyone is to catching him and putting him in jail."

"I'll look into it," Max said.

"How does Ria tie to this Enrique Valdez?" Emma asked. "Wait. She was on that island, and so were you."

"You never forget anything, do you?"

"That's why I'm good at my job."

"Yes, I met her on the island. Her sister was married to Enrique's brother. Both her sister and her sister's husband were killed in a suspicious car accident two years ago. Ria believes that Enrique is responsible for her sister's death."

"And she wants vengeance?" Max asked.

"Actually, she just wants to make sure she doesn't end up in the same kind of accident," he said, deciding not to mention Megan for the moment. "She told me that Valdez has a long reach. And that he has reason to dislike her. I don't want my questions through you to trigger anything. That's why I need this done off the record. My name can't come into it. There are people who know that Ria and I were together on the island. I can't put her in jeopardy."

Emma sighed. "I thought she was so nice, but now she sounds like a lot of trouble. Can't you find anyone trouble-free to hang out with?"

"Not anyone this beautiful, sexy or interesting," he said. "Some people are worth a little trouble. And look who's talking—a serial arsonist was stalking you when you and Max fell for each other. Talk about trouble. That word should be your middle name, Emma."

"Very funny," she said, making a face at him.

"And true," Max said.

She shot her fiancé a pointed look. "Let me give you a tip, Max. Agreeing with my brother instead of me is not the secret to a happy life."

"Got it," Max said. "What about me helping your brother?"

"That would be appreciated."

"I have a friend who should be able to help," Max said. "And I understand the need for discretion. He won't ask why I'm asking, because we do have international criminals come through San Francisco. But even if he did, I would not mention your name."

"I appreciate that," Drew said.

"I actually have to go into work for an hour," Max said.

"What? I thought we were going to the movies," Emma protested.

"Sorry, babe. I got a call. Potential witness. It won't take long," Max said, giving her a kiss. "I'll make you dinner tonight."

"I've seen you cook. We'll go out," Emma said.

Max grabbed his keys off the table. "I'll be in touch, Drew."

"Thanks."

As Max left, Drew found himself facing Emma's inquisitive gaze. She was not going to let him off as easily as Max.

"I can't tell you anything else," he said.

"You can tell me whether or not you're in love with Ria," Emma said.

His gut tightened at her question. Usually when Emma asked about his dates or his relationships, he could answer quickly and easily, but not this time.

"Well," Emma said, a thoughtful gleam in her eyes. "I think I have my answer."

"She's important to me," he said. "That's all I can say right now."

"What about Megan? She's raising her, right? Do you really want to take on a ready-made family?"

"I don't know. I'm not thinking that far ahead. But Megan is a great kid."

"I'm sure she is. And I'm sure you'd make a great father figure, if that's what you want. It would certainly be a different life than the one you've been living."

"Change is good, right?"

"Yes, just be careful. I don't want you to get hurt, Drew."

"I know you don't. You hate to see anyone in the family hurt."

"And you're the same way with your friends. I know you want to protect Ria and Megan, but if they have any kind of relationship with an international criminal, I think you're out of your league."

"That's why I came here for help."

"I'm glad you did. Don't do anything else until Max gets back to you. I know you don't like to be patient, but try."

"I will," he said. "Anyway, I have to stop by Grandpa's house, so I should go."

"What are you doing over there? Talking about the boat?"

"No, he's having some car trouble. I said I'd take a look. With all his problems with Grandma, the last thing he needs is a car that's not working."

His grandfather was in the driveway in front of his garage, his head under the hood of his 1999 BMW when Drew arrived.

"Find the problem?" Drew asked.

His grandfather started, pulled his head out from under the hood and gave him an annoyed look. "You're late."

"Ten minutes."

"Late is late," Patrick said, never one to tolerate errors of any kind.

"I'm here now. Can I take a look?"

"It's the starter. It has to be."

"Do you mind?" he asked, coming up next to him.

"Suit yourself. I have to get back inside anyway. Ellie will be wanting her lunch."

"Go ahead. I'll check things out."

As his grandfather left, Drew examined the engine. He'd always enjoyed working on engines, whether they belonged to cars or planes. After a few minutes, he found the problem, and it was not the starter.

He walked into the house and found his grandfather in the kitchen—a room that looked like it had been hit by a tornado. There were pots and pans on all the burners, as well as on the counters. There were half-eaten plates of food heaped on top of each other, glasses filled with an assortment of liquids. Most of the cupboard doors were open, as if someone had just ransacked them.

"Don't just stand there," his grandfather said gruffly. "Help me." Patrick began rinsing dishes and putting them in the dishwasher.

Drew moved over to the kitchen table and grabbed a couple of dishes, taking them over to the sink. "How long has it been since you cleaned up?" he couldn't help asking.

"About an hour."

"What?" he asked in disbelief. "All this in an hour?"

"That's how long I was outside trying to get the car to start. Now you know why late is late."

"Sorry," he muttered. "So this is Grandma's handiwork."

"She forgets where she is, what she's doing. And some

days she's filled with this almost frenetic energy. She's moving fast, trying to do a thousand things at once, like she's afraid if she doesn't get them done right away, she'll forget. Only she does forget, and then there's a thousand things all undone."

"I didn't know it was this bad," he said slowly. "But you have some help, right?"

"Sure, we have help, but it's impossible and ridiculously expensive to have anyone else here twenty-four hours a day." He paused, his eyes filling with pain. "Do you think I want to put her in a home?" He shook his head, biting down on his bottom lip. "I have loved that woman for almost sixty years of my life. I have lived with her, slept with her, eaten with her, bathed with her. I know her better than I know myself. And she used to know me." His jaw tightened. "She used to know me," he repeated, then tossed the sponge into the sink and walked out of the room.

Drew felt like he'd just been hit by a train. He didn't know what was more disturbing—that his grandmother was losing her mind, or that his gruff grandfather was capable of breaking down and being very, very human.

He let out a sigh and then finished cleaning the kitchen. He was just starting the dishwasher when his grandmother wandered into the room.

She wore a fancy silver-sequined dress and high heels, and she had a ton of makeup on her face. "I'm ready to go," she said. She stopped when she saw Drew. "Where's Patrick? We have to get to the dance."

"Uh, he must be changing," Drew replied, never sure how to talk to his grandmother when she was not herself.

"And he used to say I was the slow one," she said, sitting down at the kitchen table. "What are you doing here, Drew?"

The fact that she recognized him made him feel marginally better. Despite the odd outfit, maybe she could have a normal conversation.

"I came to help Grandpa fix the car."

"Is it broken?" she asked.

"Yeah, little bit. Can I get you something to eat?"

"I'm sure there will be food at the party. The Waltons throw the most beautiful dinner parties."

He'd never heard of the Waltons. "Well, maybe you'd like a sandwich now, just in case dinner is late."

"That might be nice. I am hungry. I don't think I've eaten in a while. Maybe some toast," she said.

"Coming right up."

He popped two pieces of bread in the toaster. His grandmother picked up the newspaper lying on the table and let out a small gasp. She put a hand to her heart.

"Oh, dear. Oh, dear," she said.

He walked around the table to see what she was looking at. "What's wrong?"

She didn't answer him, just stared at the picture.

He read the headline for the article, "Winthrop Building Gets A Second Life". An artist's rendering of a new skyscraper by the Embarcadero accompanied the article. "Winthrop," he murmured, the name sounding familiar. "Wasn't that where there was a big fire in the late seventies?"

"They're going to build it again," she murmured. "They can't do that." She looked up at Drew, panic in her blue eyes. She grabbed his arm. "They can't do that. You can't let them. Not after all this time. People will find out."

"Find out what?" he asked in confusion.

"All the secrets," she hissed. She jumped to her feet and started backing away from him.

He took a step forward, but she put up her hand. "Stay away from me. You stay away from me. I'm not going to tell you. I promised."

The kitchen door opened, and his grandfather strode in.

"What's going on?"

"He knows about the Winthrop building," she said to Patrick. "He could tell everyone."

"That's Drew, honey, your grandson," Patrick said in a rough but soothing voice. "Let me take you into the living room. We'll sit down and have some tea."

"Oh, okay," she mumbled, as Patrick led her out of the kitchen.

Drew took a breath and then slowly let it out. What the hell had just happened?

His grandfather came back into the room a moment later. "You should go home, Drew."

"What was that about?"

"I don't know," he said wearily. "It's something new every day."

He could see that his grandfather was at the end of his rope, but his vague answer bothered him. "She was reading the newspaper, and she just freaked out. Started talking about the Winthrop building."

"They're rebuilding it, I guess," Patrick said. "I saw it on the news the other day."

"Why would that upset Grandma?"

"We lost two firefighters when that building went down. Your grandmother knew one of the wives. She was distraught for days. We all were. It was a long time ago, but for some reason your grandmother seems to remember things from thirty years ago but can't recall what happened ten minutes ago."

"We need to get you more help," Drew said. "You can't do this alone."

"Your dad doesn't want me to put her in a facility."

"Then he needs to help you figure out a better way to take care of her."

"We're doing okay most days."

He gave his grandfather a disbelieving look. "I just finished cleaning the kitchen, and before she got upset, she told me you were going to a dinner party. It's the middle of the day, and she's wearing a sequined gown. That's not doing okay."

Patrick shrugged. "Thanks for coming over. I'll just take the car to a mechanic."

"That you don't have to do. I can fix the car. I just need to run down to the auto shop and pick up a part. I'll be back in a few minutes."

"I'll leave the garage door open," his grandfather said. "Maybe best not to come inside again. Ellie has had all the excitement she needs for a day."

"No problem."

He left the house, feeling incredibly sad but also angry at the illness that had literally stolen his grandmother away from him. When her brain was right, she was the person he'd loved all his life, but when the chemistry changed, she was a stranger. He supposed that was probably the way she felt, too. She just couldn't tell the difference, but he could.

How his grandfather handled it day in and day out, he didn't know, but he obviously needed more help. And he needed to talk to his father about it, too. Jack might not want to see his mother in a home, but he also wouldn't have wanted to see the kitchen the way Drew had found it.

And what about his grandmother's increasingly frequent bouts of disorientation? Her memories of terrible events that seemed to have no basis in reality—or did they?

She'd gotten agitated when she'd seen the story on the Winthrop building, and the fire that had burned down the original building had taken the lives of two firefighters. So the building had meant something to her. But what was the promise she'd made and to who? Was his grandmother lying? Were her words caused by the delusions of her illness? Or had she been involved in something shady a very long time ago?

Damn! Now he was the crazy one. His grandparents were the most honorable people he knew. He needed to stop trying to find some truth, some reality, in his grandmother's words. He had to find a way to love her the way she was now and let go of the person she used to be.

But that was all for another time. Today, he would fix their car, and be glad there was at least one problem in his life that he could resolve.

Eighteen

Ria got home from her last sailing lesson just after five o'clock on Sunday. Judging by the loud music coming from the bedroom, it was obvious that Megan was awake.

She knocked on the door, then pushed it open. Megan sat on the middle of the bed, computer in front of her, music so loud she was surprised the neighbors hadn't complained.

"Can you turn it down?" Ria asked.

"What?" Megan yelled.

She waved her hand toward the speakers.

Megan reached over and switched off the music. "Sorry. How was sailing?"

"It was fine," she said, sitting down on a corner of the bed, not willing to admit that thoughts of Drew had distracted her all day. She hadn't been able to enjoy the water the way she normally did, because her mind kept darting from joyous memories of being in Drew's arms to worrying thoughts about Drew's conversation with his friend. She wanted to believe that Tim's innocent questions wouldn't trigger interest by the wrong people on the island, but how could she be sure? She had no idea who Tim had spoken to.

"Tory," Megan said. "Is something wrong?"

"No, just a little tired," she said, not wanting to put her negative thoughts on to Megan. "How was your day?"

"I slept for most of it. Now I'm working on my essay. It's

due tomorrow."

"This is the one about the Coast Guard?"

"About Drew," Megan said. "And I want to hear all about your date last night. I can't believe he took you up in a helicopter."

"He wanted to show me his world," Ria replied. "The lights were just coming on in the city, and it was amazing. The view was incredible and Drew decided to add a little excitement by flying us under the Golden Gate Bridge."

"Was it scary?"

"It was exhilarating," Ria said, remembering the breathless feeling she'd experienced when they'd taken off. "I loved it. I can see why Drew likes to fly."

"And then you went out on his boat," Megan added. "Which is obviously your idea of the perfect date."

She smiled. "You know me too well."

"I think Drew does, too. Was it romantic?"

"To use one of your favorite words, it was awesome. Drew put together a really nice picnic—crab salad, fresh fruit, baked bread, wine. It was a beautiful night, lots of stars." Her voice drifted away, her heart aching at the memory of the night they'd shared, and the realization that it might have been their last night together.

"Did you kiss him?"

She stiffened at the question. "Megan. I'm not going to talk to you about that."

"Why not? It's just you and me. You would have told Mom, wouldn't you?"

"Because your mom was my sister, and you're my niece, not to mention the fact that you're sixteen."

Megan rolled her eyes. "I know about sex."

"Do you?" she asked tentatively. "Was this knowledge acquired last night?"

"No. No way. We were in a hotel room with five other

people," Megan said. "We just made out a little. I'm not going to have my first time be like that."

Ria felt a wave of relief that not only had Megan not had sex last night, apparently she hadn't had sex at all. "That's a good decision."

"I am capable of making them," Megan retorted.

She smiled. "You sound just like your mother. Kate had a tremendously strong will."

"Do you really think I take after her?"

"I see it more and more each day."

"Maybe being strong-willed is a family trait, because you're pretty tough, too." Megan cleared her throat. "So, you're probably going to be angry, but I have a confession to make."

Her stomach tightened. "What's that?"

"I got Drew's number off your cell phone a few days ago, and I called him this afternoon."

"Why would you call Drew?" she asked warily.

"I'm having trouble with my essay, and I have some questions."

"All right," she said slowly, sure there was more to come. "And…"

"And he's coming over for dinner," Megan said with a bright smile. "Isn't that great? He'll be able to answer my questions in person."

"You should have asked me first."

"I'm just getting a little help for school. Is it that big of a deal? You seemed like you were getting along really well this morning," she said with a gleam in her eyes.

"It's not a big deal," she said. "But I don't like you sneaking around. We have to be honest with each other, Megan. It's important."

Megan's expression grew serious. "I know. I shouldn't have looked through your phone. I'm sorry. But I think you like Drew, and I'm afraid you're going to push him away."

"If I do, that's my decision, Megan." As she finished speaking, the buzzer went off. "I guess that's him."

"He said he'd bring pizza," Megan said with a bright smile.

"Great." She got up from the bed and moved into the living room. She buzzed Drew in and then went to the door, her heart speeding up with each step. She was irritated with Megan for playing matchmaker, but deep down she was happy to see Drew again.

She opened the door as he came down the hall. A smile spread across his face when he saw her.

"Hi," he said, stopping right in front of her.

"Hi," she echoed, her stomach taking its usual nosedive.

He was holding two large pizza boxes in his hands, but he still managed to lean forward and snag a kiss off the corner of her lips. "I figured I better get that in before our chaperone joins us."

"Our chaperone is trying to be a little matchmaker."

"I know. Are you angry that she called me?"

"I should be, but I'm not. We need to talk, but it will have to be later."

"I agree."

She stepped back to let him into the apartment.

"I got four different combinations," Drew said as he set the pizza down on the table and opened the boxes. "A mix of vegetarian and meat, I wasn't sure what you liked."

"I like everything," Megan said, as she joined them at the table.

"Ria?"

She heard him call her name, but she was having trouble focusing on his question. She was too caught up in just how sexy he looked in jeans and a t-shirt with a shadow of beard along his jawline.

"Ria?" he said again.

"Oh, I like everything," she said, and she wasn't talking about the pizza.

From the intimate look he sent her, she had a feeling he could see right into her head.

"I'm going to eat in my room," Megan announced.

"You're supposed to be talking to Drew," Ria protested.

"I'll come out when you guys are done eating," Megan said. She entered the bedroom and made a point of shutting the door.

"Alone at last," Drew said with a grin. "What kind of pizza would you like?"

"Vegetarian." She grabbed plates out of the cupboard, then sat down across from him. "What did you do today?"

"I fixed my grandfather's car. Then I cleaned up their kitchen, and I watched my grandmother have a mental breakdown after reading a newspaper article." He set down his pizza and sighed. "She's really losing it."

"I'm sorry." She could see the pain in his eyes.

"It's hard to watch."

"That's the part your grandmother hates the most," Ria said.

"I know. But it's worse on my grandfather." He drew in a breath and let it out. "How was your day?"

"Better than yours." She met his gaze. "I spent most of it thinking about you."

Desire flared in his eyes. "Same here."

A long minute of shared intimacy passed between them. She wanted to talk to Drew, really talk to him, and then she wanted to kiss him, and touch him, and take off all his clothes and lose herself in his arms.

"Ria, don't look at me like that."

"I'm sorry. I don't know what is wrong with me."

"I know what's wrong with me, and that's you. We need

to talk, Ria."

"Right now I'm thinking more about getting your clothes off," she said, the words slipping out before she could stop them.

He sucked in a quick breath. "Don't tell me that."

"You said you liked it when I was direct."

"I'd like it more if we were alone."

"Right." She needed to get a grip. Her niece was in the next room. "You need to speak to Megan. She's the reason you came over."

He smiled. "A small part of the reason. If she hadn't called me, I would have called you or just showed up. But one way or the other, I was going to see you tonight. And just for the record, I've been thinking about getting your clothes off, too."

Drew paused as Megan's door opened.

Her niece took a tentative step into the room, giving them both a wary look. "Is this a good time?" she asked. "Am I interrupting anything?"

"No," Ria said, waving her into the room. "You should talk to Drew about the report so you can get it done. Nothing like leaving it til the last minute."

"I had a lot to do this weekend," Megan said defensively. "And it was so nasty of Ms. Hobbs to make us turn in a paper right after the prom."

"She gave you plenty of time to do it," Ria said.

Megan made a face at her and then said, "I'll get my computer."

Drew smiled. "You sounded just like a mom, Ria."

She shook her head in bewilderment. "Sometimes I can't believe the words that come out of my mouth. It's like I'm channeling my mother. I never did a report early in my life. So why am I expecting Megan to do so?"

"Because you're pushing her to do the right thing. It's

what parents do."

"When I was sailing around the world, I couldn't imagine myself as a parent. I wasn't sure kids were in my future."

"Really?" He raised an eyebrow. "You're great with Megan."

"Well, she's almost grown, but a baby..." She shook her head. "I could mess a kid up good."

"I don't think so. You're a natural at mothering. You have good instincts, Ria. You should listen to them."

"Except when they tell me I should get you out of my life as quickly as possible?" she challenged.

"Except then," he agreed.

"Okay," Megan said, returning to the room. "I just have a few questions."

"You can have my seat," Ria said. "I'll put the rest of this pizza away. You should take some home when you leave, Drew. Otherwise, Megan and I will be eating it for breakfast for days."

As she cleaned up, she only half-listened to Megan and Drew. Her mind drifted as she thought about what it would be like to share this kind of scene every night. To have a man in her life, a man who cared about her and about Megan—a man who could make her laugh, and make her crazy, and make her life a little bit brighter. She could see Drew in that role. He'd already insinuated himself into every aspect of her life, and now that he was in, she didn't know how to get him out. Worse, she didn't want to get him out.

But she couldn't live in her imagination. This was the real world. And the real world held danger. Getting complacent would be a huge mistake.

"I think I've got enough," Megan said a short while later. "I better start typing. Thanks, Drew. You're awesome."

"No problem. Just make sure your paper is awesome, too."

"I will."

As Megan left the room, Drew stood up. "What do you think about taking a walk, Ria?"

She hesitated. "It's late."

"It's not late. It's seven-thirty," he said dryly.

"All right, but a quick walk." She went into the bedroom. "Drew and I are going to take a walk. I won't be gone long. I'll have my phone if you need me."

Megan smiled and gave her a thumbs up. "Have fun."

—⇒⇥⇤⇐—

Drew took Ria's hand as they walked out of her apartment building. For a split second, she resisted, then her fingers curled around his. And it felt exactly right to have her hand in his. He tightened his grip on her, wanting to keep her close for as long as possible.

"I can't remember the last time I held someone's hand," she murmured as they walked down the shadowy street.

"It's nice," he said, realizing how much he liked having her at his side.

"It is," she agreed.

"Are you cold?"

"No, I'm good."

They walked for a few blocks without speaking and then Drew steered her toward a bench at the edge of a small park. He let go of her hand as they sat down, and he was surprised at how quickly he missed the contact of her skin against his. But they needed to talk.

"I went to see my sister and her fiancé today, Emma and Max," he said.

Even in the shadowy moonlight, he could see Ria tense.

"As I mentioned before, Max is a homicide detective with the SFPD. I asked him to find out whatever he could about Enrique Valdez. Specifically, I want to know if he's accused of any crimes, if there are any warrants for his arrest, and if there are, how close anyone is to catching him." He could see the anger brewing in her eyes. "I didn't tell them anything about you, Ria."

"Oh, come on, Drew. I met Emma the other night. She knows you're spending time with me, even if she doesn't know my story. Suddenly you show up at her door with questions about a drug smuggler? If she's as smart as you say she is, I'm pretty sure she already knows your questions have something to do with me."

"You're right," he admitted. "But she doesn't know the details."

"Well, that's great."

"I would trust Emma with my life."

"You're not trusting her with your life; you're trusting her with mine and with Megan's," Ria said.

"Max will be discreet," he argued. "He's not going to mention my name or yours."

"But he's going to be your brother-in-law, which connects him to you, which connects him to me. I have to be careful of every link, Drew. I have to watch my trail, and since you and I ran into each other again, my trail is covered with clues."

He heard the frustration in her voice. "I know you're worried, Ria, but I'm trying to help you. You haven't had time to think about going on the offensive. And I understand that. But you can't hide out forever. You need a long-term solution."

"This isn't a game, Drew. There isn't offense and defense; there's just staying alive, and you're making it harder."

"No," he said with an emphatic shake of his head. "If you think I'm your main problem, think again. Your biggest problem is in your apartment. Megan is a talker, and she has a boyfriend, and she's going to want to tell him things. And what about her friends, her phone, her text messages? She has a computer. She goes on the Internet. You have no idea what kind of trail she's leaving."

"Stop," she said, putting up her hand. "I hear what you're saying, but I make sure that Megan is careful."

"You can't watch her every minute, and she thinks she's safe now. You've made her believe that, and that's good, because you want her to be happy and not grow up paranoid and stressed out. But she's not safe, and someday, she's going to slip, and she's going to tell someone something. If we can find a way to get Enrique Valdez into prison, you and Megan will really be safe," Drew said.

"Enrique has a long reach and a big organization. Prison won't change that."

"At the very least, you should be able to get legal custody of Megan."

"After I'm thrown in jail for kidnapping her?" she asked sarcastically. "I'm the one who's going to end up in prison, Drew, not Enrique."

"I won't let that happen."

"Megan may think you're a superhero, but I know better." She got to her feet. "I'm going home."

"Wait." He grabbed her arm, pulling back down on the bench.

"What? Is there more? Who else did you talk to about me?"

"No one, but we're not done discussing this."

"I'm done."

He ignored her statement. "Why does Enrique want Megan?"

"What do you mean?"

"Is he after her money? Did she witness something that he wants to protect? What was his motivation for hiding her out on the island? He must have taken her away from her home, her friends, the other members of the family. Why?"

"He was afraid Megan would tell people that he killed her parents."

"Would they have believed her?"

"I don't know. Even if they did, they probably wouldn't have acted. The whole family lived in fear of Enrique."

"So there has to be something more to his motivation."

"It might be her money. She comes into an inheritance when she's twenty-five. Until then Enrique controls the money that's allegedly used for her support."

"So if he thought Megan was dead, what would happen to the money?"

"I assume the next person in line, which would have been Enrique, would get it all."

That was interesting. "Maybe Enrique is just as happy that Megan is dead then," he mused.

"I was thinking that might be a possibility," Ria agreed. "But if he finds out she's not dead, he may have to kill her in order to keep using her money. And he'll have to kill me, too, because I'll fight him til my last breath."

He heard the defiance and determination in her voice and knew she would do exactly what she'd said.

"You won't fight him alone," he promised. "Don't argue with me," he said as she opened her mouth. "You may not want me in this, but I'm in. I'm all in. I'm not leaving. I'm not turning away. I'm not pretending you're dead. So you're going to have to deal with that."

"Oh, yeah?"

"Yeah."

Tension flared between them.

"Then you're going to have to deal with this," she said. She threw her arms around his neck and planted her mouth on his.

And as he met her desperate, passion-filled kisses with his own, he knew that every word he'd just spoken was true. This woman was his woman. And he'd protect her with every last breath that he took. He just hoped it wouldn't come to that.

Nineteen

Late Monday afternoon, Drew got a call from Max just as he was getting off work, so Drew headed over to the police station. He found Max in the Investigations Unit. He was on the phone but waved Drew into the chair by his desk. A moment later, he ended his call and leaned back in his chair.

"You got here fast."

"I'm curious to hear what you learned."

"Well, Enrique Valdez is one bad ass. His official residence is in Spain, but he's wanted in three countries, including the United States, for racketeering, drug smuggling, murder and extortion."

"Then why is he free?" Drew demanded.

"He's smart, and he runs a loyal organization. A lot of men have taken the fall for him. He's also used his wealth to buy off local police in the countries where he has homes, including the island you mentioned."

"Isla de los Sueños," he said. "Island of Dreams."

"That's the one. Unfortunately, while some of his addresses are known, Valdez moves around a lot. He has private planes and luxury yachts at his disposal. He travels with bodyguards, and on one occasion he managed to escape a sting operation by using a body double."

"That's crazy," Drew said in amazement. Ria hadn't been exaggerating when she'd said Valdez was extremely dangerous.

"What's crazy is you being involved with this guy," Max

said tersely. "I did what you asked. Now I need information. What is your connection to Valdez? Or what is your girlfriend's connection?"

"I can't tell you."

"And I can't accept your answer," Max said.

"You're going to have to."

"You Callaways are so damn stubborn. You think you can handle everything on your own. Look, Drew, I'm sure you're a hell of a pilot, but chasing down criminals is not your area; it's mine."

"I made a promise."

"And I made a promise to your sister that I wouldn't let you go off half-cocked against a super criminal. Do you think I want to sleep on the couch?"

Drew let out a sigh. "As concerned as I am about your sex life, I still can't tell you the whole story. It's too dangerous."

"You have to give me something."

He hesitated, knowing he was about to cross that line Ria was so worried about. But while he knew more about Valdez now, he still knew nothing about Kate except what Ria had told him. "I've heard that Enrique had his brother and sister-in-law killed," he said slowly. "Did that come up in your notes? The brother's name was Reynoldo."

"It's my understanding the couple was killed in a car accident."

"The brakes were tampered with."

"Not according to the police report."

"Which could have been wrong if Enrique had the police department under his thumb."

Max nodded. "True. I'm assuming your girlfriend is connected to Valdez in some way. Why doesn't she want my help?"

"I can't answer that, either."

"Then let me take a guess." He leaned back in his chair, giving Drew a thoughtful look. "She's done something that could get her into trouble. You don't have to answer. I have a pretty good idea of what's going on."

"She's not a criminal, Max. She's one of Enrique's victims."

"Does she know where he is?"

"No, and she's hoping he doesn't know where she is."

"You should tell her to consider coming clean with us or the feds. If we give her protection, she'll be safer, and we might have a shot at catching him."

"Why? Because you would use her like bait?" He couldn't stand the thought of Ria and Megan being some kind of a lure.

"I never said that," Max replied. "I don't use civilians as bait."

"Maybe you don't, but I imagine others would see the situation differently."

"So what are you going to do? Be your own one-man army?"

"Believe me, I'd love to have a few more troops," he said dryly. "But I'm lucky Ria let me in at all. She doesn't trust anyone. And she'll hate that I've told you this much."

"What did she do, Drew?"

He stared back at Max. "I really can't tell you."

Max rubbed his jaw. "Did she take something or someone that belongs to Valdez? Emma told me she had her niece with her at your parents' house."

His pulse pounded at Max's sharp question. Harrison was a smart detective. He was already putting the puzzle together with the limited information that he had.

When Drew remained quiet, Max added. "If she did, Valdez won't stop at anything to get that something or that person back."

"Ria knows that," he said heavily.

"You have to let me help you, Drew. Talk to Ria. Convince her to at least speak to me. I'll do everything in my power to make sure she's safe and that the right people go to jail."

He nodded, then got to his feet. "I'll tell her. Thanks, Max."

"I wish I could do more."

"Maybe you can. I'll see what she has to say. I appreciate your discretion."

"We're going to be brothers," Max said with a smile. "Emma has been very explicit in explaining to me what Callaway family loyalty entails. You can trust me."

"I do, but I have to get Ria to trust you, too, and that will be more difficult."

"Maybe bring her by the house one day. She can talk to Emma and me in a non-threatening situation."

"That's a good idea. I'll see if I can make that happen."

"In the meantime," Max said. "Watch your back."

It wasn't his back he was concerned with; it was Ria's.

Ria worked in the yacht club office on Monday. She didn't enjoy office work usually, but she was happy to have something to take her mind off of Drew. She couldn't stop wondering what he was doing, because she was fairly certain he wasn't at all done interfering in her life. Part of her was touched that he cared enough to be that concerned about her. But the other part of her wondered if he wasn't just getting caught up in the challenge.

Drew was a rescue operative. It's what he did every day, and now he had a chance to save someone he knew, someone who wasn't a stranger, and he wanted to be successful. He wanted to pull her and Megan out of Enrique's clutches. But Drew was not used to battling someone like Valdez. She just had to convince him of that fact, which would not be an easy feat. But there was nothing she could do about it at the moment.

Megan came by the office a little before five. She'd had Lindsay's mom drop her off at the club after the school play rehearsal. Megan had won a small part in the production and was excited about being on the stage. And that school play was another reminder of how entrenched Megan was getting into life in San Francisco.

"Can we eat here?" Megan asked as Ria locked up the office. "I really like their club sandwiches."

"Sure," she said. She wasn't really in the mood to shop for groceries or to cook.

They grabbed a table in the restaurant and while they waited for their food, Megan filled her in on all the prom gossip. Ria didn't have to say much. In fact, just a nod now and then seemed to be all Megan needed to continue on to the next story, which was fine. Ria wasn't in the mood to talk anyway, and she liked the fact that Megan felt comfortable enough to confide in her.

She couldn't remember having such conversations with her mother, and Kate had been long gone by the time she was in high school.

While Ria held herself responsible for Megan's well-being, in many ways Megan felt more like a sister than a niece.

Megan paused as their food was set down before them. Then she jumped back into conversation.

"So is Drew coming over tonight?" she asked.

"I haven't spoken to him," Ria replied.

"How was your walk last night?"

"It was fine."

Megan shot her a quick look. "You seemed kind of upset when you got back."

"I don't want to talk about it."

"Did you guys have a fight?"

She sighed. "Megan. I said I don't want to talk about it."

"Well, I do. I like Drew."

"You've made that abundantly clear."

"And I think he's good for you," Megan continued. "He makes you relax. You smile when he's around. You even laugh. For a long time I thought you'd forgotten how to do that."

"Not a lot to laugh about the past few years."

"I know. And when you first took me off the island, I was really depressed and scared at first, because I didn't know what was going to happen to us. But you were so confident that we were going to be okay that I started to believe you. And you know what, Ria? We are okay."

She didn't want to take away Megan's sense of security, so she just nodded. "Yeah, we're doing good."

"But I'm not stupid, and I know that my uncle could still come after us. I just don't want to think about him every single day. I don't want to feel trapped in his prison when we're so far away from him. And I don't want you to feel that way, either."

"Thanks, Megan," she said with a soft smile. "I'll try not to be such a downer."

"Well, you're never a downer when Drew is around."

"Let it go," she said with exasperation.

Megan smiled. "I'm just looking out for you."

"Eat your dinner," she said firmly.

Thankfully, Megan picked up her sandwich and began to eat. Their conversation turned to easier topics, including which bachelor Megan thought was going to win the bachelorette's heart on her favorite television show.

Ria could barely stand to watch the show, but Megan and her friends were addicted. There was something about all those handsome men after one woman's heart that really appealed to them. She couldn't imagine trying to find love on a television show. Then again, finding love was the least of her worries right now.

When they finished eating, Megan said, "Before we go, I was wondering if you could show me Drew's boat."

Ria nodded. "I guess I could do that. It's not far." She paid the check and they headed out of the yacht club. It was past six now, and the sun was going down in the west, casting an orange pink glow over the horizon. The marina was quiet; most of the boats were packed up for the night. Mondays were usually slow days at the club.

She took Megan out to see Drew's boat, which was in a slip at the far end of the harbor.

"Who's Eleanor?" Megan asked as she looked at the sailboat.

"Drew's grandmother. It's his grandfather's boat."

"It's big," Megan said.

"Yes, it is."

As Ria looked at the deck of the boat, she couldn't help remembering the night she and Drew had made love under the stars. Drew had planned the perfect evening for her, giving her everything she loved. He knew her pretty well, which was both wonderful and terrifying.

"Are you okay?" Megan asked, giving her a thoughtful look.

"We should get home," she said briskly.

"You're thinking about Drew."

"No, I'm thinking that you're driving me crazy."

"That's because I speak the truth. But we can go home. I have homework to do."

As Megan started walking down the dock, Ria's phone

rang. She paused, wondering if it was Drew, but it was her mother's number. "Mom?" she asked. "Is something wrong?"

"I wonder if we'll ever be able to have a conversation without starting with that question," her mother said with a sigh.

"Then I'm guessing nothing is wrong."

"No. I just wanted to let you know that the car I saw in the neighborhood belonged to a realtor. There was nothing going on, no one was spying on us."

"I'm extremely relieved."

"How was Megan's prom?"

"It was good."

"That's all?"

"I can't talk right now."

"I wish we could have a real conversation," her mother complained.

"We will—someday. But I do have to go."

"Take care of yourself then and Megan, too. I love you," her mother said.

It was the first time in a very long time that her mother had ever said the words, and Ria was a bit taken aback. Before she could reply, the dial tone sounded in her ear. It was just as well. She'd forgiven her mother for a lot, but telling her she loved her wasn't going to come that easily.

As she closed her phone, she heard a scream. Her head jerked up.

Shocked, she looked down the dock and saw a man forcing Megan into a speedboat. She broke into a run as the boat started to back out of the slip.

"No," she screamed. She glanced around, but they were completely alone in the marina. There was no one to call for help. And in a few minutes, Megan would be out to sea.

She did the only thing she could think of. She took a running leap and jumped into the boat.

She landed on her knees. As she raised her head, she saw a gun pointed at her face, and Megan's terrified expression.

She tried to scramble to her feet, but something hard hit the back of her head, and everything went black.

--->>><<<---

Drew couldn't believe his eyes. He'd just gotten out of his car when he heard a scream. He'd run to the dock just in time to see Ria jump into the back of the boat. Megan was in the grip of a large man. Another man hit Ria over the back of the head, and she crumpled to the ground. Then the man gunned the motor and headed for open water.

His heart pounded with fear. He needed to go after them. He could take out his boat, but it was not going to be a match for a speedboat. He needed help.

Pulling out his phone, he called his friends at the Coast Guard Station on Yerba Buena Island. His friend, Cameron Holt, was working dispatch. He told him that he'd just witnessed a kidnapping at the San Francisco Marina. He gave dispatch what little details he had. They told him they'd send the nearest boat out to look for them.

His next call was to Tim, who had come on duty just as he'd gone off for the day. Tim was up in the air now, and Drew needed to be up there, too. He could cover more ground in the helo. He called the commander and explained the situation as quickly as he could. The commander agreed to send Tim and the helo to Crissy Field, where he could make an emergency boarding.

With the helo on the way, he drove to the nearby wide-open space just below the Golden Gate Bridge known as Crissy Field. While he was waiting, he called Max.

"Valdez's men have Ria and Megan," he said shortly, his jaw so tight it was difficult to get the words out. "They're in a speedboat. I've called the Coast Guard. But I need you to alert every law enforcement agency looking for Valdez. This is their chance to catch him. I'm going to get up in a helo in a few minutes."

"I'll make some calls," Max said. "Where do you think he's headed?"

"I have no idea." But even as he said the words, an old memory flashed through his mind, the huge luxurious yacht that he'd seen on the island. "They might be headed to a bigger boat," he said. "You mentioned Valdez has luxury yachts at his disposal. See if you can find out where those boats are."

The helo whipped his hair as it began to descend.

"I'm going out now to look for her. I have to find her, Max," he said, hearing the desperation in his own voice. "Valdez is going to kill them if I don't."

"I'll get everyone on it," Max said. "With Valdez as the prize, there should be a lot of interest in helping you track him down."

"Thanks." Drew jogged across the field and got into the helo. Along with Tim was another pilot, Erica Brent, and a flight mechanic, AJ Martin.

"What's going on?" Tim asked.

"We're looking for a speed boat." He swallowed hard. "And maybe a yacht. It's the woman from the island, Tim. It's Ria. She's alive, and she's been kidnapped by Enrique Valdez, along with her sixteen-year-old niece."

Tim stared at him in disbelief. "We're going after Valdez?"

"Yes. Let's get in the air, because if we don't find her fast…" He couldn't bring himself to finish the statement. He was not going to let Ria die. He was going to be there in time to save her. There was no other option.

Twenty

Ria woke up with a raging pain in her head just as the speedboat pulled up alongside a sixty-foot yacht. She'd seen the yacht before—in the harbor at the island.

Megan stared at her with fear in her eyes, but at least she didn't seem to be hurt.

As they anchored the boat to the yacht, the older man grabbed Megan by the arm and yanked her to her feet. In his other hand, he held a gun. He forced Megan up the stairs, and then the second man moved behind Ria.

She got to her feet, feeling dizzy and sick from the blow to her head, but there was no way she wasn't getting on the boat. As long as she stayed with Megan, she had a fighting chance of saving her.

They were led past two other men with guns, and her hope of fighting her way out of the situation dimmed, but she wasn't giving up yet. Was Valdez on board? Or had he just sent his men to get Megan back? She had a feeling she was about to find out.

They were ushered into a luxurious salon. One of the men left while the other stood guard at the door.

Ria put her arm around Megan as they sat down on the couch together. "It's going to be okay." She could feel Megan trembling, so she squeezed her tight.

"Is my uncle here?" Megan whispered.

"I don't know. He might be." She'd never met Valdez and had only seen him once on the island, and that had been from a distance. But she had a feeling she was about to come face-to-face with her brother-in-law. It was strange to think of him like that.

"How did they find us?" Megan asked.

She had no idea. Had Drew's questions triggered something, or was it the inquiries of his friend, who had spoken to someone on the island about her? Maybe the homicide cop had talked to someone in law enforcement who was linked to Valdez. Or maybe Valdez had just finally tracked them down.

What had brought them to this moment didn't matter anymore. She had to be thinking ahead, figuring a way off the boat. They were somewhere in the Pacific Ocean. She had no idea how long she'd been unconscious, or in which direction they'd gone after leaving the bay.

She looked around the room for anything that might be a possible weapon. She might be able to take out the guard, but what about all the other men on the ship? A boat this big had to be staffed by at least a half dozen people, if not more.

"How long did it take to get here?" she whispered to Megan.

"I don't know," Megan said.

"Think."

"Half an hour maybe."

"Did you see anyone following us?"

"I couldn't see anything. He made me lie face-down on the deck." Her mouth trembled. "Are they going to kill us?"

"No," she said firmly.

Megan gave her a doubtful look. "How can you be sure?"

"He didn't kill you before," she said pragmatically. "You're his family. You're blood."

"But he hates when people betray the family. That's why

he killed my parents. He said they were disloyal."

Ria didn't know how to respond to that. Megan was too smart to be reassured by false promises.

A moment later, the door opened and a short, middle-aged Hispanic male strode through the door. He had black hair, bushy eyebrows and what could only be described as evil eyes. His smile was just as slimy.

Megan snuggled in closer to Ria as he sat down in the chair across from them.

"My little one," he said to Megan. "I've missed you."

Megan didn't say a word in return.

Valdez's gaze moved to Ria, and his gaze grew speculative. "Victoria. We finally meet."

She was shocked that he knew her name.

"I must admit I am rarely surprised, but you were quite clever. I had no idea Katherine had a sister. You never came to visit. And she never went to see you. You were not at her funeral. Yet, you felt compelled to go to the island and kidnap my niece."

"My niece, too," she said. "And she came willingly. I did not kidnap her."

"That's because you lied to her about me."

"I didn't have to lie," she countered. "I only had to tell her what her mother told me."

"And what was that?"

"That you were evil, that she feared for her life, and for the life of her husband and child," she said, refusing to let this man intimidate her. If she was going down, she was going down swinging.

Anger tightened his lips. "Katherine was never in danger."

"Really, not even when you killed her?"

He stared back at her. "Katherine was not supposed to be in the car that day."

Ria was shocked by his words. "So you admit you sabotaged the car?"

His gaze moved from Ria to Megan. "You should not have run away from me, little one."

"I want to live with Ria. She's my aunt, and I want to stay with her."

"You cannot. You belong to me."

"You can have my money," Megan said. "I don't care about any of it. Just let us go."

"Your money," he said with a sneer. "Do you think I need your money? I have plenty of my own."

"Then why did you take me to the island and make me a prisoner?"

Now that Megan had found her voice, she couldn't seem to stop using it. Ria was afraid Megan would say too much. Then again, their backs were against the wall. At this point, Megan had every right to say whatever she wanted.

"I set you up in a beautiful home," Enrique said, anger in his voice. "You had everything you needed. And you were safe there, protected from my enemies. I did that for your mother."

"Don't talk about her," Megan said with fury in her eyes. "You killed her."

"I told you that was an accident. Katherine wouldn't listen. She was so stubborn and headstrong. She thought Reynoldo was the answer to her prayers, but he was nothing but a coward."

"My father was wonderful," Megan said defensively.

"I was supposed to be your father. Katherine was mine," he said forcefully. "I met her first. She came to the house at my request. Reynoldo stole her from me."

Ria was shocked at his words. Kate had never mentioned having a relationship with Enrique. Was he delusional? Or had her sister left out part of the story?

"You're lying," Megan said.

Apparently, Megan hadn't heard that part of the story, either.

Enrique laughed. "Such spirit you have—so like your mother."

"I want to go home," Megan said.

"And you will—with me." His gaze turned to Ria. "We just have to get rid of one small complication first."

Her heart skipped a beat. He was going to kill her. She knew that as certainly as she knew anything.

"The explosion was a brilliant plan," he said. "I almost believed that my niece had died in a tragic accident. But you left a clue behind—her bodyguard. When I saw him, I knew it was a setup. You should have been less squeamish and killed him. You might have gotten away with it. Or not." He smiled. "Imagine my joy when a friend told me that you had been spotted in San Francisco."

Her heart sank. Drew's friend, Tim. She'd been right to worry about the connection. But being right now didn't do any good. She should have followed her first instinct and left the city.

"How did you find me?" she asked, stalling for time. She needed to figure a way out of this impossible situation before Enrique killed her.

"It wasn't difficult. I simply tracked down your friend and then followed him."

Drew would hate that he'd been the one to bring them down. If she didn't make it off this boat alive, she hoped he would never find out what inadvertent part he had played in her death. It would destroy him.

"Please let us go," Megan said. She grabbed Ria's hand. "I love her. If you care about me at all, let us go home. We won't tell anyone about you. We'll never talk about you again."

"That is not what I want," he said. "You are a Valdez. You belong with the family."

"I hate you."

"You will learn to love me, little one. Everyone does." He got to his feet. "You will come with me now."

"No," Megan said, desperation in her voice. Her hand tightened around Ria's.

"Don't touch her," Ria said, feeling completely helpless but refusing to give up yet.

"I give the orders on this boat."

He'd barely finished speaking when several blasts filled the air.

Gunshots!

Enrique turned toward the man at the door. As the guard left the salon, Ria grabbed the lamp off the side table and brought it crashing down on the back of Enrique's head.

He staggered, clutching his head. She hit him again for good measure, and he fell to the ground. She grabbed Megan's hand and ran for the door.

When they reached the deck, Ria was shocked to see gunfire being exchanged between three men on the deck and a Coast Guard helicopter. Drew?

One of the men on deck clutched his chest and fell to the ground.

More gunfire.

"Stay here," Ria said, pushing Megan into the shadows. She needed to get the gun lying on the ground by the man who'd been shot.

As she moved towards him, she saw a man coming down from the helicopter on a rope. What the hell was Drew doing?

One of the guards lifted his gun and took aim.

She rushed towards him, tackling him from the back, hurtling her body on top of his. His gun skidded across the deck.

She ran for it, but he was after her, shoving her hard against the rail. She lost her breath for a moment. And then Megan jumped on his back, and the two struggled.

Ria wanted to help. She just needed to breathe, to move. As she staggered to her feet, Drew landed on the deck of the boat.

He took out the other guard with a shot through the chest.

Two more men came around the corner.

Drew shot twice more, each bullet finding its target.

Ria tried to pull Megan away from her attacker, but the man kicked her in the stomach, and she fell to her knees again.

Then Drew jumped into the fray, pulling the man off Megan, and then smashing his fist into the guard's face.

Megan stumbled backwards on the deck.

The two men fought for their lives.

Ria searched for the gun, something she could use to help Drew. She finally found it against the rail. As she reached for it, she heard Megan scream.

Whirling around, she saw that Enrique had come back to life. He had his arm around Megan's neck and his gun pointed at her head.

She raised the gun in her hand and aimed it at him. "Let her go."

"Lower your gun, or she's dead," Valdez said.

"Then you'll be dead, too," she said, praying Drew would win the fight he was engaged in.

She met Megan's terrified gaze, but saw determination in her niece's eyes.

A second later, Megan sank to the ground the way they'd been taught in self-defense class, bringing Enrique's arm down with her.

As Megan slid from Enrique's grip, Ria fired.

Enrique stumbled backward, blood spreading across his

shirt. He looked at her in shock.

She fired again—for her sister.

And a third—for Reynoldo.

She couldn't stop pulling the trigger. She wanted him dead. She wanted to be free. She wanted Megan to be able to grow up away from this evil man.

"Ria, stop," Drew said, grabbing her arm. "He's dead."

She could barely hear him.

"Stop."

She stared at him in confusion.

"He's dead," Drew repeated.

"Are you sure?"

"Yes," he said, taking the gun out of her hand.

She glanced past Drew to see the man he'd been fighting unconscious on the ground. The deck was littered with bodies, and yet somehow they were still standing.

Megan ran to her, and Ria threw her arms around her niece as a Coast Guard cutter pulled up alongside the boat.

"It's over," she told Megan. "It's all over."

--->>><<<--

Within minutes the Coast Guard boarded the yacht. Drew hustled Ria and Megan onto the cutter. They went inside and sat down together on a bench. Drew squatted in front of them, giving them each a sharp look. His gaze settled on Ria, and he frowned. "He hurt you."

"I'm fine," she said, shivering with the after effects of the adrenaline rush and the cool night air. Parts of her body throbbed with pain, but the feeling of being free of Enrique was so great that she didn't care about the physical injuries. She was alive, and so was Megan.

"You're cold," Drew said. He jumped up and grabbed two blankets from a member of the crew, wrapping one around Megan and the other around Ria.

"Thank you," she whispered, meeting his gaze.

"You're welcome."

"I couldn't believe it when I saw you coming down that rope. My God, Drew, they were shooting at you. Are you completely crazy?"

"We were shooting at them. My crew had my back," he said.

"It was still a crazy stunt," she said.

"I told you he was a superhero," Megan said.

Drew smiled at Megan. "I'm more impressed by you, kid. The way you tackled that guard was beyond awesome."

Megan smiled shakily. "I tried to remember the self-defense stuff, but those guys were big, and they had guns."

"You did everything right," Ria assured her. "I'm very proud of you." She turned back to Drew. "And don't try to downplay your heroics. You saved our lives tonight, and I will be forever grateful. I honestly didn't think we were going to make it off that boat alive."

"You're the one who took out Valdez, Ria."

She drew in a difficult breath at the memories of those few terrifying moments. "I can't believe I shot him. I've never shot anyone before."

"Is he really dead?" Megan interrupted, uncertainty in her voice. "You don't think he survived?"

"No, he's dead," Drew said. "He can't hurt either of you anymore. You're both going to get your lives back."

After so many months of living in fear, it was almost impossible for Ria to believe that. It would take some time to sink in. She glanced past Drew, seeing the action going on outside and between the boats. "What will they do with them?"

"The ones that are alive will be arrested and tried."

"What about me?" Ria said. "I—I killed Enrique, and I

took Megan away from her legal guardian."

"We'll sort it out," he said with confidence.

She wanted to believe him.

He met her questioning gaze. "Trust me," he added.

"I do," she said, knowing it was the complete and utter truth.

"I need to talk to the captain," Drew said. "Can I get either of you anything right now?"

Megan shook her head.

"We're good," Ria said. And for the first time in a very long time, she wasn't lying.

⟶⟫⟪⟵

It was almost three o'clock in the morning before Ria walked back through her apartment door. She'd been to the hospital to get her head checked out and was relieved to have only a painful bump on her head and not a concussion. She had abrasions on her face and hands and a sprained finger as well as several bruises on other parts of her body, but she counted herself lucky to have gotten off so easily. And she was more than grateful that Megan was completely fine.

While she was in the emergency room, Drew had stayed with Megan, watching over her like a guard dog. Then he'd accompanied them both to a series of interviews and intense conversations with various agencies ranging from the Coast Guard to the DEA, FBI and local police.

Max Harrison was in charge of the police investigation, and he had assured Ria that while custody issues would have to be resolved, he would do everything in his power to help her and Megan stay together. His resolve had been strengthened by the arrival of Emma, who had told Max in no uncertain terms that he better make sure that happened.

Ria had been extremely grateful to have so much

support, not just from Drew, Max and Emma, but also Drew's friends at the Coast Guard. Drew's friend, Tim, had apologized to her for any part he had played in alerting Valdez to her whereabouts. Drew had also asked her if his questions had led Valdez to her and Megan.

She'd downplayed their involvement, because she didn't want anyone else to feel guilty or responsible. Both Drew and Tim had risked their lives for her. And without them, the night would have had a far different ending.

"I'm going to lie down," Megan said, her face pale, as she paused outside her bedroom door.

"Are you okay?" Ria asked.

Megan hesitated. "I want to be happy, but it doesn't seem real."

"I know."

"And what about you?" Megan asked. "I heard you talking about custody. I don't want them to take me away from you. I don't want to go back to Spain, and I don't want to see anyone in the Valdez family. You're my family now."

Ria saw the fear in her eyes and wished she could erase it completely, but they had some hurdles still to clear.

"Don't worry about that now," she said. "Max said he would help us."

"And he will," Drew interjected. "And so will I. The Callaways have a lot of connections, and I'll use every one I have to in order to make sure that you two aren't split up."

Megan nodded, reassured by Drew's words. And why not? The man was a superhero in Megan's eyes—in Ria's eyes, too.

"Okay. Are you going to stay here tonight, Drew?" Megan asked.

"Absolutely. There's no place I'd rather be."

Relief filled Megan's eyes that Drew's strong presence would be right outside her bedroom door.

As Megan went into her room, Drew turned to Ria. "You should go to sleep, too. It's been a long night."

"It has," she agreed. "But I feel tired and wired at the same time. On one hand, I think I could sleep for a week, but on the other hand I'm not sure I can close my eyes. I keep reliving every moment of the night. I don't know how to let it go."

"Breathe deep. Adrenaline packs a big punch, but the downside is usually utter exhaustion. Once you lie down, you'll start to relax."

"Relax—what a concept," she said with a bewildered shake of her head. "It's been so long. I'm not sure I even know how."

He smiled and put his arms around her. "You're safe now. I've got you, and I'm not letting you go."

"I may not let you go, either," she said, sliding her arms around his waist. She rested her head on his shoulder. He squeezed her tight, burying his face in her hair. And for several long minutes they just held each other. "I was afraid I'd never see you again," she murmured, lifting her head to look at him.

"I felt the same way, Ria," he said heavily. "I've never been that scared."

It was hard to believe that anything scared this man.

I have so many things I want to ask you," she said. "I don't even know how you knew where we were."

"I arrived at the docks just in time to see a man grab Megan and throw her into a boat. Then I saw you jump in after her. I couldn't believe it."

"I couldn't let Megan go without me," she said.

"You're incredibly brave."

"I was acting on instinct." Her eyes blurred. "I love that kid, you know."

He gave her a tender smile. "I know. I'm quite fond of

her myself."

"So what happened next?"

"I called in the Coast Guard and Max. I told Max to get every agency he could think of involved. And he did. Then I had Tim pick me up and we went looking for you."

"How did you know where to look?"

"I didn't. We flew around for far too long before we spotted the yacht. I remembered seeing one that looked a lot like it on the island. When we got closer, someone took a shot at us. I knew we were in the right place."

She thought again about his daring rescue from the helicopter. "I couldn't believe it when I saw you coming out of the helicopter with people shooting at you. What the hell were you thinking?"

"That I wasn't going to lose you again. It almost killed me the last time, and I barely knew you." He paused, his gaze darkening with emotion. "I love you, Ria. I have from the first minute I saw you."

Her heart turned over at the truth in his eyes. "Oh, Drew, I love you, too."

"Thank God," he said with relief.

She licked her lips. "But—"

He put a finger against her lips. "No *buts*, not tonight. In fact, I don't want to talk anymore. I just want to hold you. We'll figure out the rest later."

"All I have to offer you is a pullout couch," she said apologetically.

"I don't care where I sleep, as long as you're next to me."

They pulled out the couch, kicked off their shoes, and stretched out on the bumpy mattress. Drew rolled on to his back, and Ria curled up next to him, her face resting on his chest, his arm around her waist. She could hear his heart beating, and his solid, warm length made her feel safe and protected. She closed her eyes and let the rest of the world fade away.

⸻⸻

Drew couldn't sleep. The events of the night replayed over and over again in his head. He remembered the gut-wrenching fear he'd experienced when he's seen Ria and Megan on the yacht, fighting for their lives. He'd had only one thought—to get down to that boat and save them. He was more than grateful to his team for providing backup. But the real heroes of the night were truly Megan and Ria.

Ria had taken on bodyguards twice her size. And Megan had not hesitated to do the same. Both women had tremendous will and emotional strength. They hadn't cowered and cried; they'd fought back. Ria had grabbed a gun and shot Enrique in order to protect herself and her niece and also him. She was one hell of a woman. He'd never met anyone like her. He doubted he ever would again.

He tightened his arm around her as she shifted in sleep. He didn't want to let her go, not tonight, not tomorrow, not ever.

But would things change in the morning, after the adrenaline burned off? The night had always been their time, the mornings not so much. Would she push him away again as soon as the sun rose?

She was independent, and she had Megan to raise. She'd no doubt try to make it sound like he'd be better off dating a woman without baggage. He didn't care about her baggage. Actually, he did care. He was crazy about Megan, and watching the kid in action tonight had only left him in awe of her resilience. She'd lost her parents. She'd been hidden away on an island with bodyguards, then she'd been taken away by an aunt she barely knew and forced to live a life of deception.

But Megan hadn't broken under the stress, and she'd never lost her hope, her faith in a better future. She'd called him a superhero, but his actions didn't compare to what she'd done, or what Ria had done.

Megan was a special kid, and he was happy that she was finally going to get to be a kid. She wouldn't have to look over her shoulder anymore. She could get a permanent phone, spend hours on it texting her friends. She could get a driver's license. Go to college. Have a life.

And Ria could have a life, too.

Maybe a life with him.

He tensed a little at the thought. He'd never told a woman he loved her, never. Something had always stopped him. He couldn't tell someone they had his heart unless it was true, and it had never been true—until now.

Closing his eyes, he blew out a sigh and let his mind drift. It took him right where he wanted to go, to memories of Ria, kissing her, running his hands through her hair, making love to her.

As she snuggled against him, he was tempted to wake her up. But he couldn't do that to her. She needed to sleep, to heal. For now, he would just hold her, and that would be enough.

———»«———

Ria woke up alone. She sat up in bed, realizing that the sun was brighter than when she normally got up. The clock on the wall read ten past nine, and the apartment was really quiet.

She was a little surprised that Drew would leave without telling her. Had he had second thoughts about telling her he loved her? Perhaps he regretted his words now that the danger had passed. Drew had been determined to save them, and he'd done that. So what now? They were safe. They were free.

She knew he cared about her, and the chemistry between them was unmistakable. But Drew was a hotshot helicopter pilot who could have any woman he wanted—women who weren't raising sixteen-year-olds.

With a sigh, she got out of bed. That's when she realized the bedroom door was ajar. She pushed it open. The room was empty. Megan was gone.

She felt a familiar surge of panic. Then she heard voices out in the hall. She returned to the living room as the apartment door swung open. Megan and Drew walked in with coffees and grocery bags.

She let a breath of relief. "I was just wondering where you were."

Drew's gaze met hers, and he must have seen the fear in her eyes. "Sorry, Ria. We thought we'd be back before you woke up."

"It's fine." She tried to slow her breathing and calm her racing heart.

"We're safe now," Megan reminded her.

"I keep telling myself that. I guess it will take a while for reality to sink in. A part of me still thinks it was a dream."

"It wasn't a dream," Drew said forcefully. "Enrique is gone. He'll never threaten or hurt either of you again. Today you start over."

"Yes, we do," she agreed. "I assume you have some food in those bags."

"We're going to make a huge breakfast," Megan announced, dropping the bags on the kitchen counter. "And then…" She glanced over at Drew. "Maybe you should tell her. She might take it better."

"Tell me what?" she asked suspiciously.

"I think we should celebrate your first day of freedom," Drew said. "I've taken the day off work. Megan has already missed the start of school, and I think you're free as well, aren't you?"

"I do have Tuesdays off," she admitted.

"So let's play tourist," Drew said. "We can walk around the city, see the sights, eat great food and not look over our shoulders."

"That sounds wonderful, but I think I have to meet with Max today."

"I already called him. He said we can meet him this evening. He wants to get a little further in the investigation before he talks to you again."

"Is he investigating me?" she asked, unable to get rid of the lingering fear that she might still be facing some charges.

"He's investigating Valdez along with everyone else we spoke to last night. And I've also asked Sara to get involved. She's an excellent attorney, and you may need one."

Ria was touched by his family's support. "Everyone is being so generous; they barely know me."

"But they know me. And they want to help. I'll start breakfast. Megan requested French toast and bacon."

"What can I do?"

"Nothing."

She watched them unpack the groceries then said, "If you don't need me, I'll take a shower."

"I need you, Ria," he said with a teasing smile. "But not for breakfast."

Megan clapped her hands over her ears. "I am not listening to this."

Drew laughed. "Don't worry, I'm done."

Ria headed into the bathroom with a smile. She felt so much lighter this morning and listening to Drew and Megan bicker over who was making the egg batter warmed her heart. She felt like she was part of a family again, and that was both wonderful and a little scary. She didn't want Drew to break her heart, but if there was a man who was worth the risk, it was Drew.

An hour later, after a delicious breakfast, they took a

brisk walk to the nearest cable car stop. They hopped on one of San Francisco's famous trolley cars for a somewhat harrowing climb up and down the steepest hills in the city. They got off the cable car by Union Square and roamed around the big department stores. Then it was on to Chinatown for Dim Sum and fresh fortune cookies.

As the hours passed, Ria felt the tension drain from her body. Two long years of fear had put permanent knots in her neck and shoulders, but now her muscles were starting to let go of the need to be ready to run or to fight. She'd done her fighting last night. Now they were free to walk around without constantly looking behind them.

After Chinatown, they went down to the water, visiting the sea lions outside Pier 39, and buying touristy stuff like t-shirts and hats.

They finally went home tired and happy just after three o'clock. Ria flopped onto the couch while Drew took the chair across from her.

"That was fun," she told him. "I needed that."

"We all did," he said.

"Hey, you two," Megan interrupted, looking up from her cell phone. "Lindsay just got home from school, and she wants me to come over to her house. Can I go, and can I walk there by myself?"

Ria stiffened, realizing that Megan was about to force her to put their sense of freedom to the test. "Yes," she said, although it took a lot of strength to get the word out.

Lindsay lived two blocks away, so she wasn't exactly sending Megan into the panhandle but it was still an important step—for both of them.

"Thanks," Megan said, meeting her gaze. "I know that was hard for you." She paused. "Can I tell her everything?"

"You can tell her whatever you want," Ria said. "We have no more secrets." She just hoped that Megan's past and her ties to a drug smuggler wouldn't affect her relationship with her friends. But she didn't want Megan to have to hide her true self anymore.

"Can I stay for dinner, too?"

"If Lindsay's mom is okay with it, but you still have to be home by nine," she added. "I don't want you walking alone after dark, so I'll meet you. And that fear has nothing to do with Enrique."

"Fine," Megan said with a little exasperated sigh. "But I am sixteen you know."

"Believe me, I never forget," Ria said dryly. "Text me when you get to Lindsay's."

Megan rolled her eyes, then headed out the door.

"I never understood why my mother got so nervous when I was a teenager," Ria said to Drew. "Now I do. I thought I was invincible. She knew I wasn't."

"Megan will be careful. But it's important for her to feel her independence," he said quietly.

"That's why I let her go." She swallowed, knowing that the conversation she'd been putting off all day really needed to begin. "About what you said last night, Drew. If you got caught up in the moment, I would understand."

"I didn't get caught up in a moment," he said, tenderness in his gaze. "I meant every word." He got up from the chair and sat down next to her on the couch. He took her hand in his. "Let me say it again. I love you, Ria. I fell for you the first time we met. That night in the bar, I had no idea that a beautiful stranger was about to steal my heart."

"You stole mine, too," she said, looking into his eyes. "But I have Megan. We're a package deal. Where she goes, I go."

"I think Megan likes me."

"She adores you, but that's not the point. Actually, it *is* the point. I don't want her to get hurt if you decide later on that you don't want this kind of relationship or life."

"I want you and I want Megan. I'm not afraid of a sixteen-year-old, especially one as great as Megan."

"Are you sure? Our life is not very exciting—homework, school nights, parent-teacher conferences. Is that really the kind of life you want to lead?"

"Yes. In fact, what you just described sounds damn good to me."

"Really?" she asked doubtfully.

He laughed. "Why are you always trying to get rid of me?"

"You seem a little too good to be true."

"I'm not." His expression grew more serious. "But is it me you're worried about? Or is it you? You're free now. You could grab a boat and hit the high seas. You could hand Megan over to your mom, or even take her with you."

She shook her head. "No, I'll never turn Megan over to anyone. And I've been all over the world, Drew, searching for a place to call home. I finally found it. It's here." She put her hand on his heart. "Wherever you are, I want to be."

He put his hand over hers. "I feel the same way, Ria." He took a breath. "When we first met, you told me that you needed the sea to be happy."

She nodded. "And you said you needed the sky."

"But the truth is all I really need is you. I'm never letting you go, Ria. This is it for me."

"Me, too." Her gaze fell to his lips. "I haven't kissed you in way too long. What time do we have to meet your family?"

"Not for a couple of hours."

She smiled into his eyes. "What will we do with the time?"

"I have a few ideas."

"Show me."

Epilogue

Six weeks later

"I can't believe we're in a wedding," Megan whispered to Ria as they posed on the steps of the church for bridal party pictures with Sara and her other bridesmaids.

"I know," Ria said, adjusting the bouquet in her hand as the photographer set up his camera.

In six weeks, their entire lives had changed. They were no longer on the run, no longer worried about getting caught by Valdez or law enforcement, and they had been welcomed into the Callaway family with warmth and love.

The photographer snapped several shots, then said, "Now, just the sisters."

Megan and Ria stepped away from the group as the bride, Sara, posed with the Callaway women, her maid of honor, Emma, and her two future sisters-in-law, Nicole and Shayla, on the steps of the chapel. Behind the church was a wide grassy area and a gorgeous view of the Golden Gate Bridge and the San Francisco Bay.

The women were just as beautiful as the view, Ria thought. Sara with her dark hair and white gown stood out in the middle of the three sisters with their varying shades of blonde hair and pink dresses. With only a few weeks to plan the wedding before Sara started to show her pregnancy, they'd foregone the matching dresses and instead had decided on a theme of short, silky cocktail dresses in some shade of pink.

Ria had tried to decline when Sara first approached her with the idea of being a bridesmaid, but she'd lost that battle in about two minutes, especially since Megan was thrilled by the idea. Sara was also very persuasive in her arguments. She was an excellent lawyer who knew how to win a case. So Ria had agreed to be part of the wedding party. How could she say no after Sara helped her navigate murky legal waters with both local and international law enforcement? With Sara's help, Ria's name had been cleared, and she'd been granted legal custody of Megan.

The Valdez family had been shattered by Enrique's death, and also the death of his right-hand man, who'd been one of the victims on the yacht that terrible night. With their leader gone, the rest of the Valdez family just wanted to live in peace. No one had come forward to challenge Ria for Megan's care, and as far as Ria and Megan were concerned, they were completely done with that part of their lives. They were concentrating on the future now, a future that looked nothing but bright and hopeful.

"Phew," Emma said, coming over to Ria. "I'm already tired of smiling, and we haven't even gotten to the ceremony yet."

"I know what you mean," Ria said.

"Sara looks beautiful, doesn't she?"

She followed Emma's gaze to Sara, who was now caught up in conversation with Megan.

"She does," Ria agreed.

"And Megan looks happy, too. So do you," Emma added. "I'm so glad everything worked out."

"Thanks to all of you, I have my life back. Actually, that's not true, because my life now is much, much better than any other life I've lived."

"I have a feeling my brother has something to do with

that."

"Everything," she admitted.

"So maybe this wedding is a good time for you two to make an announcement," Emma said with a sparkle in her eyes.

"No announcements. This is Sara's day. And we have your wedding coming up in August, so I think there's enough action happening for a while."

"Actually, we're pushing our date back to the fall," Emma said.

"Really? Why?" she asked in surprise.

"The venue we had selected for August is too expensive for me and Max on our own. We had originally planned to share it with Sara and Aiden, so we had to let it go. Unfortunately, it's been difficult to find another place in the summer. But now I'm thinking maybe a Christmas wedding."

"That sounds lovely, if you don't mind waiting."

"Max and I are so happy together that it doesn't really matter. We want the marriage, of course, but we already have the most important things, love and a life together." Emma blinked moisture out of her eyes. "Good grief, I can't believe I'm tearing up already. I'm not usually the girl in the family who cries. That's Nicole."

"Are you talking about me?" Nicole asked, as she joined them.

"Yes, I said you're usually the one who cries at these things," Emma said, dabbing her eyes with a tissue.

"True," Nicole admitted. "But I think I'll wait until the actual ceremony to start weeping. Are you all right, Emma?"

"I'm just happy," Emma said. "Sara has loved Aiden for so long. They're finally going to seal the deal after all these years."

"I think the baby-on-the-way has already done that," Nicole said dryly. She glanced over her shoulder at the parking lot. "I wonder where the guys are. Shouldn't they be here by now?"

Ria smiled, and Nicole gave her a curious look. So did Emma.

"What do you know, Ria?" Emma demanded.

"I think your brothers want to arrive in style," she said, the sound of an approaching helicopter drowning out the end of her sentence.

Megan, Sara and Shayla joined them as the helicopter came in for a landing on the grass beyond the church.

"Oh, wow," Megan muttered.

"Wow is right," Sara said, as Aiden hopped out of the helicopter in a black tuxedo.

"It's like James Bond," Megan added.

"Damn those boys. They always outshine us," Emma complained as the rest of the Callaway men made their way off the helicopter.

Following Aiden were Burke, Sean, Colton, Max, and finally Drew.

Her own personal James Bond, Ria thought, her eyes on the ruggedly handsome man who was heading directly for her.

"Aiden cannot see the bride," Emma said suddenly, grabbing Sara's arm.

"I think he already has," Sara said, her gaze on her fiancé.

"Not up close," Emma replied. "Let's get you back to the dressing room."

While the other bridesmaids hustled Sara away, Ria waited for Drew.

He gave her a smile and a warm kiss. "What did you think of our entrance?"

"Very impressive. My heart skipped a beat. But then it seems to do that every time I see you," she admitted, gazing into his eyes.

He put his hands on her waist and kissed her again. "This wedding is giving me some ideas."

Her breath caught in her throat. "I think you're getting caught up in the moment again, Drew."

"You always think that, but it's never true. It's not about the moment; it's about you. I love you, Ria. And I want to marry you. But this is not the official proposal, he added quickly. "I need to do that in a much more exciting way. There will be flowers and candles and romance. Megan would kill me if I didn't do it right. She's given me very firm instructions, and I do not want to let her down."

She smiled, happy that the relationship between Megan and Drew was so strong. But she needed to set him straight on one thing. "I'm glad that you're taking Megan into consideration, but I don't need candles or flowers, Drew."

"But you're going to get them," he said, cutting her off. "Because you deserve the best."

"I have the best. I have you," she said with a smile. "And just so you know—
whenever you ask me, however you ask me, the answer will be yes."

"Good, because I don't take no for an answer."

"Don't I know it," she said with a laugh. "You're the most stubborn man I have ever met."

"Which makes me the perfect match for you," he retorted. "We're going to have a good life together, Ria."

"I'm absolutely certain of that," she said as she threw her arms around his neck and pulled his head down to hers for a long and loving kiss.

THE END

Keep reading for an excerpt from

the next book in the Callaway series

BETWEEN NOW AND FOREVER
(Coming July 2015!)

ONE

It felt like earthquake weather. Nicole Prescott slipped off her bright orange sweater and tied it loosely around the waist of her jeans. It was unseasonably warm for the last day of October, not a trace of breeze blowing off the bay, not a hint of fog sweeping across the tall red spires of the Golden Gate Bridge, just blue skies, and an eerie stillness, as if something momentous was about to happen.

It was just her imagination, she told herself, heightened by the ghosts and goblins running through the Halloween carnival at Washington Elementary School. The school sat at the top of one of San Francisco's many steep hills and overlooked the bay and marina.

The auditorium had been turned into a haunted house, and wooden booths dotted the playground offering games ranging from darts to a water balloon toss and a cakewalk. Smells of popcorn, hot dogs with mustard and salty pretzels warmed the air while children in costumes roamed the playground. Everything seemed normal, and yet it wasn't—at least not in Nicole's quiet corner of the yard.

Glancing at her six-year-old son, Brandon, Nicole bit back a sigh of frustration. She'd hoped that Brandon would find a way to join in the carnival fun. She'd dressed him up as Hercules, with a chest plate, a black cape and some muscled armbands. She'd even given him a sword to carry. Her son had ditched the sword upon arrival, and a few minutes ago had tossed the chest plate onto the ground. Instead of playing games with the other children, Brandon knelt by the line of rosebushes that ran along the fence at the furthest end of the school property and as far away from the carnival action as he could get.

Digging into the dirt, he pulled out pebble after pebble, his entire being focused on the stones as he arranged and rearranged them in patterns on the cement path. Every few minutes, he would swap one rock with another, his small fingers moving with a passion and a purpose Nicole could not begin to understand. She watched as Brandon picked up a stone, sweeping his finger across the surface, tracing the rough edge, as if he were memorizing the curves, the cracks, the weight. Then he set the stone down and picked up another one, seeking a pattern, a conclusion, that would bring some sort of closure to his obsession, but the end never came. Even when he seemed to find the perfect match, he was never completely satisfied with the result. Lately, there appeared to be a greater urgency to his movements, as if he thought he was running out of time.

Nicole yearned for some way to connect with her only child, but most days Brandon seemed unaware of her presence, his focus so pure, so single, and so solitary. His world was his own, and she had no place in it. When she tried to interfere or help, he would go into an angry, agitated frenzy, hitting his forehead with the palm of his hand over and over again until she backed away.

For three years she'd battled her son's diagnosis of autism, researching every new therapy, constantly changing his diet, taking him to doctor after doctor, but while she'd seen small changes in his behavior, nothing significant had occurred. Her son was trapped in his own head, and she couldn't find a way to get through to him. The pain of that broken connection was relentless.

While Brandon might not remember the first few years of his life, she had forgotten nothing, from the sweetness of his joyous smile when he woke up in the morning, to the feel of his soft arms around her neck when he'd hugged her, the sound of his laugh—half snort, half giggle—and the touch of his hand in hers. He'd been perfect for two years, eleven months, and six days, and then he'd changed. He'd become withdrawn, isolated, and unresponsive. It was as if the light in his brain had gone out.

Terrified, she'd fought desperately to find first a diagnosis and then a cure. But the enemy she fought was winning the war, invincible at every turn. She'd prayed for a miracle, but none had come. She'd put Brandon before everything and everyone else in her life, including her soon-to-be ex-husband, Ryan.

Another ache filled her heart, this one having nothing to do with her son, and everything to do with the man she'd vowed to love for all time. She tried to shake Ryan out of her mind. There were only so many emotions she could handle at one time.

Brandon paused, his body stiffening as he stared down at the two stones in front of him. He glanced over at her, and Nicole's heart stopped in amazement. There was a rare spark in his blue eyes, a moment of triumph, satisfaction, and in that brief glance he connected with her in a way he hadn't done in a long time. He had looked to her to see his achievement.

Her eyes blurred with shocked tears. Maybe this was the momentous thing she'd been anticipating. But the moment vanished as quickly as it had come.

Brandon's gaze dropped away, and he sat back on his heels. After a moment, he picked up the rocks and put them in the pocket of his jeans. Then he scampered down the path, searching for more stones among the rose bushes. Even though he had found the perfect pair, he would have to do it again and again and again.

She wanted to take him by the hand and lead him over to

one of the game booths, get him involved in the world around him, but she wouldn't be doing it for him; she'd be doing it for herself. Brandon had no interest in playing with the other children. And while she could interact with the mothers, the truth was—she rarely did. The moms were always polite to her, but they were often wary, as if they thought their kids could somehow catch autism from Brandon. They wanted distance, and most days she let them have it.

She glanced across the playground, seeing Theresa and Kathleen organizing the cakewalk. At one time they'd all been so close. They'd taken walks together, bought strollers, complained about sleepless nights. They'd looked to each other for advice about pacifiers, night terrors, and thumb sucking. Seeing them huddling together now, she could imagine their conversation. They were probably planning their evening. They'd gather at Kathleen's house before trick-or-treating, share wine and appetizers while the children ate pizza. The men would take the kids through the neighborhood while the women stayed behind to hand out candy. Kathleen's husband, Patrick, would take pictures.

Patrick, she thought with a sigh, another good friend gone. Since she and Ryan had separated, Patrick had chosen to stick with Ryan. It was no surprise. Patrick and Ryan had grown up together. She couldn't blame Patrick; she couldn't really blame anyone. A lot of the distance was her fault. She'd drifted away, and they'd let her go. That was the way of relationships. If no one fought for them, they ended. Or maybe that was just the way of her relationships. She had only so much fight in her; what she had left she saved for Brandon.

Taking a seat on a nearby bench, she reached into her purse and pulled out the folder of essays she needed to grade. She'd cut back on her teaching in the past three years, but she still taught a class in Greek Mythology at San Francisco City

College three mornings a week. The Gods had always fascinated her. They represented the best and the worst of humankind. While they rose to heroic proportions, they also battled deep and sometimes fatal flaws within themselves, representing the good and bad within each individual.

A passion for history and mythology was something she'd inherited from her biological father, David Kane, who was a professor of history at UC Berkeley. Her love of learning was the only thing David had given her before he divorced her mother, Lynda, when she was six years old. Everything else she'd gotten from her stepfather, Jack Callaway, a man who had given her love and treated her like his own daughter.

A soccer ball came rolling towards her. She put down her folder and grabbed it. Then she stood up as Derek, Kathleen's three-year-old son came running over, followed by his mother.

"Sorry about that," Kathleen said, her cheeks red from chasing after Derek. She was a tall, slim woman with blond hair and a lightly freckled complexion.

"No problem." Nicole tossed the ball back to Derek, who squealed with delight. "Your baby is getting big."

"That's for sure, and he's hard to keep up with. He has so much more energy and stubbornness than William did at this age," she finished, referring to her six-year-old, who was in the same class as Brandon.

Derek dropped the soccer ball and kicked it in Nicole's direction. It took her a second to realize that Derek was playing a game with her. It had been a long time since a child had played with her. It felt surprisingly good and ridiculously sad all at the same time. She kicked the ball back to him.

"Don't encourage him," Kathleen warned. "He'll never leave you alone."

She wanted to encourage Derek. She wanted to keep on

playing. She just wished it was Brandon who was the child kicking the ball to her.

Kathleen snagged the ball. "Sorry to break this up, but I have to do my duty in the haunted house. Why don't you and Brandon come by tonight, Nicole?" Her gaze softened. "We miss you. Everyone would love to see you."

"I miss you all, too," Nicole admitted.

A guilty expression flashed in Kathleen's eyes. "I know I haven't been in touch since you and Ryan split up. It's not because I don't care. It's just—"

"It's fine," Nicole said, cutting her off. "You're busy. We're all busy."

"It is that time of the year."

Kathleen had barely finished speaking when the buzz of a small plane drew Nicole's head upward. It was a reflex she couldn't quite shake. The plane dipped its wings as if it were saying hello. Her heart skipped a beat, an old memory of Ryan, seventeen years old, cocky as hell, taking off at the small airport in Half Moon Bay with his flight instructor. Back then he'd thought he could conquer the world; she'd thought the same thing.

With a sigh she lowered her gaze from the sky. Kathleen gave her a speculative look. "Do you miss Ryan?"

More than she'd ever imagined.

"It's complicated." She looked past Kathleen to see Joni waving at them, and she was relieved at the interruption. "Joni is calling you."

Kathleen turned her head and groaned. "I have to go. Sorry."

"No problem."

"We need to catch up, Nicole. Let's make it happen before too much more time passes."

Nicole nodded. "See you later."

As Kathleen and Derek returned to the carnival, Nicole

thought about trying to take Brandon through the haunted house. Even as the thought crossed her mind, she immediately dismissed it. Brandon would hate it. He'd throw a screaming fit, and everyone would be uncomfortable.

Enough was enough. It was time to put an end to yet another moment of wishful thinking that this day would be different—normal. She had to accept the fact that this version of her life was normal.

She could put Brandon in a costume. She could bring him to a carnival, but she couldn't make him care about Halloween. She couldn't really make him care about anything. It wasn't his fault. It just wasn't in him.

She turned around to see what Brandon was doing, and it took a moment for her to register the fact that Brandon wasn't playing in the rosebushes where she'd last seen him. Her gaze moved down the fence. Brandon wasn't there. Had he gone over to the carnival on his own while she was talking to Kathleen and Derek? She looked around the playground, trying to catch a glimpse of Brandon's tousled blonde hair, his black cape, but all she could see was a blur of costumes and children in the playground, and none of them were her son.

Her heart began to pound against her chest, her breath coming short and fast. She told herself to calm down. Everything was fine. This was Brandon's school. He knew his way around; he'd probably just gone to the bathroom.

The sound of a car speeding down the street brought her head around. She caught a glimpse of the tail end of a white SUV. Then her gaze fell on the black cape lying on the ground by the gate.

Had Brandon left the yard?

It seemed to take forever to get her feet to move. She was frozen in fear, a terrible certainty ripping through her soul. Brandon had gone through that gate. But why?

He didn't like change, new environments, or strangers. He wouldn't leave on his own.

Her feet finally took flight. She ran across the yard and picked up the cape. It was still warm from the heat of Brandon's body. She walked through the gate to the sidewalk, looking in either direction. There was no sign of her son. Where was he?

She ran back into the playground, calling Brandon's name. She searched every game booth, every corner, running into the halls of the school. A couple of the other moms came over to help her search. The principal made an announcement over the loudspeaker. Everyone started looking for Brandon.

Forty-five minutes later it became clear that Brandon wasn't in the school or the yard. She'd checked under every desk, looked in every closet. The lights had been turned on in the haunted house to make sure Brandon hadn't gotten lost in the cobwebbed maze.

And then the police arrived.

She answered their questions with what little knowledge she had and took them out to the spot where Brandon had been playing. Then she saw something she'd missed before— a small trail of rocks leading down the sidewalk. They must have fallen out of Brandon's pockets. The trail ended at the curb. She looked up and down the street again.

The two cops were talking to her, but she couldn't hear what they were saying. The fear was overwhelming.

The scream came from down deep in her soul, the raw agony of the torn connection between mother and child.

Her baby was gone!

The ground shook beneath her feet. It wasn't an earthquake – it was worse.

Between Now And Forever Releases July 2015!

About The Author

Barbara Freethy is a #1 New York Times Bestselling Author of 42 novels ranging from contemporary romance to romantic suspense and women's fiction. Traditionally published for many years, Barbara opened her own publishing company in 2011 and has since sold over 5 million books! Nineteen of her titles have appeared on the New York Times and USA Today Bestseller Lists.

Known for her emotional and compelling stories of love, family, mystery and romance, Barbara enjoys writing about ordinary people caught up in extraordinary adventures. Barbara's books have won numerous awards. She is a six-time finalist for the RITA for best contemporary romance from Romance Writers of America and a two-time winner for DANIEL'S GIFT and THE WAY BACK HOME.

Barbara has lived all over the state of California and currently resides in Northern California where she draws much of her inspiration from the beautiful bay area.

For a complete listing of books, as well as excerpts and contests, and to connect with Barbara:

Visit Barbara's Website:
www.barbarafreethy.com

Join Barbara on Facebook:
www.facebook.com/barbarafreethybooks

Follow Barbara on Twitter:
www.twitter.com/barbarafreethy

CPSIA information can be obtained at www.ICGtesting.com
Printed in the USA
BVOW08s0116050515

398970BV00002B/2/P